A DANGEROUS WAGER . . .

"No, no. I make you a good bet. I am rich man and I am sporting man also. Listen to me. Outside de hotel iss my car. Iss very fine car. American car from your country. Cadillac—"

"Hey, now. Wait a minute." The boy leaned back in his deck chair and he laughed. "I can't put up that sort of property. This is crazy."

"Not crazy at all. You strike lighter ten times running and Cadillac is yours. You like to have dis Cadillac, yes?"

"Sure, I'd like to have a Cadillac." The boy was still grinning.

"All right. Fine. We make a bet and I put up my Cadillac."

"And what do I put up?"

The little man carefully removed the red band from his still unlighted cigar. "I never ask you, my friend, to bet something you cannot afford. You understand?"

"Then what do I bet?"

"I make it very easy for you, yes?"

"OK. You make it easy."

"Some small ting you can afford to give away, and if you happen to lose it you would not feel too bad. Right?"

"Such as what?"

"Such as, perhaps, the little finger on your left hand."

"My what?" The boy stopped grinning.

—from "Man from the South"

Books by Roald Dahl

The BFG
Boy: Tales of Childhood
Charlie and the Chocolate Factory
Charlie and the Great Glass Elevator
Danny the Champion of the World
Dirty Beasts
The Enormous Crocodile
Esio Trot
Fantastic Mr. Fox
George's Marvelous Medicine
The Giraffe and the Pelly and Me
Going Solo
James and the Giant Peach
The Magic Finger
Matilda
The Minpins
The Missing Golden Ticket and Other Splendiferous Secrets
Roald Dahl's Revolting Rhymes
Skin and Other Stories
The Twits
The Umbrella Man and Other Stories
The Vicar of Nibbleswicke
The Witches
The Wonderful Story of Henry Sugar and Six More

Roald Dahl

The Umbrella Man
and Other Stories

speak

An Imprint of Penguin Group (USA) Inc.

Speak
Published by the Penguin Group
Penguin Group (USA) Inc., 345 Hudson Street, New York, New York 10014, U.S.A.
Penguin Group (Canada), 90 Eglinton Avenue East, Suite 700, Toronto, Ontario, Canada M4P 2Y3
(a division of Pearson Penguin Canada Inc.)
Penguin Books Ltd, 80 Strand, London WC2R 0RL, England
Penguin Ireland, 25 St Stephen's Green, Dublin 2, Ireland (a division of Penguin Books Ltd)
Penguin Group (Australia), 250 Camberwell Road, Camberwell, Victoria 3124, Australia
(a division of Pearson Australia Group Pty Ltd)
Penguin Books India Pvt Ltd, 11 Community Centre, Panchsheel Park, New Delhi - 110 017, India
Penguin Group (NZ), 67 Apollo Drive, Rosedale, North Shore 0632, New Zealand
(a division of Pearson New Zealand Ltd)
Penguin Books (South Africa) (Pty) Ltd, 24 Sturdee Avenue,
Rosebank, Johannesburg 2196, South Africa

Registered Offices: Penguin Books Ltd, 80 Strand, London WC2R 0RL, England

First published in Great Britain as *The Great Automatic Grammatizator*
by Hamish Hamilton Limited, 1996
First published in the United States of America by Viking, a member of Penguin Putnam Inc., 1998
Published by Puffin Books, a division of Penguin Putnam Books for Young Readers, 2000
This edition published by Speak, an imprint of Penguin Group (USA) Inc., 2003, 2010

17 19 20 18

Copyright © Roald Dahl Nominee Limited, 1996
All rights reserved

Grateful acknowledgment is made for permission to reprint the following stories from *Kiss Kiss*:
"Mrs Bixby and the Colonel's Coat," "The Landlady," and "Royal Jelly," copyright © 1959 by Roald
Dahl; copyright renewed 1987 by Roald Dahl. "Parson's Pleasure," copyright © 1958 by Roald Dahl;
copyright renewed 1986 by Roald Dahl. "The Way Up to Heaven," copyright © 1954 by Roald Dahl;
copyright renewed 1982 by Roald Dahl. By permission of Alfred A. Knopf, Inc.

"The Great Automatic Grammatizator," "Man from the South," "Taste," and "Neck" were published in *Someone Like You* (Knopf). Copyright © 1948, 1949, 1950, 1952, 1953, 1961 by Roald Dahl.

"The Butler," "The Umbrella Man," and "Vengeance Is Mine Inc." were published in *More Tales of
the Unexpected* (Michael Joseph, London). Copyright © 1973, 1980 by Roald Dahl.

"Katina" was published in *Over to You* (Reynal & Hitchcock). Copyright © 1946 by Roald Dahl.

THE LIBRARY OF CONGRESS HAS CATALOGED THE VIKING EDITION AS FOLLOWS:
Dahl, Roald
The umbrella man and other stories / Roald Dahl.
p.   cm.
Summary: Thirteen stories, selected for teenagers, from Dahl's adult writings, including "The Great
Automatic Grammatizator," "Mrs. Bixby and the Colonel's Coat," and "Vengeance Is Mine Inc."
ISBN: 0-670-87854-5 (hc)
1. Short stories, English. [1. Short stories.] I. Title.
PZ7.D1515Um 1998 97-32549 CIP AC

Speak ISBN 978-0-14-240087-6

Printed in the United States of America

CONTENTS

CONTENTS

"Well, Knipe, my boy. Now that it's finished, I just called you in to tell you I think you've done a fine job."

Adolph Knipe stood still in front of Mr. Bohlen's desk. There seemed to be no enthusiasm in him at all.

"Aren't you pleased?"

"Oh yes, Mr. Bohlen."

"Did you see what the papers said this morning?"

"No sir, I didn't."

The man behind the desk pulled a folded newspaper towards him, and began to read: "The building of the great automatic computing engine, ordered by the government some time ago, is now complete. It is probably the fastest electronic calculating machine in the world today. Its function is to satisfy the ever-increasing need of science, industry, and administration for rapid mathematical calculation which, in the past, by traditional methods, would have been physically impossible, or would have required more time than the problems justified. The speed with which the new engine works, said Mr. John Bohlen, head of the firm of electrical engineers mainly responsible for its construction, may be grasped by the fact that it can provide the correct answer in five seconds to a problem that would occupy a mathematician for a month. In three minutes, it can produce a calculation that by hand (if it were possible) would fill half a million sheets of foolscap paper. The automatic computing engine uses pulses of electricity, generated at the rate of a million a second, to solve all calculations that resolve themselves into addition, subtraction, multiplication, and division. For practical purposes there is no limit to what it can do . . ."

Mr. Bohlen glanced up at the long, melancholy face of the younger man. "Aren't you proud, Knipe? Aren't you pleased?"

"Of course, Mr. Bohlen."

"I don't think I have to remind you that your own contribution, especially to the original plans, was an important one. In fact, I might go so far as to say that without you and some of your ideas, this project might still be on the drawing boards today."

Adolph Knipe moved his feet on the carpet, and he watched the two small white hands of his chief, the nervous fingers playing with a paper clip, unbending it, straightening out the hairpin curves. He didn't like the man's hands. He didn't like his face either, with the tiny mouth and the narrow purple-coloured lips. It was unpleasant the way only the lower lip moved when he talked.

"Is anything bothering you, Knipe? Anything on your mind?"

"Oh no, Mr. Bohlen. No."

"How would you like to take a week's holiday? Do you good. You've earned it."

"Oh, I don't know, sir."

The older man waited, watching this tall, thin person who stood so sloppily before him. He was a difficult boy. Why couldn't he stand up straight? Always drooping and untidy, with spots on his jacket, and hair falling all over his face.

"I'd like you to take a holiday, Knipe. You need it."

"All right, sir. If you wish."

"Take a week. Two weeks if you like. Go somewhere warm. Get some sunshine. Swim. Relax. Sleep. Then come back, and we'll have another talk about the future."

Adolph Knipe went home by bus to his two-room apartment. He threw his coat on the sofa, poured himself a drink of whisky, and sat down in front of the typewriter that was on the table. Mr. Bohlen was right. Of course he was right. Except that he didn't know the half of it. He probably thought it was a woman. Whenever a young man gets depressed, everybody thinks it's a woman.

He leaned forward and began to read through the half-finished sheet of typing still in the machine. It was headed "A Narrow Escape," and it began "The night was dark and stormy, the wind whistled in the trees, the rain poured down like cats and dogs . . ."

Adolph Knipe took a sip of whisky, tasting the malty-bitter flavour, feeling the trickle of cold liquid as it travelled down his throat and settled in the top of his stomach, cool at first, then spreading and becoming warm, making a little area of warmness in the gut. To hell with Mr. John Bohlen anyway. And to hell with the great electrical computing machine. To hell with . . .

At exactly that moment, his eyes and mouth began slowly to open, in a sort of wonder, and slowly he raised his head and became still, absolutely motionless, gazing at the wall opposite with this look that was more perhaps of astonishment than of wonder, but quite fixed now, unmoving, and remaining thus for forty, fifty, sixty seconds. Then gradually (the head still motionless), a subtle change spreading over the face, astonishment becoming pleasure, very slight at first, only around the corners of the mouth, increasing gradually, spreading out until at last the whole face was open wide and shining with extreme delight. It was the first time Adolph Knipe had smiled in many, many months.

"Of course," he said, speaking aloud, "it's completely ridiculous." Again he smiled, raising his upper lip and baring his teeth in a queerly sensual manner.

"It's a delicious idea, but so impracticable it doesn't really bear thinking about at all."

From then on, Adolph Knipe began to think about nothing else. The idea fascinated him enormously, at first because it gave him a promise—however remote—of revenging himself in a most devilish manner upon his greatest enemies. From this angle alone, he toyed idly with it for perhaps ten or fifteen minutes; then all at once he found himself examining it quite seriously as a practical possibility. He took paper and made some preliminary notes. But he didn't get far. He found himself, almost immediately, up against the old truth that a machine, however ingenious, is incapable of original thought. It can handle no problems except those that resolve themselves into mathematical terms—problems that contain one, and only one, correct answer.

This was a stumper. There didn't seem any way around it. A machine cannot have a brain. On the other hand, it *can* have a memory, can it not? Their own electronic calculator had a marvellous memory. Simply by converting electric pulses, through a column of mercury, into supersonic waves, it could store away at least a thousand numbers at a time, extracting any one of them at the precise moment it was needed. Would it not be possible, therefore, on this principle, to build a memory section of almost unlimited size?

Now what about that?

Then suddenly, he was struck by a powerful but simple little truth, and it was this: *that English grammar is governed by rules that are almost mathematical in their strictness!* Given the words, and given the sense of what is to be said, then there is only one correct order in which those words can be arranged.

No, he thought, that isn't quite accurate. In many sentences there are several alternative positions for words and phrases, all of which may be grammatically correct. But what the hell. The theory itself is basically true. Therefore, it stands to reason that an engine built along the lines of the electric computer could be adjusted to arrange words (instead of numbers) in their right order according to the rules of grammar. Give it the verbs, the nouns, the adjectives, the pronouns, store them in the memory section as a vocabulary, and arrange for them to be extracted as required. Then feed it with plots and leave it to write the sentences.

There was no stopping Knipe now. He went to work immediately, and there followed during the next few days a period of intense labour. The living room became littered with sheets of paper: formulae and calculations; lists of words, thousands and thousands of words; the plots of stories, curiously broken up and subdivided; huge extracts from *Roget's Thesaurus*; pages filled with the first names of men and women; hundreds of surnames taken from the telephone directory; intricate drawings of wires and circuits and switches and thermionic valves; drawings of machines that could punch holes of different shapes in little cards, and of a strange electric typewriter that could type ten thousand words a minute. Also a kind of control panel with a series of small push buttons, each one labelled with the name of a famous American magazine.

He was working in a mood of exultation, prowling around the room amidst this littering of paper, rubbing his hands together, talking out loud to himself; and sometimes, with a sly curl of the nose he would mutter a series of murderous imprecations in which the word "editor" seemed always to be present. On the fifteenth day of continuous work, he collected the papers into two large folders which he carried—almost at a run—to the offices of John Bohlen Inc., electrical engineers.

Mr. Bohlen was pleased to see him back.

"Well Knipe, good gracious me, you look a hundred per cent better. You have a good holiday? Where'd you go?"

He's just as ugly and untidy as ever, Mr. Bohlen thought. Why doesn't he stand up straight? He looks like a bent stick. "You look a hundred per cent better, my boy." I wonder what he's grinning about. Every time I see him, his ears seem to have got larger.

Adolph Knipe placed the folders on the desk. "Look, Mr. Bohlen!" he cried. "Look at these!"

Then he poured out his story. He opened the folders and pushed the plans in front of the astonished little man. He talked for over an hour, explaining everything, and when he had finished, he stepped back, breathless, flushed, waiting for the verdict.

"You know what I think, Knipe? I think you're nuts." Careful now, Mr. Bohlen told himself. Treat him carefully. He's valuable, this one is. If only he didn't look so awful, with that long horse face and the big teeth. The fellow had ears as big as rhubarb leaves.

"But Mr. Bohlen! It'll work! I've proved to you it'll work! You can't deny that!"

"Take it easy now, Knipe. Take it easy, and listen to me."

Adolph Knipe watched his man, disliking him more every second.

"This idea," Mr. Bohlen's lower lip was saying, "is very ingenious—I might almost say brilliant—and it only goes to confirm my opinion of your abilities, Knipe. But don't take it too seriously. After all, my boy, what possible use can it be to us? Who on earth wants a machine for writing stories? And where's the money in it, anyway? Just tell me that."

"May I sit down, sir?"

"Sure, take a seat."

Adolph Knipe seated himself on the edge of a chair. The older man watched him with alert brown eyes, wondering what was coming now.

"I would like to explain something Mr. Bohlen, if I may, about how I came to do all this."

"Go right ahead, Knipe." He would have to be humoured a little now, Mr. Bohlen told himself. The boy was really valuable—a sort of genius, almost—worth his weight in gold to the firm. Just look at these papers here. Darndest thing you ever saw. Astonishing piece of work. Quite useless, of course. No commercial value. But it proved again the boy's ability.

"It's a sort of confession, I suppose, Mr. Bohlen. I think it explains why I've always been so . . . so kind of worried."

"You tell me anything you want, Knipe. I'm here to help you—you know that."

The young man clasped his hands together tight on his lap, hugging himself with his elbows. It seemed as though suddenly he was feeling very cold.

"You see, Mr. Bohlen, to tell the honest truth, I don't really care much for my work here. I know I'm good at it and all that sort of thing, but my heart's not in it. It's not what I want to do most."

Up went Mr. Bohlen's eyebrows, quick like a spring. His whole body became very still.

"You see, sir, all my life I've wanted to be a writer."

"A writer!"

"Yes, Mr. Bohlen. You may not believe it, but every bit of spare time I've had, I've spent writing stories. In the last ten years I've written hundreds, literally hundreds of short stories. Five hundred and sixty-six, to be precise. Approximately one a week."

"Good heavens, man! What on earth did you do that for?"

"All I know, sir, is I have the urge."

"What sort of urge?"

"The creative urge, Mr. Bohlen." Every time he looked up he saw Mr. Bohlen's lips. They were growing thinner and thinner, more and more purple.

"And may I ask you what you do with these stories, Knipe?"

"Well sir, that's the trouble. No one will buy them. Each time I finish one, I send it out on the rounds. It goes to one magazine after another. That's all that happens, Mr. Bohlen, and they simply send them back. It's very depressing."

Mr. Bohlen relaxed. "I can see quite well how you feel, my boy." His voice was dripping with sympathy. "We all go through it one time or another in our lives. But now—now that you've had proof—positive proof—from the experts themselves, from the editors, that your stories are—what shall I say—rather unsuccessful, it's time to leave off. Forget it, my boy. Just forget all about it."

"No, Mr. Bohlen! No! That's not true! I *know* my stories are good. My heavens, when you compare them with the stuff some of those magazines print—oh my word, Mr. Bohlen!—the sloppy, boring stuff that you see in the magazines week after week—why, it drives me mad!"

"Now wait a minute, my boy . . ."

"Do you ever read the magazines, Mr. Bohlen?"

"You'll pardon me, Knipe, but what's all this got to do with your machine?"

"Everything, Mr. Bohlen, absolutely everything! What I want to tell you is, I've made a study of magazines, and it seems that each one tends to have its own particular type of story. The writers—the successful ones—know this, and they write accordingly."

"Just a minute, my boy. Calm yourself down, will you. I don't think all this is getting us anywhere."

"*Please*, Mr. Bohlen, hear me through. It's all terribly important." He paused to catch his breath. He was properly worked up now, throwing his hands around as he talked. The long, toothy face, with the big ears on either side, simply shone with enthusiasm, and there was an excess of saliva in his mouth which caused him to speak his words wet. "So you see, on my machine, by having an adjustable coordinator between the 'plot-memory' section and the 'word-memory' section I am able to produce any type of story I desire simply by pressing the required button."

"Yes, I know, Knipe, I know. This is all very interesting, but what's the point of it?"

"Just this, Mr. Bohlen. The market is limited. We've got to be able to produce the right stuff, at the right time, whenever we want it. It's a matter of business, that's all. I'm looking at it from *your* point of view now—as a commercial proposition."

"My dear boy, it can't possibly be a commercial proposition— ever. You know as well as I do what it costs to build one of these machines."

"Yes sir, I do. But with due respect, I don't believe you know what the magazines pay writers for stories."

"What do they pay?"

"Anything up to twenty-five hundred dollars. It probably averages around a thousand."

Mr. Bohlen jumped.

"Yes *sir*, it's true."

"Absolutely impossible, Knipe! Ridiculous!"

"No sir, it's true."

"You mean to sit there and tell me that these magazines pay out money like that to a man for . . . just for scribbling off a story! Good heavens, Knipe! Whatever next! Writers must all be millionaires!"

"That's exactly it, Mr. Bohlen! That's where the machine comes in. Listen a minute, sir, while I tell you some more. I've got it all worked out. The big magazines are carrying approximately three fiction stories in each issue. Now, take the fifteen most important magazines—the ones paying the most money. A few of them are monthlies, but most of them come out every week. All right. That makes, let us say, around forty big stories being bought each week. That's forty thousand dollars. So with our machine—when we get it working properly—we can collar nearly the whole of this market!"

"My dear boy, you're mad!"

"No sir, honestly, it's true what I say. Don't you see that with volume alone we'll completely overwhelm them! This machine can produce a five-thousand-word story, all typed and ready for dispatch, in thirty seconds. How can the writers compete with that? I ask you, Mr. Bohlen, *how?*"

At that point, Adolph Knipe noticed a slight change in the man's expression, an extra brightness in the eyes, the nostrils distending, the whole face becoming still, almost rigid. Quickly, he continued. "Nowadays, Mr. Bohlen, the handmade article hasn't a hope. It can't possibly compete with mass production, especially in this country—you know that. Carpets . . . chairs . . . shoes . . . bricks . . . crockery . . . anything you like to mention—they're all made by machinery now. The quality may be inferior, but that doesn't matter. It's the cost of production that counts. And stories—well—they're just another product, like carpets and chairs, and no one cares how you produce them so long as you deliver the goods. We'll sell them wholesale, Mr. Bohlen! We'll undercut every writer in the country! We'll corner the market!"

Mr. Bohlen edged up straighter in his chair. He was leaning forward now, both elbows on the desk, the face alert, the small brown eyes resting on the speaker.

"I still think it's impracticable, Knipe."

"Forty thousand a week!" cried Adolph Knipe. "And if we halve the price, making it twenty thousand a week, that's still a million a year!" And softly he added, "You didn't get any million a year for building the old electronic calculator, did you, Mr. Bohlen?"

"But seriously now, Knipe. D'you really think they'd buy them?"

"Listen, Mr. Bohlen. Who on earth is going to want custommade stories when they can get the other kind at half the price? It stands to reason, doesn't it?"

"And how will you sell them? Who will you say has written them?"

"We'll set up our own literary agency, and we'll distribute them through that. And we'll invent all the names we want for the writers."

"I don't like it, Knipe. To me, that smacks of trickery, does it not?"

"And another thing, Mr. Bohlen. There's all manner of valuable by-products once you've got started. Take advertising, for example. Beer manufacturers and people like that are willing to pay good money these days if famous writers will lend their names to their products. Why, my heavens, Mr. Bohlen! This isn't any children's plaything we're talking about. It's big business."

"Don't get too ambitious, my boy."

"And another thing. There isn't any reason why we shouldn't put *your* name, Mr. Bohlen, on some of the better stories, if you wished it."

"My goodness, Knipe. What should I want that for?"

"I don't know, sir, except that some writers get to be very much respected—like Mr. Erle Gardner or Kathleen Morris, for example. We've got to have names, and I was certainly thinking of using my own on one or two stories, just to help out."

"A writer, eh?" Mr. Bohlen said, musing. "Well, it would surely surprise them over at the club when they saw my name in the magazines—the good magazines."

"That's right, Mr. Bohlen!"

For a moment, a dreamy, faraway look came into Mr. Bohlen's eyes, and he smiled. Then he stirred himself and began leafing through the plans that lay before him.

"One thing I don't quite understand, Knipe. Where do the plots come from? The machine can't possibly invent plots."

"We feed those in, sir. That's no problem at all. Everyone has plots. There's three or four hundred of them written down in that folder there on your left. Feed them straight into the 'plot-memory' section of the machine."

"Go on."

"There are many other little refinements too, Mr. Bohlen. You'll see them all when you study the plans carefully. For example, there's a trick that nearly every writer uses, of inserting at least one long, obscure word into each story. This makes the reader think that the man is very wise and clever. So I have the machine do the

13

same thing. There'll be a whole stack of long words stored away just for this purpose."

"Where?"

"In the 'word-memory' section," he said, epexegetically.

Through most of that day the two men discussed the possibilities of the new engine. In the end, Mr. Bohlen said he would have to think about it some more. The next morning, he was quietly enthusiastic. Within a week, he was completely sold on the idea.

"What we'll have to do, Knipe, is to say that we're merely building another mathematical calculator, but of a new type. That'll keep the secret."

"Exactly, Mr. Bohlen."

And in six months the machine was completed. It was housed in a separate brick building at the back of the premises, and now that it was ready for action, no one was allowed near it excepting Mr. Bohlen and Adolph Knipe.

It was an exciting moment when the two men—the one, short, plump, breviped—the other tall, thin and toothy—stood in the corridor before the control panel and got ready to run off the first story. All around them were walls dividing up into many small corridors, and the walls were covered with wiring and plugs and switches and huge glass valves. They were both nervous, Mr. Bohlen hopping from one foot to the other, quite unable to keep still.

"Which button?" Adolph Knipe asked, eyeing a row of small white discs that resembled the keys of a typewriter. "You choose, Mr. Bohlen. Lots of magazines to pick from—*Saturday Evening Post, Collier's, Ladies' Home Journal*—any one you like."

"Goodness me, boy! How do I know?" He was jumping up and down like a man with hives.

"Mr. Bohlen," Adolph Knipe said gravely, "do you realize that at this moment, with your little finger alone, you have it in your power to become the most versatile writer on this continent?"

"Listen Knipe, just get on with it, will you please—and cut out the preliminaries."

"Okay, Mr. Bohlen. Then we'll make it . . . let me see—this one. How's that?" He extended one finger and pressed down a button with the name TODAY'S WOMAN printed across it in diminutive black type. There was a sharp click, and when he took his finger away, the button remained down, below the level of the others.

"So much for the selection," he said. "Now—here we go!" He reached up and pulled a switch on the panel. Immediately, the room was filled with a loud humming noise, and a crackling of electric sparks, and the jingle of many tiny, quickly moving levers; and almost in the same instant, sheets of quarto paper began sliding out from a slot to the right of the control panel and dropping into a basket below. They came out quick, one sheet a second, and in less than half a minute it was all over. The sheets stopped coming.

"That's it!" Adolph Knipe cried. "There's your story!"

They grabbed the sheets and began to read. The first one they picked up started as follows: "Aifkjmbsaoegweztpplnvoqudskigt&,-fuhpekanvbertyuio lkjhgfdsazxcvbnm,peru itrehdjkg mvnb,wmsuy . . . " They looked at the others. The style was roughly similar in all of them. Mr. Bohlen began to shout. The younger man tried to calm him down.

"It's all right, sir. Really it is. It only needs a little adjustment. We've got a connection wrong somewhere, that's all. You must remember, Mr. Bohlen, there's over a million feet of wiring in this room. You can't expect everything to be right first time."

"It'll never work," Mr. Bohlen said.

"Be patient, sir. Be patient."

Adolph Knipe set out to discover the fault, and in four days' time he announced that all was ready for the next try.

"It'll never work," Mr. Bohlen said. "I know it'll never work."

Knipe smiled and pressed the selector button marked READER'S DIGEST. Then he pulled the switch, and again the strange, exciting, humming sound filled the room. One page of typescript flew out of the slot into the basket.

"Where's the rest?" Mr. Bohlen cried. "It's stopped! It's gone wrong!"

"No sir, it hasn't. It's exactly right. It's for the *Digest*, don't you see?"

This time it began. "Few people yet know thatarevolutionary-newcurehasbeendiscoveredwhichmaywellbringpermanentreliefto-sufferersofthemostdreadeddiseaseofourtime . . ." And so on.

"It's gibberish!" Mr. Bohlen shouted.

"No sir, it's fine. Can't you see? It's simply that she's not breaking up the words. That's an easy adjustment. But the story's there. Look, Mr. Bohlen, look! It's all there except that the words are joined together."

And indeed it was.

On the next try a few days later, everything was perfect, even the punctuation. The first story they ran off, for a famous women's magazine, was a solid, plotty story of a boy who wanted to better himself with his rich employer. This boy arranged, so that story went, for a friend to hold up the rich man's daughter on a dark night when she was driving home. Then the boy himself, happening by, knocked the gun out of his friend's hand and rescued the girl. The girl was grateful. But the father was suspicious. He questioned the boy sharply. The boy broke down and confessed. Then the father, instead of kicking him out of the house, said that he admired the boy's resourcefulness. The girl admired his honesty—and his looks. The father promised him to be head of the Accounts Department. The girl married him.

"It's tremendous, Mr. Bohlen! It's exactly right!"

"Seems a bit sloppy to me, my boy!"

"No sir, it's a seller, a real seller!"

In his excitement, Adolph Knipe promptly ran off six more stories in as many minutes. All of them—except one, which for some reason came out a trifle lewd—seemed entirely satisfactory.

Mr. Bohlen was now mollified. He agreed to set up a literary agency in an office downtown, and to put Knipe in charge. In a couple of weeks, this was accomplished. Then Knipe mailed out the first dozen stories. He put his own name to four of them, Mr. Bohlen's to one, and for the others he simply invented names.

Five of these stories were promptly accepted. The one with Mr. Bohlen's name on it was turned down with a letter from the fiction editor saying, "This is a skilful job, but in our opinion it doesn't quite come off. We would like to see more of this writer's work . . . " Adolph Knipe took a cab out to the factory and ran off another story for the same magazine. He again put Mr.

Bohlen's name to it, and mailed it immediately. That one they bought.

The money started pouring in. Knipe slowly and carefully stepped up the output, and in six months' time he was delivering thirty stories a week, and selling about half.

He began to make a name for himself in literary circles as a prolific and successful writer. So did Mr. Bohlen; but not quite such a good name, although he didn't know it. At the same time, Knipe was building up a dozen or more fictitious persons as promising young authors. Everything was going fine.

At this point it was decided to adapt the machine for writing novels as well as stories. Mr. Bohlen, thirsting now for greater honours in the literary world, insisted that Knipe go to work at once on this prodigious task.

"I want to do a novel," he kept saying. "I want to do a novel."

"And so you will, sir. And so you will. But please be patient. This is a very complicated adjustment I have to make."

"Everyone tells me I ought to do a novel," Mr. Bohlen cried. "All sorts of publishers are chasing after me day and night begging me to stop fooling around with stories and do something really important instead. A novel's the only thing that counts—that's what they say."

"We're going to do novels," Knipe told him. "Just as many as we want. But please be patient."

"Now listen to me, Knipe. What I'm going to do is a *serious* novel, something that'll make 'em sit up and take notice. I've been getting rather tired of the sort of stories you've been putting my name to lately. As a matter of fact, I'm none too sure you haven't been trying to make a monkey out of me."

"A monkey, Mr. Bohlen?"

"Keeping all the best ones for yourself, that's what you've been doing."

"Oh no, Mr. Bohlen! No!"

"So this time I'm going to make damn sure I write a high class intelligent book. You understand that."

"Look, Mr. Bohlen. With the sort of switchboard I'm rigging up, you'll be able to write any sort of book you want."

And this was true, for within another couple of months, the genius of Adolph Knipe had not only adapted the machine for novel writing, but had constructed a marvellous new control system which enabled the author to pre-select literally any type of plot and any style of writing he desired. There were so many dials and levers on the thing, it looked like the instrument panel of some enormous aeroplane.

First, by depressing one of a series of master buttons, the writer made his primary decision; historical, satirical, philosophical, political, romantic, erotic, humorous or straight. Then, from the second row (the basic buttons), he chose his theme: army life, pioneer days, civil war, world war, racial problem, wild west, country life, childhood memories, seafaring, the sea bottom and many, many more. The third row of buttons gave a choice of literary style: classical, whimsical, racy, Hemingway, Faulkner, Joyce, feminine, etc. The fourth row was for characters, the fifth for wordage—and so on and so on—ten long rows of pre-selector buttons.

But that wasn't all. Control had also to be exercised during the actual writing process (which took about fifteen minutes per novel), and to do this the author had to sit, as it were, in the driver's seat, and pull (or push) a battery of labelled stops, as on an organ. By so doing, he was able continually to modulate or merge fifty different and variable qualities such as tension, surprise, humour, pathos, and mystery. Numerous dials and gauges on the dashboard itself told him throughout exactly how far along he was with his work.

Finally, there was the question of "passion." From a careful study of the books at the top of the best-seller lists for the past year, Adolph Knipe had decided that this was the most important ingredient of all—a magical catalyst that somehow or other could transform the dullest novel into a howling success—at any rate financially. But Knipe also knew that passion was powerful, heady stuff, and must be prudently dispensed—the right proportions at the right moments; and to ensure this, he had devised an independent control consisting of two sensitive sliding adjustors operated by foot pedals, similar to the throttle and brake in a car. One pedal governed the per centage of passion to be injected, the other regulated its intensity. There was no doubt, of course—and this was the only drawback—that the writing of a novel by the Knipe methods was going to be rather like flying a plane and driving a car and playing an organ all at the same time, but this did not trouble the inventor. When all was ready, he proudly escorted Mr. Bohlen into the machine house and began to explain the operating procedure for the new wonder.

"Good God, Knipe! I'll never be able to do all that! Dammit man, it'd be easier to write the thing by hand!"

"You'll soon get used to it, Mr. Bohlen, I promise you. In a week or two, you'll be doing it without hardly thinking. It's just like learning to drive."

Well, it wasn't quite as easy as that, but after many hours of practice, Mr. Bohlen began to get the hang of it, and finally, late one evening, he told Knipe to make ready for running off the first novel. It was a tense moment, with the fat little man crouching nervously in the driver's seat, and the tall toothy Knipe fussing excitedly around him.

"I intend to write an important novel, Knipe."

"I'm sure you will, sir. I'm sure you will."

With one finger, Mr. Bohlen carefully pressed the necessary preselector buttons:

Master button—*satirical*

Subject—*racial problem*

Style—*classical*

Characters—*six men, four women, one infant*

Length—*fifteen chapters.*

At the same time he had his eye particularly upon three organ stops marked *power, mystery, profundity.*

"Are you ready, sir?"

"Yes, yes, I'm ready."

Knipe pulled the switch. The great engine hummed. There was a deep whirring sound from the oiled movement of fifty thousand cogs and rods and levers; then came the drumming of the rapid electrical typewriter, setting up a shrill, almost intolerable clatter. Out into the basket flew the typewritten pages—one every two seconds. But what with the noise and the excitement and having to play upon the stops, and watch the chapter-counter and the pace-indicator and the passion-gauge, Mr. Bohlen began to panic. He reacted in precisely the way a learner driver does in a car—by pressing both feet hard down on the pedals and keeping them there until the thing stopped.

"Congratulations on your first novel," Knipe said, picking up the great bundle of typed pages from the basket.

Little pearls of sweat were oozing out all over Mr. Bohlen's face. "It sure was hard work, my boy."

"But you got it done, sir. You got it done."

"Let me see it, Knipe. How does it read?"

He started to go through the first chapter, passing each finished page to the younger man.

"Good heavens, Knipe! What's this!" Mr. Bohlen's thin purple fish-lip was moving slightly as it mouthed the words, his cheeks were beginning slowly to inflate.

"But look here, Knipe! This is outrageous!"

"I must say it's a bit fruity, sir."

"*Fruity*! It's perfectly revolting! I can't possibly put my name to this!"

"Quite right, sir. Quite right!"

"Knipe! Is this some nasty trick you've been playing on me?"

"Oh no, sir! No!"

"It certainly looks like it."

"You don't think, Mr. Bohlen, that you mightn't have been pressing a little hard on the passion-control pedals, do you?"

"My dear boy, how should I know."

"Why don't you try another?"

So Mr. Bohlen ran off a second novel, and this time it went according to plan.

Within a week, the manuscript had been read and accepted by an enthusiastic publisher. Knipe followed with one in his own name, then made a dozen more for good measure. In no time at all, Adolph Knipe's Literary Agency had become famous for its large stable of promising young novelists. And once again the money started rolling in.

It was at this stage that young Knipe began to display a real talent for big business.

"See here, Mr. Bohlen," he said. "We still got too much competition. Why don't we just absorb all the other writers in the country?"

Mr. Bohlen, who now sported a bottle-green velvet jacket and allowed his hair to cover two-thirds of his ears, was quite content with things the way they were. "Don't know what you mean, my boy. You can't just absorb writers."

"Of course you can, sir. Exactly like Rockefeller did with his oil companies. Simply buy 'em out, and if they won't sell, squeeze 'em out. It's easy!"

"Careful now, Knipe. Be careful."

"I've got a list here sir, of fifty of the most successful writers in the country, and what I intend to do is offer each one of them a lifetime contract with pay. All *they* have to do is undertake never to write another word; and, of course, to let us use their names on our own stuff. How about that?"

"They'll never agree."

"You don't know writers, Mr. Bohlen. You watch and see."

"What about the creative urge, Knipe?"

"It's bunk! All they're really interested in is the money—just like everybody else."

In the end, Mr. Bohlen reluctantly agreed to give it a try, and Knipe, with his list of writers in his pocket, went off in a large chauffeur-driven Cadillac to make his calls.

He journeyed first to the man at the top of the list, a very great and wonderful writer, and he had no trouble getting into the house. He told his story and produced a suitcase full of sample novels, and a contract for the man to sign which guaranteed him so much a year for life. The man listened politely, decided he was dealing with a lunatic, gave him a drink, then firmly showed him to the door.

The second writer on the list, when he saw Knipe was serious, actually attacked him with a large metal paperweight, and the inventor had to flee down the garden followed by such a torrent of abuse and obscenity as he had never heard before.

But it took more than this to discourage Adolph Knipe. He was disappointed but not dismayed, and off he went in his big car to seek his next client. This one was a female, famous and popular, whose fat romantic books sold by the million across the country. She received Knipe graciously, gave him tea, and listened attentively to his story.

"It all sounds very fascinating," she said. "But of course I find it a little hard to believe."

"Madam," Knipe answered. "Come with me and see it with your own eyes. My car awaits you."

So off they went, and in due course, the astonished lady was ushered into the machine house where the wonder was kept. Eagerly,

Knipe explained its workings, and after a while he even permitted her to sit in the driver's seat and practise with the buttons.

"All right," he said suddenly, "you want to do a book now?"

"Oh yes!" she cried. "Please!"

She was very competent and seemed to know exactly what she wanted. She made her own pre-selections, then ran off a long, romantic, passion-filled novel. She read through the first chapter and became so enthusiastic that she signed up on the spot.

"That's one of them out of the way," Knipe said to Mr. Bohlen afterwards. "A pretty big one too."

"Nice work, my boy."

"And you know *why* she signed?"

"Why?"

"It wasn't the money. She's got plenty of that."

"Then why?"

Knipe grinned, lifting his lip and baring a long pale upper gum. "Simply because she saw the machine-made stuff was better than her own."

Thereafter, Knipe wisely decided to concentrate only upon mediocrity. Anything better than that—and there were so few it didn't matter much—was apparently not quite so easy to seduce.

In the end, after several months of work, he had persuaded something like seventy per cent of the writers on his list to sign the contract. He found that the older ones, those who were running out of ideas and had taken to drink, were the easiest to handle. The younger people were more troublesome. They were apt to become abusive, sometimes violent when he approached them; and more than once Knipe was slightly injured on his rounds.

But on the whole, it was a satisfactory beginning. This last year—the first full year of the machine's operation—it was estimated that at least one half of all the novels and stories published in the English language were produced by Adolph Knipe upon the Great Automatic Grammatizator.

Does this surprise you?

I doubt it.

And worse is yet to come. Today, as the secret spreads, many more are hurrying to tie up with Mr. Knipe. And all the time the screw turns tighter for those who hesitate to sign their names.

This very moment, as I sit here listening to the howling of my nine starving children in the other room, I can feel my own hand creeping closer and closer to that golden contract that lies over on the other side of the desk.

Give us strength, Oh Lord, to let our children starve.

MRS. BIXBY AND THE COLONEL'S COAT

America is the land of opportunities for women. Already they own about eighty-five per cent of the wealth of the nation. Soon they will have it all. Divorce has become a lucrative process, simple to arrange and easy to forget; and ambitious females can repeat it as often as they please and parlay their winnings to astronomical figures. The husband's death also brings satisfactory rewards and some ladies prefer to rely upon this method. They know that the waiting period will not be unduly protracted, for overwork and hypertension are bound to get the poor devil before long, and he will die at his desk with a bottle of Benzedrines in one hand and a packet of tranquillizers in the other.

Succeeding generations of youthful American males are not deterred in the slightest by this terrifying pattern of divorce and death. The higher the divorce rate climbs, the more eager they become. Young men marry like mice, almost before they have reached the age of puberty, and a large proportion of them have at least two ex-wives on the payroll by the time they are thirty-six years old. To support these ladies in the manner to which they are accustomed, the men must work like slaves, which is of course precisely what they are. But now at last, as they approach their premature middle age, a sense of disillusionment and fear begins to creep slowly into their hearts, and in the evenings they take to huddling together in little groups, in clubs and bars, drinking their whiskies and swallowing their pills, and trying to comfort one another with stories.

The basic theme of these stories never varies. There are always three main characters—the husband, the wife, and the dirty dog. The husband is a decent clean-living man, working hard at his job. The wife is cunning, deceitful, and lecherous, and she is invariably up to some sort of jiggery-pokery with the dirty dog. The husband is too good a man even to suspect her. Things look black for the husband. Will the poor man ever find out? Must he be a cuckold for the rest of his life? Yes, he must. But wait! Suddenly, by a brilliant manoeuvre, the husband completely turns the tables on his monstrous spouse. The woman is flabbergasted, stupefied, humiliated, defeated. The audience of men around the bar smiles quietly to itself and takes a little comfort from the fantasy.

There are many of these stories going around, these wonderful wishful thinking dreamworld inventions of the unhappy male, but most of them are too fatuous to be worth repeating, and far too fruity to be put down on paper. There is one, however, that seems to be superior to the rest, particularly as it has the merit of being true. It is extremely popular with twice- or thrice-bitten males in search of solace, and if you are one of them, and if you haven't heard it before, you may enjoy the way it comes out. The story is called "Mrs. Bixby and the Colonel's Coat," and it goes something like this:

Mr. and Mrs. Bixby lived in a smallish apartment somewhere in New York City. Mr. Bixby was a dentist who made an average income. Mrs. Bixby was a big vigorous woman with a wet mouth. Once a month, always on Friday afternoons, Mrs. Bixby would board the train at Pennsylvania Station and travel to Baltimore to visit her old aunt. She would spend the night with the aunt and return to New York on the following day in time to cook supper for her husband. Mr. Bixby accepted this arrangement good-naturedly. He knew that Aunt Maude lived in Baltimore, and that his wife was very fond of the old lady, and certainly it would be unreasonable to deny either of them the pleasure of a monthly meeting.

"Just so long as you don't ever expect me to accompany you," Mr. Bixby had said in the beginning.

"Of course not, darling," Mrs. Bixby had answered. "After all, she is not *your* aunt. She's mine."

So far so good.

As it turned out, however, the aunt was little more than a convenient alibi for Mrs. Bixby. The dirty dog, in the shape of a gentleman known as the Colonel, was lurking slyly in the background, and our heroine spent the greater part of her Baltimore time in this scoundrel's company. The Colonel was exceedingly wealthy. He lived in a charming house on the outskirts of town. No wife or family encumbered him, only a few discreet and loyal servants, and in Mrs. Bixby's absence he consoled himself by riding his horses and hunting the fox.

Year after year, this pleasant alliance between Mrs. Bixby and the Colonel continued without a hitch. They met so seldom—twelve times a year is not much when you come to think of it—that there was little or no chance of their growing bored with one another. On the contrary, the long wait between meetings only made the heart grow fonder, and each separate occasion became an exciting reunion.

"Tally-ho!" the Colonel would cry each time he met her at the station in the big car. "My dear, I'd almost forgotten how ravishing you looked. Let's go to earth."

Eight years went by.

It was just before Christmas, and Mrs. Bixby was standing on the station in Baltimore waiting for the train to take her back to New York. This particular visit which had just ended had been more than usually agreeable, and she was in a cheerful mood. But then the Colonel's company always did that to her these days. The man had a way of making her feel that she was altogether a rather remarkable woman, a person of subtle and exotic talents, fascinating beyond measure; and what a very different thing that was from the dentist husband at home who never succeeded in making her feel that she was anything but a sort of eternal patient, someone who dwelt in the waiting room, silent among the magazines, seldom if ever nowadays to be called in to suffer the finicky precise ministrations of those clean pink hands.

"The Colonel asked me to give you this," a voice beside her said. She turned and saw Wilkins, the Colonel's groom, a small wizened dwarf with grey skin, and he was pushing a large flattish cardboard box into her arms.

"Good gracious me!" she cried, all of a flutter. "My heavens, what an enormous box! What is it, Wilkins? Was there a message? Did he send me a message?"

"No message," the groom said, and he walked away.

As soon as she was on the train, Mrs. Bixby carried the box into the privacy of the Ladies' Room and locked the door. How exciting this was! A Christmas present from the Colonel. She started to undo the string. "I'll bet it's a dress," she said aloud. "It might even be two dresses. Or it might be a whole lot of beautiful under-clothes. I won't look. I'll just feel around and try to guess what it is. I'll try to guess the colour as well, and exactly what it looks like. Also how much it cost."

She shut her eyes tight and slowly lifted off the lid. Then she put one hand down into the box. There was some tissue paper on top; she could feel it and hear it rustling. There was also an envelope or a card of some sort. She ignored this and began burrowing underneath the tissue paper, the fingers reaching out delicately, like tendrils.

"My God," she cried suddenly. "It can't be true!"

She opened her eyes wide and stared at the coat. Then she pounced on it and lifted it out of the box. Thick layers of fur made a lovely noise against the tissue paper as they unfolded, and when she held it up and saw it hanging to its full length, it was so beautiful it took her breath away.

Never had she seen mink like this before. It *was* mink, wasn't it? Yes, of course it was. But what a glorious colour! The fur was al-most pure black. At first she thought it *was* black; but when she held it closer to the window she saw that there was a touch of blue in it as well, a deep rich blue, like cobalt. Quickly she looked at the label. It said simply, WILD LABRADOR MINK. There was nothing else, no sign of where it had been bought or anything. But that, she told herself, was probably the Colonel's doing. The wily old fox was making darn sure he didn't leave any tracks. Good for him. But what in the world could it have cost? She hardly dared to think. Four, five, six thousand dollars? Possibly more.

She just couldn't take her eyes off it. Nor, for that matter, could she wait to try it on. Quickly she slipped off her own plain red coat. She was panting a little now, she couldn't help it, and her eyes were stretched very wide. But oh God, the feel of that fur! And those huge wide sleeves with their thick turned-up cuffs! Who was it had once told her that they always used female skins for the arms and male skins for the rest of the coat? Someone had told her that. Joan Rutfield, probably; though how *Joan* would know anything about *mink* she couldn't imagine.

The great black coat seemed to slide on to her almost of its own accord, like a second skin. Oh boy! It was the queerest feeling! She glanced into the mirror. It was fantastic. Her whole personality had suddenly changed completely. She looked dazzling, radiant, rich, brilliant, voluptuous, all at the same time. And the sense of power that it gave her! In this coat she could walk into any place she wanted and people would come scurrying around her like rabbits. The whole thing was just too wonderful for words!

Mrs. Bixby picked up the envelope that was still lying in the box. She opened it and pulled out the Colonel's letter:

I once heard you saying you were fond of mink so I got you this. I'm told it's a good one. Please accept it with my sincere good wishes as a parting gift. For my own personal reasons I shall not be able to see you anymore. Good-bye and good luck.

Well!

Imagine that!

Right out of the blue, just when she was feeling so happy.

No more Colonel.

What a dreadful shock.

She would miss him enormously.

Slowly, Mrs. Bixby began stroking the lovely soft black fur of the coat.

What you lose on the swings you get back on the roundabouts.

She smiled and folded the letter, meaning to tear it up and throw it out of the window, but in folding it she noticed that there was something written on the other side:

P.S. Just tell them that nice generous aunt of yours gave it to you for Christmas.

Mrs. Bixby's mouth, at that moment stretched wide in a silky smile, snapped back like a piece of elastic.

"The man must be mad!" she cried. "Aunt Maude doesn't have that sort of money. She couldn't possibly give me this."

But if Aunt Maude didn't give it to her, then who did?

Oh God! In the excitement of finding the coat and trying it on, she had completely overlooked this vital aspect.

In a couple of hours she would be in New York. Ten minutes after that she would be home, and the husband would be there to greet her; and even a man like Cyril, dwelling as he did in a dark phlegmy world of root canals, bicuspids, and caries, would start asking a few questions if his wife suddenly waltzed in from a week-end wearing a six-thousand-dollar mink coat.

You know what I think, she told herself. I think that goddamn Colonel has done this on purpose just to torture me. He knew perfectly well Aunt Maude didn't have enough money to buy this. He knew I wouldn't be able to keep it.

But the thought of parting with it now was more than Mrs. Bixby could bear.

"I've *got* to have this coat!" she said aloud. "I've got to have this coat! I've got to have this coat!"

Very well, my dear. You shall have the coat. But don't panic. Sit still and keep calm and start thinking. You're a clever girl, aren't you? You've fooled him before. The man never has been able to see much further than the end of his own probe, you know that. So just sit absolutely still and *think*. There's lots of time.

Two and a half hours later, Mrs. Bixby stepped off the train at Pennsylvania Station and walked quietly to the exit. She was wearing her old red coat again now and carrying the cardboard box in her arms. She signalled for a taxi.

"Driver," she said, "would you know of a pawnbroker that's still open around here?"

The man behind the wheel raised his brows and looked back at her, amused.

"Plenty along Sixth Avenue," he answered.

"Stop at the first one you see, then, will you please?" She got in and was driven away.

Soon the taxi pulled up outside a shop that had three brass balls hanging over the entrance.

"Wait for me, please," Mrs. Bixby said to the driver, and she got out of the taxi and entered the shop.

There was an enormous cat crouching on the counter eating fish-heads out of a white saucer. The animal looked up at Mrs. Bixby with bright yellow eyes, then looked away again and went on eating. Mrs. Bixby stood by the counter, as far away from the cat as possible, waiting for someone to come, staring at the watches, the shoe buckles, the enamel brooches, the old binoculars, the broken spectacles, the false teeth. Why did they always pawn their teeth, she wondered.

"Yes?" the proprietor said, emerging from a dark place in the back of the shop.

"Oh, good evening," Mrs. Bixby said. She began to untie the string around the box. The man went up to the cat and started stroking it along the top of its back, and the cat went on eating the fishheads.

"Isn't it silly of me?" Mrs. Bixby said. "I've gone and lost my pocket book, and this being Saturday, the banks are all closed until Monday and I've simply got to have some money for the weekend. This is quite a valuable coat, but I'm not asking much. I only want to borrow enough on it to tide me over till Monday. Then I'll come back and redeem it."

The man waited, and said nothing. But when she pulled out the mink and allowed the beautiful thick fur to fall over the counter, his eyebrows went up and he drew his hand away from the cat and came over to look at it. He picked it up and held it out in front of him.

"If only I had a watch on me or a ring," Mrs. Bixby said, "I'd give you that instead. But the fact is I don't have a thing with me other than this coat." She spread out her fingers for him to see.

"It looks new," the man said, fondling the soft fur.

"Oh yes, it is. But, as I said, I only want to borrow enough to tide me over till Monday. How about fifty dollars?"

"I'll loan you fifty dollars."

"It's worth a hundred times more than that, but I know you'll take good care of it until I return."

The man went over to a drawer and fetched a ticket and placed it on the counter. The ticket looked like one of those labels you tie on to the handle of your suitcase, the same shape and size exactly, and the same stiff brownish paper. But it was perforated across the middle so that you could tear it in two, and both halves were identical.

"Name?" he asked.

"Leave that out. And the address."

She saw the man pause, and she saw the nib of the pen hovering over the dotted line, waiting.

"You don't *have* to put the name and address, do you?"

The man shrugged and shook his head and the pen nib moved on down to the next line.

"It's just that I'd rather not," Mrs. Bixby said. "It's purely personal."

"You'd better not lose this ticket, then."

"I won't lose it."

"You realize that anyone who gets hold of it can come in and claim the article?"

"Yes, I know that."

"Simply on the number."

"Yes, I know."

"What do you want me to put for a description?"

"No description either, thank you. It's not necessary. Just put the amount I'm borrowing."

The pen nib hesitated again, hovering over the dotted line beside the word ARTICLE.

"I think you ought to put a description. A description is always a help if you want to sell the ticket. You never know, you might want to sell it sometime."

"I don't want to sell it."

"You might have to. Lots of people do."

"Look," Mrs. Bixby said. "I'm not broke, if that's what you mean. I simply lost my purse. Don't you understand?"

"You have it your own way then," the man said. "It's your coat."

At this point an unpleasant thought struck Mrs. Bixby. "Tell me something," she said. "If I don't have a description on my ticket, how can I be sure you'll give me back the coat and not something else when I return?"

"It goes in the books."

"But all I've got is a number. So actually you could hand me any old thing you wanted, isn't that so?"

"Do you want a description or don't you?" the man asked.

"No," she said. "I trust you."

The man wrote "fifty dollars" opposite the word VALUE on both sections of the ticket, then he tore it in half along the perforations and slid the lower portion across the counter. He took a wallet from the inside pocket of his jacket and extracted five ten-dollar bills. "The interest is three per cent a month," he said.

"Yes, all right. And thank you. You'll take good care of it, won't you?"

The man nodded but said nothing.

"Shall I put it back in the box for you?"

"No," the man said.

Mrs. Bixby turned and went out of the shop on to the street where the taxi was waiting. Ten minutes later, she was home.

"Darling," she said as she bent over and kissed her husband. "Did you miss me?"

Cyril Bixby laid down the evening paper and glanced at the watch on his wrist. "It's twelve and a half minutes past six," he said. "You're a bit late, aren't you?"

"I know. It's those dreadful trains. Aunt Maude sent you her love as usual. I'm dying for a drink, aren't you?"

The husband folded his newspaper into a neat rectangle and placed it on the arm of his chair. Then he stood up and crossed over to the sideboard. His wife remained in the centre of the room pulling off her gloves, watching him carefully, wondering how long she ought to wait. He had his back to her now, bending forward to measure the gin, putting his face right up close to the measurer and peering into it as though it were a patient's mouth.

It was funny how small he always looked after the Colonel. The Colonel was huge and bristly, and when you were near to him he smelled faintly of horseradish. This one was small and neat and bony and he didn't really smell of anything at all, except peppermint drops, which he sucked to keep his breath nice for the patients.

"See what I've bought for measuring the vermouth," he said, holding up a calibrated glass beaker. "I can get it to the nearest milligram with this."

"Darling, how clever."

I really must try to make him change the way he dresses, she told herself. His suits are just too ridiculous for words. There had been a time when she thought they were wonderful, those Edwardian jackets with high lapels and six buttons down the front, but now they merely seemed absurd. So did the narrow stovepipe trousers. You had to have a special sort of face to wear things like that, and Cyril just didn't have it. His was a long bony countenance with a narrow nose and a slightly prognathous jaw, and when you saw it coming up out of the top of one of those tightly fitting old-fashioned suits it looked like a caricature of Sam Weller. He probably thought it looked like Beau Brummel. It was a fact that in the office he invariably greeted female patients with his white coat unbuttoned so that they would catch a glimpse of the trappings underneath; and in some obscure way this was obviously meant to convey the impression that he was a bit of a dog. But Mrs. Bixby knew better. The plumage was a bluff. It meant nothing. It reminded her of an ageing peacock strutting on the lawn with only half its feathers left. Or one of those fatuous self-fertilizing flowers—like the dandelion. A dandelion never has to get fertilized for the setting of its seed, and all those brilliant yellow petals are just a waste of time, a boast, a masquerade. What's the word the biologists use? Subsexual. A dandelion is subsexual. So, for that matter, are the summer broods of water fleas. It sounds a bit like Lewis Carroll, she thought—water fleas and dandelions and dentists.

"Thank you, darling," she said, taking the martini and seating herself on the sofa with her handbag on her lap. "And what did *you* do last night?"

"I stayed on in the office and cast a few inlays. I also got my accounts up to date."

"Now really, Cyril, I think it's high time you let other people do your donkey work for you. You're much too important for that sort of thing. Why don't you give the inlays to the mechanic?"

"I prefer to do them myself. I'm extremely proud of my inlays."

"I know you are, darling, and I think they're absolutely wonderful. They're the best inlays in the whole world. But I don't want you to burn yourself out. And why doesn't that Pulteney woman do the accounts? That's part of her job, isn't it?"

"She does do them. But I have to price everything up first. She doesn't know who's rich and who isn't."

"This martini is perfect," Mrs. Bixby said, setting down her glass on the side table. "Quite perfect." She opened her bag and took out a handkerchief as if to blow her nose. "Oh look!" she cried, seeing the ticket. "I forgot to show you this! I found it just now on the seat of my taxi. It's got a number on it, and I thought it might be a lottery ticket or something, so I kept it."

She handed the small piece of stiff brown paper to her husband, who took it in his fingers and began examining it minutely from all angles, as though it were a suspect tooth.

"You know what this is?" he said slowly.

"No dear, I don't."

"It's a pawn ticket."

"A what?"

"A ticket from a pawnbroker. Here's the name and address of the shop—somewhere on Sixth Avenue."

"Oh dear, I *am* disappointed. I was hoping it might be a ticket for the Irish Sweep."

"There's no reason to be disappointed," Cyril Bixby said. "As a matter of fact this could be rather amusing."

"Why could it be amusing, darling?"

He began explaining to her exactly how a pawn ticket worked, with particular reference to the fact that anyone possessing the ticket was entitled to claim the article. She listened patiently until he had finished his lecture.

"You think it's worth claiming?" she asked.

"I think it's worth finding out what it is. You see this figure of fifty dollars that's written here? You know what that means?"

"No, dear, what does it mean?"

"It means that the item in question is almost certain to be something quite valuable."

"You mean it'll be worth fifty dollars?"

"More like five hundred."

"Five hundred!"

"Don't you understand?" he said. "A pawnbroker never gives you more than about a tenth of the real value."

"Good gracious! I never knew that."

"There's a lot of things you don't know, my dear. Now you listen to me. Seeing that there's no name and address of the owner . . ."

"But surely there's something to say who it belongs to?"

"Not a thing. People often do that. They don't want anyone to know they've been to a pawnbroker. They're ashamed of it."

"Then you think we can keep it?"

"Of course we can keep it. This is now *our* ticket."

"You mean *my* ticket," Mrs. Bixby said firmly. "I found it."

"My dear girl, what *does* it matter? The important thing is that we are now in a position to go and redeem it any time we like for only fifty dollars. How about that?"

"Oh, what fun!" she cried. "I think it's terribly exciting, especially when we don't even know what it is. It could be *anything*, isn't that right, Cyril? Absolutely anything!"

"It could indeed, although it's most likely to be either a ring or a watch."

"But wouldn't it be marvellous if it was a *real* treasure? I mean something *really* old, like a wonderful old vase or a Roman statue."

"There's no knowing what it might be, my dear. We shall just have to wait and see."

"I think it's absolutely fascinating! Give me the ticket and I'll rush over first thing Monday morning and find out!"

"I think I'd better do that."

"Oh no!" she cried. "Let *me* do it!"

"I think not. I'll pick it up on my way to work."

"But it's *my* ticket! *Please* let me do it, Cyril! Why should *you* have all the fun?"

"You don't know these pawnbrokers, my dear. You're liable to get cheated."

"I wouldn't get cheated, honestly I wouldn't. Give the ticket to me, please."

"Also you have to have fifty dollars," he said, smiling. "You have to pay out fifty dollars in cash before they'll give it to you."

"I've got that," she said. "I think."

"I'd rather you didn't handle it, if you don't mind."

"But Cyril, I *found* it. It's mine. Whatever it is, it's mine, isn't that right?"

"Of course it's yours, my dear. There's no need to get so worked up about it."

"I'm not. I'm just excited, that's all."

"I suppose it hasn't occurred to you that this might be something entirely masculine—a pocket watch, for example, or a set of shirt-studs. It isn't only women that go to pawnbrokers, you know."

"In that case I'll give it to you for Christmas," Mrs. Bixby said magnanimously. "I'll be delighted. But if it's a woman's thing, I want it myself. Is that agreed?"

"That sounds very fair. Why don't you come with me when I collect it?"

Mrs. Bixby was about to say yes to this, but caught herself just in time. She had no wish to be greeted like an old customer by the pawnbroker in her husband's presence.

"No," she said slowly. "I don't think I will. You see, it'll be even more thrilling if I stay behind and wait. Oh, I do hope it isn't going to be something that neither of us wants."

"You've got a point there," he said. "If I don't think it's worth fifty dollars, I won't even take it."

"But you said it would be worth five hundred."

"I'm quite sure it will. Don't worry."

"Oh, Cyril. I can hardly wait! Isn't it exciting?"

"It's amusing," he said, slipping the ticket into his waistcoat pocket. "There's no doubt about that."

Monday morning came at last, and after breakfast Mrs. Bixby followed her husband to the door and helped him on with his coat.

"Don't work too hard, darling," she said.

"No, all right."

"Home at six?"

"I hope so."

"Are you going to have time to go to that pawnbroker?" she asked.

"My God, I forgot all about it. I'll take a cab and go there now. It's on my way."

"You haven't lost the ticket, have you?"

"I hope not," he said, feeling in his waistcoat pocket. "No, here it is."

"And you have enough money?"

"Just about."

"Darling," she said, standing close to him and straightening his tie, which was perfectly straight. "If it happens to be something nice, something you think I might like, will you telephone me as soon as you get to the office?"

"If you want me to, yes."

"You know, I'm sort of hoping it'll be something for you, Cyril. I'd much rather it was for you than for me."

"That's very generous of you, my dear. Now I must run."

About an hour later, when the telephone rang, Mrs. Bixby was across the room so fast she had the receiver off the hook before the first ring had finished.

"I got it!" he said.

"You did! Oh, Cyril, what was it? Was it something good?"

"Good!" he cried. "It's fantastic! You wait till you get your eyes on this! You'll swoon!"

"Darling, what is it? Tell me quick!"

"You're a lucky girl, that's what you are."

"It's for me, then?"

"Of course it's for you. Though how in the world it ever got to be pawned for fifty dollars I'll be damned if I know. Someone's crazy."

"Cyril! Stop keeping me in suspense! I can't bear it!"

"You'll go mad when you see it."

"What is it?"

"Try to guess."

Mrs. Bixby paused. Be careful, she told herself. Be very careful now.

"A necklace," she said.

"Wrong."

"A diamond ring."

"You're not even warm. I'll give you a hint. It's something you can wear."

"Something I can wear? You mean like a hat?"

"No, it's not a hat," he said, laughing.

"For goodness' sake, Cyril! Why don't you tell me?"

"Because I want it to be a surprise. I'll bring it home with me this evening."

"You'll do nothing of the sort!" she cried. "I'm coming right down there to get it now!"

"I'd rather you didn't do that."

"Don't be so silly, darling. Why shouldn't I come?"

"Because I'm too busy. You'll disorganize my whole morning schedule. I'm half an hour behind already." ⸱

"Then I'll come in the lunch hour. All right?"

"I'm not having a lunch hour. Oh well, come at one-thirty then, while I'm having a sandwich. Good-bye."

At half past one precisely, Mrs. Bixby arrived at Mr. Bixby's place of business and rang the bell. Her husband, in his white dentist's coat, opened the door himself.

"Oh, Cyril, I'm so excited!"

"So you should be. You're a lucky girl, did you know that?" He led her down the passage and into the surgery.

"Go and have your lunch, Miss Pulteney," he said to the assistant, who was busy putting instruments into the sterilizer. "You can finish that when you come back." He waited until the girl had gone, then he walked over to a closet that he used for hanging up his clothes and stood in front of it, pointing with his finger. "It's in there," he said. "Now—shut your eyes."

Mrs. Bixby did as she was told. Then she took a deep breath and held it, and in the silence that followed she could hear him opening the cupboard door and there was a soft swishing sound as he pulled out a garment from among the other things hanging there.

"All right! You can look!"

"I don't dare to," she said, laughing.

"Go on. Take a peek."

Coyly, beginning to giggle, she raised one eyelid a fraction of an inch, just enough to give her a dark blurry view of the man standing there in his white overalls holding something up in the air.

"Mink!" he cried. "Real mink!"

At the sound of the magic word she opened her eyes quick, and at the same time she actually started forward in order to clasp the coat in her arms.

But there was no coat. There was only a ridiculous little fur neckpiece dangling from her husband's hand.

"Feast your eyes on that!" he said, waving it in front of her face.

Mrs. Bixby put a hand up to her mouth and started backing away. I'm going to scream, she told herself. I just know it. I'm going to scream.

"What's the matter, my dear? Don't you like it?" He stopped waving the fur and stood staring at her, waiting for her to say something.

"Why yes," she stammered. "I . . . I . . . think it's . . . it's lovely . . . really lovely."

"Quite took your breath away for a moment there, didn't it?"

"Yes, it did."

"Magnificent quality," he said. "Fine colour, too. You know something, my dear? I reckon a piece like this would cost you two or three hundred dollars at least if you had to buy it in a shop."

"I don't doubt it."

There were two skins, two narrow mangy-looking skins with their heads still on them and glass beads in their eye sockets and little paws hanging down. One of them had the rear end of the other in its mouth, biting it.

"Here," he said. "Try it on." He leaned forward and draped the thing around her neck, then stepped back to admire. "It's perfect. It really suits you. It isn't everyone who has mink, my dear."

"No, it isn't."

"Better leave it behind when you go shopping or they'll all think we're millionaires and start charging us double."

"I'll try to remember that, Cyril."

"I'm afraid you mustn't expect anything else for Christmas. Fifty dollars was rather more than I was going to spend anyway."

He turned away and went over to the basin and began washing his hands. "Run along now, my dear, and buy yourself a nice lunch. I'd take you out myself but I've got old man Gorman in the waiting room with a broken clasp on his denture."

Mrs. Bixby moved towards the door.

I'm going to kill that pawnbroker, she told herself. I'm going right back there to the shop this very minute and I'm going to throw this filthy neckpiece right in his face and if he refuses to give me back my coat I'm going to kill him.

"Did I tell you I was going to be late home tonight?" Cyril Bixby said, still washing his hands.

"No."

"It'll probably be at least eight-thirty the way things look at the moment. It may even be nine."

"Yes, all right. Good-bye." Mrs. Bixby went out, slamming the door behind her.

At that precise moment, Miss Pulteney, the secretary-assistant, came sailing past her down the corridor on her way to lunch.

"Isn't it a gorgeous day?" Miss Pulteney said as she went by, flashing a smile. There was a lilt in her walk, a little whiff of perfume attending her, and she looked like a queen, just exactly like a queen in the beautiful black mink coat that the Colonel had given to Mrs. Bixby.

As soon as George Cleaver had made his first million, he and Mrs. Cleaver moved out of their small suburban villa into an elegant London house. They acquired a French chef called Monsieur Estragon and an English butler called Tibbs, both wildly expensive. With the help of these two experts, the Cleavers set out to climb the social ladder and began to give dinner parties several times a week on a lavish scale.

But these dinners never seemed quite to come off. There was no animation, no spark to set the conversation alight, no style at all. Yet the food was superb and the service faultless.

"What the heck's wrong with our parties, Tibbs?" Mr. Cleaver said to the butler. "Why don't nobody never loosen up and let themselves go?"

Tibbs inclined his head to one side and looked at the ceiling. "I hope, sir, you will not be offended if I offer a small suggestion."

"What is it?"

"It's the wine, sir."

"What about the wine?"

"Well, sir, Monsieur Estragon serves superb food. Superb food should be accompanied by superb wine. But you serve them a cheap and very odious Spanish red."

"Then why in heaven's name didn't you say so before, you twit?" cried Mr. Cleaver. "I'm not short of money. I'll give them the best flipping wine in the world if that's what they want! What is the best wine in the world?"

"Claret, sir," the butler replied, "from the greatest *châteaux* in Bordeaux—Lafite, Latour, Haut-Brion, Margaux, Mouton-Rothschild and Cheval Blanc. And from only the very greatest vintage years, which are, in my opinion, 1906, 1914, 1929 and 1945. Cheval Blanc was also magnificent in 1895 and 1921, and Haut-Brion in 1906."

"Buy them all!" said Mr. Cleaver. "Fill the flipping cellar from top to bottom!"

"I can try, sir," the butler said. "But wines like these are extremely rare and cost a fortune."

"I don't give a hoot what they cost!" said Mr. Cleaver. "Just go out and get them!"

That was easier said than done. Nowhere in England or in France could Tibbs find any wine from 1895, 1906, 1914 or 1921. But he did manage to get hold of some twenty-nines and forty-fives. The bills for these wines were astronomical. They were in fact so huge that even Mr. Cleaver began to sit up and take notice. And his interest quickly turned into outright enthusiasm when the butler suggested to him that a knowledge of wine was a very considerable social asset. Mr. Cleaver bought books on the subject and read them from cover to cover. He also learned a great deal from Tibbs himself, who taught him, among other things, just how wine should be properly tasted. "First, sir, you sniff it long and deep, with your nose right inside the top of the glass, like this. Then you take a mouthful and you open your lips a tiny bit and suck in air, letting the air bubble through the wine. Watch me do it. Then you roll it vigorously around your mouth. And finally you swallow it."

In due course, Mr. Cleaver came to regard himself as an expert on wine, and inevitably he turned into a colossal bore. "Ladies and gentlemen," he would announce at dinner, holding up his glass, "this is a Margaux '29! The greatest year of the century! Fantastic bouquet! Smells of cowslips! And notice especially the aftertaste and how the tiny trace of tannin gives it that glorious astringent quality! Terrific, ain't it?"

The guests would nod and sip and mumble a few praises, but that was all.

"What's the matter with the silly twerps?" Mr. Cleaver said to Tibbs after this had gone on for some time. "Don't none of them appreciate a great wine?"

The butler laid his head to one side and gazed upward. "I think they *would* appreciate it, sir," he said, "if they were able to taste it. But they can't."

"What the heck d'you mean, they can't taste it?"

"I believe, sir, that you have instructed Monsieur Estragon to put liberal quantities of vinegar in the salad dressing."

"What's wrong with that? I like vinegar."

"Vinegar," the butler said, "is the enemy of wine. It destroys the palate. The dressing should be made of pure olive oil and a little lemon juice. Nothing else."

"Hogwash!" said Mr. Cleaver.

"As you wish, sir."

"I'll say it again, Tibbs. You're talking hogwash. The vinegar don't spoil my palate one bit."

"You are very fortunate, sir," the butler murmured, backing out of the room.

That night at dinner, the host began to mock his butler in front of the guests. "Mister Tibbs," he said, "has been trying to tell me I can't taste my wine if I put vinegar in the salad dressing. Right, Tibbs?"

"Yes, sir," Tibbs replied gravely.

"And I told him hogwash. Didn't I, Tibbs?"

"Yes, sir."

"This wine," Mr. Cleaver went on, raising his glass, "tastes to me exactly like a Château Lafite '45, and what's more it is a Château Lafite '45."

Tibbs, the butler, stood very still and erect near the sideboard, his face pale. "If you'll forgive me, sir," he said, "that is not a Lafite '45."

Mr. Cleaver swung round in his chair and stared at the butler. "What the heck d'you mean," he said. "There's the empty bottles beside you to prove it!"

These great clarets, being old and full of sediment, were always decanted by Tibbs before dinner. They were served in cut-glass decanters, while the empty bottles, as is the custom, were placed on the sideboard. Right now, two empty bottles of Lafite '45 were standing on the sideboard for all to see.

"The wine you are drinking, sir," the butler said quietly, "happens to be that cheap and rather odious Spanish red."

Mr. Cleaver looked at the wine in his glass, then at the butler. The blood was coming to his face now, his skin was turning scarlet. "You're lying, Tibbs!" he said.

"No sir, I'm not lying," the butler said. "As a matter of fact, I have never served you any other wine but Spanish red since I've been here. It seemed to suit you very well."

"I don't believe him!" Mr. Cleaver cried out to his guests. "The man's gone mad."

"Great wines," the butler said, "should be treated with reverence. It is bad enough to destroy the palate with three or four cocktails before dinner, as you people do, but when you slosh vinegar over your food into the bargain, then you might just as well be drinking dishwater."

Ten outraged faces around the table stared at the butler. He had caught them off balance. They were speechless.

"This," the butler said, reaching out and touching one of the empty bottles lovingly with his fingers, "this is the last of the forty-fives. The twenty-nines have already been finished. But they were glorious wines. Monsieur Estragon and I enjoyed them immensely."

The butler bowed and walked quite slowly from the room. He crossed the hall and went out of the front door of the house into the street where Monsieur Estragon was already loading their suitcases into the boot of the small car which they owned together.

It was getting on towards six o'clock so I thought I'd buy myself a beer and go out and sit in a deck chair by the swimming pool and have a little evening sun.

I went to the bar and got the beer and carried it outside and wandered down the garden towards the pool.

It was a fine garden with lawns and beds of azaleas and tall coconut palms, and the wind was blowing strongly through the tops of the palm trees, making the leaves hiss and crackle as though they were on fire. I could see the clusters of big brown nuts hanging down underneath the leaves.

There were plenty of deck chairs around the swimming pool and there were white tables and huge brightly coloured umbrellas and sunburned men and women sitting around in bathing suits. In the pool itself there were three or four girls and about a dozen boys, all splashing about and making a lot of noise and throwing a large rubber ball at one another.

I stood watching them. The girls were English girls from the hotel. The boys I didn't know about, but they sounded American, and

I thought they were probably naval cadets who'd come ashore from the U.S. naval training vessel which had arrived in harbour that morning.

I went over and sat down under a yellow umbrella where there were four empty seats, and I poured my beer and settled back comfortably with a cigarette.

It was very pleasant sitting there in the sunshine with beer and cigarette. It was pleasant to sit and watch the bathers splashing about in the green water.

The American sailors were getting on nicely with the English girls. They'd reached the stage where they were diving under the water and tipping them up by their legs.

Just then I noticed a small, oldish man walking briskly around the edge of the pool. He was immaculately dressed in a white suit and he walked very quickly with little bouncing strides, pushing himself high up on to his toes with each step. He had on a large creamy Panama hat, and he came bouncing along the side of the pool, looking at the people and the chairs.

He stopped beside me and smiled, showing two rows of very small, uneven teeth, slightly tarnished. I smiled back.

"Excuse pleess, but may I sit here?"

"Certainly," I said. "Go ahead."

He bobbed around to the back of the chair and inspected it for safety, then he sat down and crossed his legs. His white buckskin shoes had little holes punched all over them for ventilation.

"A fine evening," he said. "They are all evenings fine here in Jamaica." I couldn't tell if the accent were Italian or Spanish, but I felt fairly sure he was some sort of a South American. And old too, when you saw him close. Probably around sixty-eight or seventy.

"Yes," I said. "It is wonderful here, isn't it."

"And who, might I ask, are all dese? Dese is no hotel people." He was pointing at the bathers in the pool.

"I think they're American sailors," I told him. "They're Americans who are learning to be sailors."

"Of course dey are Americans. Who else in de world is going to make as much noise as dat? You are not American no?"

"No," I said. "I am not."

Suddenly one of the American cadets was standing in front of us. He was dripping wet from the pool and one of the English girls was standing there with him.

"Are these chairs taken?" he said.

"No," I answered.

"Mind if I sit down?"

"Go ahead."

"Thanks," he said. He had a towel in his hand and when he sat down he unrolled it and produced a pack of cigarettes and a lighter. He offered the cigarettes to the girl and she refused; then he offered them to me and I took one. The little man said, "Tank you, no, but I tink I have a cigar." He pulled out a crocodile case and got himself a cigar, then he produced a knife which had a small scissors in it and he snipped the end off the cigar.

"Here, let me give you a light." The American boy held up his lighter.

"Dat will not work in dis wind."

"Sure it'll work. It always works."

The little man removed his unlighted cigar from his mouth, cocked his head on one side and looked at the boy.

"*All*-ways?" he said slowly.

"Sure, it never fails. Not with me anyway."

The little man's head was still cocked over on one side and he was still watching the boy. "Well, well. So you say dis famous lighter it never fails. Iss dat you say?"

"Sure," the boy said. "That's right." He was about nineteen or twenty with a long freckled face and a rather sharp birdlike nose. His chest was not very sunburned and there were freckles there too, and a few wisps of pale-reddish hair. He was holding the lighter in his right hand, ready to flip the wheel. "It never fails," he said, smiling now because he was purposely exaggerating his little boast. "I promise you it never fails."

"One momint, pleess." The hand that held the cigar came up high, palm outward, as though it were stopping traffic. "Now juss one momint." He had a curiously soft, toneless voice and he kept looking at the boy all the time.

"Shall we not perhaps make a little bet on dat?" He smiled at the boy. "Shall we not make a little bet on whether your lighter lights?"

"Sure, I'll bet," the boy said. "Why not?"

"You like to bet?"

"Sure, I'll always bet."

The man paused and examined his cigar, and I must say I didn't much like the way he was behaving. It seemed he was already trying to make something out of this, and to embarrass the boy, and at the same time I had the feeling he was relishing a private little secret all his own.

He looked up again at the boy and said slowly, "I like to bet, too. Why we don't have a good bet on dis ting? A good big bet."

"Now wait a minute," the boy said. "I can't do that. But I'll bet you a quarter. I'll even bet you a dollar, or whatever it is over here—some shillings, I guess."

The little man waved his hand again. "Listen to me. Now we have some fun. We make a bet. Den we go up to my room here in de hotel where iss no wind and I bet you you cannot light dis famous lighter of yours ten times running without missing once."

"I'll bet I can," the boy said.

"All right. Good. We make a bet, yes?"

"Sure, I'll bet you a buck."

"No, no. I make you a very good bet. I am rich man and I am sporting man also. Listen to me. Outside de hotel iss my car. Iss very fine car. American car from your country. Cadillac —"

"Hey, now. Wait a minute." The boy leaned back in his deck chair and he laughed. "I can't put up that sort of property. This is crazy."

"Not crazy at all. You strike lighter successfully ten times running and Cadillac is yours. You like to have dis Cadillac, yes?"

"Sure, I'd like to have a Cadillac." The boy was still grinning.

"All right. Fine. We make a bet and I put up my Cadillac."

"And what do I put up?"

The little man carefully removed the red band from his still un-lighted cigar. "I never ask you, my friend, to bet something you cannot afford. You understand?"

"Then what do I bet?"

"I make it very easy for you, yes?"

"OK. You make it easy."

"Some small ting you can afford to give away, and if you did hap-pen to lose it you would not feel too bad. Right?"

"Such as what?"

"Such as, perhaps, de little finger on your left hand."

"My *what*?" The boy stopped grinning.

"Yes. Why not? You win, you take de car. You looss, I take de finger."

"I don't get it. How d'you mean, you take the finger?"

"I chop it off."

"Jumping jeepers! That's a crazy bet. I think I'll just make it a dollar."

The little man leaned back, spread out his hands palms upwards and gave a tiny contemptuous shrug of the shoulders, "Well, well, well," he said. "I do not understand. You say it lights but you will not bet. Den we forget it, yes?"

The boy sat quite still, staring at the bathers in the pool. Then he remembered suddenly he hadn't lighted his cigarette. He put it between his lips, cupped his hands around the lighter and flipped the wheel. The wick lighted and burned with a small, steady, yel-low flame and the way he held his hands the wind didn't get to it at all.

"Could I have a light, too?" I said.

"God, I'm sorry, I forgot you didn't have one."

I held out my hand for the lighter, but he stood up and came over to do it for me.

"Thank you," I said, and he returned to his seat.

"You having a good time?" I asked.

"Fine," he answered. "It's pretty nice here."

There was a silence then, and I could see that the little man had succeeded in disturbing the boy with his absurd proposal. He was sitting there very still, and it was obvious that a small tension was beginning to build up inside him. Then he started shifting about in his seat, and rubbing his chest, and stroking the back of his neck, and finally he placed both hands on his knees and began tap-tapping with his fingers against the kneecaps. Soon he was tapping with one of his feet as well.

"Now just let me check up on this bet of yours," he said at last. "You say we go up to your room and if I make this lighter light ten times running I win a Cadillac. If it misses just once then I forfeit the little finger of my left hand. Is that right?"

"Certainly. Dat is de bet. But I tink you are afraid."

"What do we do if I lose? Do I have to hold my finger out while you chop it off?"

"Oh, no! Dat would be no good. And you might be tempted to refuse to hold it out. What I should do I should tie one of your hands to de table before we started and I should stand dere with a knife ready to go *chop* de momint your lighter missed."

"What year is the Cadillac?" the boy asked.

"Excuse. I not understand."

"What year—how old is the Cadillac?"

"Ah! How old? Yes. It is last year. Quite new car. But I see you are not betting man. Americans never are."

The boy paused for just a moment and he glanced first at the English girl, then at me. "Yes," he said sharply. "I'll bet you."

"Good!" The little man clapped his hands together quietly, once. "Fine," he said. "We do it now. And you, sir," he turned to me, "you would perhaps be good enough to, what you call it, to—to referee." He had pale, almost colourless eyes with tiny bright black pupils.

"Well," I said. "I think it's a crazy bet. I don't think I like it very much."

"Nor do I," said the English girl. It was the first time she'd spoken. "I think it's a stupid, ridiculous bet."

"Are you serious about cutting off this boy's finger if he loses?" I said.

"Certainly I am. Also about giving him Cadillac if he win. Come now. We go to my room."

He stood up. "You like to put on some clothes first?" he said.

"No," the boy answered. "I'll come like this." Then he turned to me. "I'd consider it a favour if you'd come along and referee."

"All right," I said. "I'll come along, but I don't like the bet."

"You come too," he said to the girl. "You come and watch."

The little man led the way back through the garden to the hotel. He was animated now, and excited, and that seemed to make him bounce up higher than ever on his toes as he walked along.

"I live in annexe," he said. "You like to see car first? Iss just here."

He took us to where we could see the front driveway of the hotel and he stopped and pointed to a sleek pale-green Cadillac parked close by.

"Dere she iss. De green one. You like?"

"Say, that's a nice car," the boy said.

"All right. Now we go up and see if you can win her."

We followed him into the annexe and up one flight of stairs. He unlocked his door and we all trooped into what was a large pleasant double bedroom. There was a woman's dressing gown lying across the bottom of one of the beds.

"First," he said, "we 'ave a little martini."

The drinks were on a small table in the far corner, all ready to be mixed, and there was a shaker and ice and plenty of glasses. He began to make the martini, but meanwhile he'd rung the bell and now there was a knock on the door and a coloured maid came in.

"Ah!" he said, putting down the bottle of gin, taking a wallet from his pocket and pulling out a pound note. "You will do something for me now, pleess." He gave the maid the pound.

"You keep dat," he said. "And now we are going to play a little game in here and I want you to go off and find for me two—no tree tings. I want some nails, I want a hammer, and I want a chopping knife, a butcher's chopping knife which you can borrow from de kitchen. You can get, yes?"

"A *chopping knife!*" The maid opened her eyes wide and clasped her hands in front of her. "You mean a *real* chopping knife?"

"Yes, yes, of course. Come on now, pleess. You can find dose tings surely for me."

"Yes, sir, I'll try, sir. Surely I'll try to get them." And she went.

The little man handed round the martinis. We stood there and sipped them, the boy with the long freckled face and the pointed nose, bare-bodied except for a pair of faded brown bathing shorts; the English girl, a large-boned fair-haired girl wearing a pale blue bathing suit, who watched the boy over the top of her glass all the time; the little man with the colourless eyes standing there in his immaculate white suit drinking his martini and looking at the girl in her pale blue bathing dress. I didn't know what to make of it all. The man seemed serious about the bet and he seemed serious about the business of cutting off the finger. But hell, what if the boy lost? Then we'd have to rush him to the hospital in the Cadillac that he hadn't won. That would be a fine thing. Now wouldn't that be a really fine thing? It would be a damn silly unnecessary thing so far as I could see.

"Don't you think this is rather a silly bet?" I said.

"I think it's a fine bet," the boy answered. He had already downed one large martini.

"I think it's a stupid, ridiculous bet," the girl said. "What'll happen if you lose?"

"It won't matter. Come to think of it, I can't remember ever in my life having had any use for the little finger on my left hand. Here he is." The boy took hold of the finger. "Here he is and he hasn't ever done a thing for me yet. So why shouldn't I bet him? I think it's a fine bet."

The little man smiled and picked up the shaker and refilled our glasses.

"Before we begin," he said, "I will present to de—to de referee de key of de car." He produced a car key from his pocket and gave it to me. "De papers," he said, "de owning papers and insurance are in de pocket of de car."

Then the coloured maid came in again. In one hand she carried a small chopper, the kind used by butchers for chopping meat bones, and in the other a hammer and a bag of nails.

"Good! You get dem all. Tank you, tank you. Now you can go." He waited until the maid had closed the door, then he put the implements on one of the beds and said, "Now we prepare ourselves, yes?" And to the boy, "Help me, pleess, with dis table. We carry it out a little."

It was the usual kind of hotel writing desk, just a plain rectangular table about four feet by three with a blotting pad, ink, pens and paper. They carried it out into the room away from the wall, and removed the writing things.

"And now," he said, "a chair." He picked up a chair and placed it beside the table. He was very brisk and very animated, like a person organizing games at a children's party. "And now de nails. I must put in de nails." He fetched the nails and he began to hammer them into the top of the table.

We stood there, the boy, the girl, and I, holding Martinis in our hands, watching the little man at work. We watched him hammer two nails into the table, about six inches apart. He didn't hammer them right home; he allowed a small part of each one to stick up. Then he tested them for firmness with his fingers.

Anyone would think the son of a bitch had done this before, I told myself. He never hesitates. Table, nails, hammer, kitchen chopper. He knows exactly what he needs and how to arrange it.

"And now," he said, "all we want is some string." He found some string. "All right, at last we are ready. Will you pleess to sit here at de table?" he said to the boy.

The boy put his glass away and sat down.

"Now place de left hand between dese two nails. De nails are only so I can tie your hand in place. All right, good. Now I tie your hand secure to de table—so."

He wound the string around the boy's wrist, then several times around the wide part of the hand, then he fastened it tight to the nails. He made a good job of it and when he'd finished there wasn't any question about the boy being able to draw his hand away. But he could move his fingers.

"Now pleess, clench de fist, all except for de little finger. You must leave de little finger sticking out, lying on de table."

"*Ex*-cellent! *Ex*-cellent! Now we are ready. Wid your right hand you manipulate de lighter. But one moment, pleess."

He skipped over to the bed and picked up the chopper. He came back and stood beside the table with the chopper in his hand.

"We are all ready?" he said. "Mister referee, you must say to begin."

The English girl was standing there in her pale blue bathing costume right behind the boy's chair. She was just standing there, not saying anything. The boy was sitting quite still holding the lighter in his right hand, looking at the chopper. The little man was looking at me.

"Are you ready?" I asked the boy.

"I'm ready."

"And you?" to the little man.

"Quite ready," he said and he lifted the chopper up in the air and held it there about two feet above the boy's finger, ready to chop. The boy watched it, but didn't flinch and his mouth didn't move at all. He merely raised his eyebrows and frowned.

"All right," I said. "Go ahead."

The boy said, "Will you please count aloud the number of times I light it."

"Yes," I said. "I'll do that."

With his thumb he raised the top of the lighter, and again with the thumb he gave the wheel a sharp flick. The flint sparked and the wick caught fire and burned with a small yellow flame.

"One!" I called.

He didn't blow the flame out; he closed the top of the lighter on it and he waited for perhaps five seconds before opening it again.

He flicked the wheel very strongly and once more there was a small flame burning on the wick.

"Two!"

No one else said anything. The boy kept his eyes on the lighter. The little man held the chopper up in the air and he too was watching the lighter.

"Three!"

"Four!"

"Five!"

"Six!"

"Seven!" Obviously it was one of those lighters that worked. The flint gave a big spark and the wick was the right length. I watched the thumb snapping the top down on to the flame. Then a pause.

Then the thumb raising the top once more. This was an all-thumb operation. The thumb did everything. I took a breath, ready to say eight. The thumb flicked the wheel. The flint sparked. The little flame appeared.

"Eight!" I said, and as I said it the door opened. We all turned and we saw a woman standing in the doorway, a small, black-haired woman, rather old, who stood there for about two seconds then rushed forward, shouting, "Carlos! Carlos!" She grabbed his wrist, took the chopper from him, threw it on the bed, took hold of the little man by the lapels of his white suit and began shaking him very vigorously, talking to him fast and loud and fiercely all the time in some Spanish-sounding language. She shook him so fast you couldn't see him any more. He became a faint, misty, quickly moving outline, like the spokes of a turning wheel.

Then she slowed down and the little man came into view again and she hauled him across the room and pushed him backwards on to one of the beds. He sat on the edge of it blinking his eyes and testing his head to see if it would still turn on his neck.

"I am sorry," the woman said. "I am so terribly sorry that this should happen." She spoke almost perfect English.

"It is too bad," she went on. "I suppose it is really my fault. For ten minutes I leave him alone to go and have my hair washed and I come back and he is at it again." She looked sorry and deeply concerned.

The boy was untying his hand from the table. The English girl and I stood there and said nothing.

"He is a menace," the woman said. "Down where we live at home he has taken altogether forty-seven fingers from different people, and has lost eleven cars. In the end they threatened to have him put away somewhere. That's why I brought him up here."

"We were only having a little bet," mumbled the little man from the bed.

"I suppose he bet you a car," the woman said.

"Yes," the boy answered. "A Cadillac."

"He has no car. It's mine. And that makes it worse," she said, "that he should bet you when he has nothing to bet with. I am ashamed and very sorry about it all." She seemed an awfully nice woman.

"Well," I said, "then here's the key of your car." I put it on the table.

"We were only having a little bet," mumbled the little man.

"He hasn't anything left to bet with," the woman said. "He hasn't a thing in the world. Not a thing. As a matter of fact I myself won it all from him a long while ago. It took time, a lot of time, and it was hard work, but I won it all in the end." She looked up at the boy and she smiled, a slow sad smile, and she came over and put out a hand to take the key from the table.

I can see it now, that hand of hers; it had only one finger on it, and a thumb.

Billy Weaver had travelled down from London on the slow after-noon train, with a change at Swindon on the way, and by the time he got to Bath it was about nine o'clock in the evening and the moon was coming up out of a clear starry sky over the houses op-posite the station entrance. But the air was deadly cold and the wind was like a flat blade of ice on his cheeks.

"Excuse me," he said, "but is there a fairly cheap hotel not too far away from here?"

"Try The Bell and Dragon," the porter answered, pointing down the road. "They might take you in. It's about a quarter of a mile along on the other side."

Billy thanked him and picked up his suitcase and set out to walk the quarter-mile to The Bell and Dragon. He had never been to Bath before. He didn't know anyone who lived there. But Mr. Greenslade at the Head Office in London had told him it was a splendid city. "Find your own lodgings," he had said, "and then go along and report to the Branch Manager as soon as you've got your-self settled."

Billy was seventeen years old. He was wearing a new navy-blue overcoat, a new brown trilby hat, and a new brown suit, and he was feeling fine. He walked briskly down the street. He was trying to do everything briskly these days. Briskness, he had decided, was *the* one common characteristic of all successful businessmen. The big shots up at Head Office were absolutely fantastically brisk all the time. They were amazing.

There were no shops in this wide street that he was walking along, only a line of tall houses on each side, all of them identical. They had porches and pillars and four or five steps going up to their front doors, and it was obvious that once upon a time they had been very swanky residences. But now, even in the darkness, he could see that the paint was peeling from the woodwork on their doors and windows, and that the handsome white façades were cracked and blotchy from neglect.

Suddenly, in a downstairs window that was brilliantly illuminated by a street lamp not six yards away, Billy caught sight of a printed notice propped up against the glass in one of the upper panes. It said BED AND BREAKFAST. There was a vase of pussy willows, tall and beautiful, standing just underneath the notice.

He stopped walking. He moved a bit closer. Green curtains (some sort of velvety material) were hanging down on either side of the window. The pussy willows looked wonderful beside them. He went right up and peered through the glass into the room, and the first thing he saw was a bright fire burning in the hearth. On the carpet in front of the fire, a pretty little dachshund was curled up asleep with its nose tucked into its belly. The room itself, so far as he could see in the half-darkness, was filled with pleasant furniture.

There was a baby-grand piano and a big sofa and several plump armchairs; and in one corner he spotted a large parrot in a cage. Animals were usually a good sign in a place like this, Billy told himself; and all in all, it looked to him as though it would be a pretty decent house to stay in. Certainly it would be more comfortable than The Bell and Dragon.

On the other hand, a pub would be more congenial than a boardinghouse. There would be beer and darts in the evenings, and lots of people to talk to, and it would probably be a good bit cheaper, too. He had stayed a couple of nights in a pub once before and he had liked it. He had never stayed in any boardinghouses, and, to be perfectly honest, he was a tiny bit frightened of them. The name itself conjured up images of watery cabbage, rapacious landladies, and a powerful smell of kippers in the living room.

After dithering about like this in the cold for two or three minutes, Billy decided that he would walk on and take a look at The Bell and Dragon before making up his mind. He turned to go.

And now a queer thing happened to him. He was in the act of stepping back and turning away from the window when all at once his eye was caught and held in the most peculiar manner by the small notice that was there. BED AND BREAKFAST, it said. BED AND BREAKFAST, BED AND BREAKFAST, BED AND BREAKFAST. Each word was like a large black eye staring at him through the glass, holding him, compelling him, forcing him to stay where he was and not to walk away from that house, and the next thing he knew, he was actually moving across from the window to the front door of the house, climbing the steps that led up to it, and reaching for the bell.

He pressed the bell. Far away in a back room he heard it ringing, and then *at once*—it must have been at once because he hadn't even had time to take his finger from the bell button—the door swung open and a woman was standing there.

Normally you ring the bell and you have at least a half-minute's wait before the door opens. But this dame was like a jack-in-the-box. He pressed the bell—and out she popped! It made him jump.

She was about forty-five or fifty years old, and the moment she saw him, she gave him a warm welcoming smile.

"*Please* come in," she said pleasantly. She stepped aside, holding the door wide open, and Billy found himself automatically starting forward into the house. The compulsion or, more accurately, the desire to follow after her into that house was extraordinarily strong.

"I saw the notice in the window," he said, holding himself back.

"Yes, I know."

"I was wondering about a room."

"It's *all* ready for you, my dear," she said. She had a round pink face and very gentle blue eyes.

"I was on my way to The Bell and Dragon," Billy told her. "But the notice in your window just happened to catch my eye."

"My dear boy," she said, "why don't you come in out of the cold?"

"How much do you charge?"

"Five and sixpence a night, including breakfast."

It was fantastically cheap. It was less than half of what he had been willing to pay.

"If that is too much," she added, "then perhaps I can reduce it just a tiny bit. Do you desire an egg for breakfast? Eggs are expensive at the moment. It would be sixpence less without the egg."

"Five and sixpence is fine," he answered. "I should like very much to stay here."

"I knew you would. Do come in."

She seemed terribly nice. She looked exactly like the mother of one's best school-friend welcoming one into the house to stay for the Christmas holidays. Billy took off his hat, and stepped over the threshold.

"Just hang it there," she said, "and let me help you with your coat."

There were no other hats or coats in the hall. There were no umbrellas, no walking sticks—nothing.

"We have it *all* to ourselves," she said, smiling at him over her shoulder as she led the way upstairs. "You see, it isn't very often I have the pleasure of taki .g a visitor into my little nest."

The old girl is slightly dotty, Billy told himself. But at five and sixpence a night, who gives a damn about that? "I should've thought you'd be simply swamped with applicants," he said politely.

"Oh, I am, my dear, I am, of course I am. But the trouble is that I'm inclined to be just a teeny weeny bit choosey and particular—if you see what I mean."

"Ah, yes."

"But I'm always ready. Everything is always ready day and night in this house just on the off-chance that an acceptable young gentleman will come along. And it is such a pleasure, my dear, such a very great pleasure when now and again I open the door and I see someone standing there who is just *exactly* right." She was halfway up the stairs, and she paused with one hand on the stair rail, turning her head and smiling down at him with pale lips. "Like you," she added, and her blue eyes travelled slowly all the way down the length of Billy's body, to his feet, and then up again.

On the first-floor landing she said to him, "This floor is mine."

They climbed up a second flight. "And this one is *all* yours," she said. "Here's your room. I do hope you'll like it." She took him into a small but charming front bedroom, switching on the light as she went in.

"The morning sun comes right in the window, Mr. Perkins. It *is* Mr. Perkins, isn't it?"

"No," he said. "It's Weaver."

"Mr. Weaver. How nice. I've put a water bottle between the sheets to air them out, Mr. Weaver. It's such a comfort to have a hot water bottle in a strange bed with clean sheets, don't you agree? And you may light the gas fire at any time if you feel chilly."

"Thank you," Billy said. "Thank you ever so much." He noticed that the bedspread had been taken off the bed, and that the bedclothes had been neatly turned back on one side, all ready for someone to get in.

"I'm so glad you appeared," she said, looking earnestly into his face. "I was beginning to get worried."

"That's all right," Billy answered brightly. "You mustn't worry about me." He put his suitcase on the chair and started to open it.

"And what about supper, my dear? Did you manage to get anything to eat before you came here?"

"I'm not a bit hungry, thank you," he said. "I think I'll just go to bed as soon as possible because tomorrow I've got to get up rather early and report to the office."

"Very well, then. I'll leave you now so that you can unpack. But before you go to bed, would you be kind enough to pop into the sitting room on the ground floor and sign the book? Everyone has to do that because it's the law of the land, and we don't want to go breaking any laws at *this* stage in the proceedings, do we?" She gave him a little wave of the hand and went quickly out of the room and closed the door.

Now, the fact that his landlady appeared to be slightly off her rocker didn't worry Billy in the least. After all, she was not only harmless—there was no question about that—but she was also quite obviously a kind and generous soul. He guessed that she had probably lost a son in the war, or something like that, and had never got over it.

So a few minutes later, after unpacking his suitcase and washing his hands, he trotted downstairs to the ground floor and entered the living room. His landlady wasn't there, but the fire was glowing in the hearth, and the little dachshund was still sleeping in front of it. The room was wonderfully warm and cosy. I'm a lucky fellow, he thought, rubbing his hands. This is a bit of all right.

He found the guest book lying open on the piano, so he took out his pen and wrote down his name and address. There were only two other entries above his on the page, and, as one always does with guest books, he started to read them. One was a Christopher Mulholland from Cardiff. The other was Gregory W. Temple from Bristol.

That's funny, he thought suddenly. Christopher Mulholland. It rings a bell.

Now where on earth had he heard that rather unusual name before?

Was he a boy at school? No. Was it one of his sister's numerous young men, perhaps, or a friend of his father's? No, no, it wasn't any of those. He glanced down again at the book.

Christopher Mulholland	*231 Cathedral Road, Cardiff*
Gregory W. Temple	*27 Sycamore Drive, Bristol*

As a matter of fact, now he came to think of it, he wasn't at all sure that the second name didn't have almost as much of a familiar ring about it as the first.

"Gregory Temple?" he said aloud, searching his memory. "Christopher Mulholland? . . ."

"Such charming boys," a voice behind him answered, and he turned and saw his landlady sailing into the room with a large silver tea tray in her hands. She was holding it well out in front of her, and rather high up, as though the tray were a pair of reins on a frisky horse.

"They sound somehow familiar," he said.

"They do? How interesting."

"I'm almost positive I've heard those names before somewhere. Isn't that queer? Maybe it was in the newspapers. They weren't famous in any way, were they? I mean famous cricketers or footballers or something like that?"

"Famous," she said, setting the tea tray down on the low table in front of the sofa. "Oh no, I don't think they were famous. But they were extraordinarily handsome, both of them, I can promise you that. They were tall and young and handsome, my dear, just exactly like you."

Once more, Billy glanced down at the book. "Look here," he said, noticing the dates. "This last entry is over two years old."

"It is?"

"Yes, indeed. And Christopher Mulholland's is nearly a year before that—more than *three years* ago."

"Dear me," she said, shaking her head and heaving a dainty little sigh. "I would never have thought it. How time does fly away from us all, doesn't it, Mr. Wilkins?"

"It's Weaver," Billy said. "W-e-a-v-e-r."

"Oh, of course it is!" she cried, sitting down on the sofa. "How silly of me. I do apologize. In one ear and out the other, that's me, Mr. Weaver."

"You know something?" Billy said. "Something that's really quite extraordinary about all this?"

"No, dear, I don't."

"Well, you see—both of these names, Mulholland and Temple, I not only seem to remember each of them separately, so to speak, but somehow or other, in some peculiar way, they both appear to be sort of connected together as well. As though they were both famous for the same sort of thing, if you see what I mean—like . . . like Dempsey and Tunney, for example, or Churchill and Roosevelt."

"How amusing," she said. "But come over here now, dear, and sit down beside me on the sofa and I'll give you a nice cup of tea and a ginger biscuit before you go to bed."

"You really shouldn't bother," Billy said. "I didn't mean you to do anything like that." He stood by the piano, watching her as she fussed about with the cups and saucers. He noticed that she had small, white, quickly moving hands, and red fingernails.

"I'm almost positive it was in the newspapers I saw them," Billy said. "I'll think of it in a second. I'm sure I will."

There is nothing more tantalizing than a thing like this which lingers just outside the borders of one's memory. He hated to give up.

"Now wait a minute," he said. "Wait just a minute. Mulholland . . . Christopher Mulholland . . . wasn't *that* the name of the Eton schoolboy who was on a walking tour through the West Country, and then all of a sudden . . ."

"Milk?" she said. "And sugar?"

"Yes, please. And then all of a sudden . . ."

"Eton schoolboy?" she said. "Oh no, my dear, that can't possibly be right because *my* Mr. Mulholland was certainly not an Eton schoolboy when he came to me. He was a Cambridge undergraduate. Come over here now and sit next to me and warm yourself in front of this lovely fire. Come on. Your tea's all ready for you." She patted the empty place beside her on the sofa, and she sat there smiling at Billy and waiting for him to come over.

He crossed the room slowly, and sat down on the edge of the sofa. She placed his teacup on the table in front of him.

"*There* we are," she said. "How nice and cosy this is, isn't it?"

Billy started sipping his tea. She did the same. For half a minute or so, neither of them spoke. But Billy knew that she was looking at him. Her body was half-turned towards him, and he could feel her eyes resting on his face, watching him over the rim of her teacup. Now and again, he caught a whiff of a peculiar smell that seemed to emanate directly from her person. It was not in the least unpleasant, and it reminded him—well, he wasn't quite sure what it reminded him of. Pickled walnuts? New leather? Or was it the corridors of a hospital?

"Mr. Mulholland was a great one for his tea," she said at length. "Never in my life have I seen anyone drink as much tea as dear, sweet Mr. Mulholland."

"I suppose he left fairly recently," Billy said. He was still puzzling his head about the two names. He was positive now that he had seen them in the newspapers—in the headlines.

"Left?" she said, arching her brows. "But my dear boy, he never left. He's still here. Mr. Temple is also here. They're on the third floor, both of them together."

Billy set down his cup slowly on the table, and stared at his landlady. She smiled back at him, and then she put out one of her white hands and patted him comfortingly on the knee. "How old are you, my dear?" she asked.

"Seventeen."

"Seventeen!" she cried. "Oh, it's the perfect age! Mr. Mulholland was also seventeen. But I think he was a trifle shorter than you are, in fact I'm sure he was, and his teeth weren't *quite* so white. You have the most beautiful teeth, Mr. Weaver, did you know that?"

"They're not as good as they look," Billy said. "They've got simply masses of fillings in them at the back."

"Mr. Temple, of course, was a little older," she said, ignoring his remark. "He was actually twenty-eight. And yet I never would have guessed it if he hadn't told me, never in my whole life. There wasn't a *blemish* on his body."

"A what?" Billy said.

"His skin was *just* like a baby's."

There was a pause. Billy picked up his teacup and took another sip of his tea, then he set it down again gently in its saucer. He waited for her to say something else, but she seemed to have lapsed into another of her silences. He sat there staring straight ahead of him into the far corner of the room, biting his lower lip.

"That parrot," he said at last. "You know something? It had me completely fooled when I first saw it through the window from the street. I could have sworn it was alive."

"Alas, no longer."

"It's most terribly clever the way it's been done," he said. "It doesn't look in the least bit dead. Who did it?"

"I did."

"*You* did?"

"Of course," she said. "And have you met my little Basil as well?" She nodded towards the dachshund curled up so comfortably in front of the fire. Billy looked at it. And suddenly, he realized that this animal had all the time been just as silent and motionless as the parrot. He put out a hand and touched it gently on the top of its back. The back was hard and cold, and when he pushed the hair to one side with his fingers, he could see the skin underneath, greyish-black and dry and perfectly preserved.

"Good gracious me," he said. "How absolutely fascinating." He turned away from the dog and stared with deep admiration at the little woman beside him on the sofa. "It must be most awfully difficult to do a thing like that."

"Not in the least," she said. "I stuff *all* my little pets myself when they pass away. Will you have another cup of tea?"

"No, thank you," Billy said. The tea tasted faintly of bitter almonds, and he didn't much care for it.

"You did sign the book, didn't you?"

"Oh, yes."

"That's good. Because later on, if I happen to forget what you were called, then I can always come down here and look it up. I still do that almost every day with Mr. Mulholland and Mr. . . . Mr. . . . ."

"Temple," Billy said. "Gregory Temple. Excuse my asking, but haven't there been *any* other guests here except them in the last two or three years?"

Holding her teacup high in one hand, inclining her head slightly to the left, she looked up at him out of the corners of her eyes and gave him another gentle little smile.

"No, my dear," she said. "Only you."

Mr. Boggis was driving the car slowly, leaning back comfortably in the seat with one elbow resting on the sill of the open window. How beautiful the countryside, he thought; how pleasant to see a sign or two of summer once again. The primr.oses especially. And the hawthorn. The hawthorn was exploding white and pink and red along the hedges and the primr.oses were growing underneath in little clumps, and it was beautiful.

He took one hand off the wheel and lit himself a cigarette. The best thing now, he told himself, would be to make for the top of Brill Hill. He could see it about half a mile ahead. And that must be the village of Brill, that cluster of cottages among the trees right on the very summit. Excellent. Not many of his Sunday sections had a nice elevation like that to work from.

He drove up the hill and stopped the car just short of the summit on the outskirts of the village. Then he got out and looked around. Down below, the countryside was spread out before him like a huge green carpet. He could see for miles. It was perfect. He took a pad and pencil from his pocket, leaned against the back of the car, and allowed his practised eye to travel slowly over the landscape.

He could see one medium farmhouse over on the right, back in the fields, with a track leading to it from the road. There was another larger one beyond it. There was a house surrounded by tall elms that looked as though it might be a Queen Anne, and there were two likely farms away over on the left. Five places in all. That was about the lot in this direction.

Mr. Boggis drew a rough sketch on his pad showing the position of each so that he'd be able to find them easily when he was down below, then he got back into the car and drove up through the village to the other side of the hill. From there he spotted six more possibles—five farms and one big white Georgian house. He studied the Georgian house through his binoculars. It had a clean prosperous look, and the garden was well ordered. That was a pity. He ruled it out immediately. There was no point in calling on the prosperous.

In this square then, in this section, there were ten possibles in all. Ten was a nice number, Mr. Boggis told himself. Just the right amount for a leisurely afternoon's work. What time was it now? Twelve o'clock. He would have liked a pint of beer in the pub before he started, but on Sundays they didn't open until one. Very well, he would have it later. He glanced at the notes on his pad. He decided to take the Queen Anne first, the house with the elms. It had looked nicely dilapidated through the binoculars. The people there could probably do with some money. He was always lucky with Queen Annes, anyway. Mr. Boggis climbed back into the car, released the handbrake, and began cruising slowly down the hill without the engine.

Apart from the fact that he was at this moment disguised in the uniform of a clergyman, there was nothing very sinister about Mr. Cyril Boggis. By trade he was a dealer in antique furniture, with his own shop and showroom in the King's Road, Chelsea. His premises were not large, and generally he didn't do a great deal of business, but because he always bought cheap, very very cheap, and sold very very dear, he managed to make quite a tidy little income every year. He was a talented salesman, and when buying or selling a piece he could slide smoothly into whichever mood suited the client best. He could become grave and charming for the aged, obsequious for the rich, sober for the godly, masterful for the weak, mischievous for the widow, arch and saucy for the spinster. He was well aware of his gift, using it shamelessly on every possible occasion; and often, at the end of an unusually good performance, it was as much as he could do to prevent himself from turning aside and taking a bow or two as the thundering applause of the audience went rolling through the theatre.

In spite of this rather clownish quality of his, Mr. Boggis was not a fool. In fact, it was said of him by some that he probably knew as much about French, English, and Italian furniture as anyone else in London. He also had surprisingly good taste, and he was quick to recognize and reject an ungraceful design, however genuine the article might be. His real love, naturally, was for the work of the great eighteenth-century English designers, Ince, Mayhew, Chippendale, Robert Adam, Manwaring, Inigo Jones, Hepplewhite,

Kent, Johnson, George Smith, Lock, Sheraton, and the rest of them, but even with these he occasionally drew the line. He refused, for example, to allow a single piece from Chippendale's Chinese or Gothic period to come into his showroom, and the same was true of some of the heavier Italian designs of Robert Adam.

During the past few years, Mr. Boggis had achieved considerable fame among his friends in the trade by his ability to produce unusual and often quite rare items with astonishing regularity. Apparently the man had a source of supply that was almost inexhaustible, a sort of private warehouse, and it seemed that all he had to do was to drive out to it once a week and help himself. Whenever they asked him where he got the stuff, he would smile knowingly and wink and murmur something about a little secret.

The idea behind Mr. Boggis's little secret was a simple one, and it had come to him as a result of something that had happened on a certain Sunday afternoon nearly nine years before, while he was driving in the country.

He had gone out in the morning to visit his old mother, who lived in Sevenoaks, and on the way back the fanbelt on his car had broken, causing the engine to overheat and the water to boil away. He had got out of the car and walked to the nearest house, a smallish farm building about fifty yards off the road, and had asked the woman who answered the door if he could please have a jug of water.

While he was waiting for her to fetch it, he happened to glance in through the door to the living room, and there, not five yards from where he was standing, he spotted something that made him so excited the sweat began to come out all over the top of his head.

It was a large oak armchair of a type that he had only seen once before in his life. Each arm, as well as the panel at the back, was supported by a row of eight beautifully turned spindles. The back panel itself was decorated by an inlay of the most delicate floral design, and the head of a duck was carved to lie along half the length of either arm. Good God, he thought. This thing is late fifteenth century!

He poked his head in further through the door, and there, by heavens, was another of them on the other side of the fireplace!

He couldn't be sure, but two chairs like that must be worth at least a thousand pounds up in London. And oh, what beauties they were!

When the woman returned, Mr. Boggis introduced himself and straight away asked if she would like to sell her chairs.

Dear me, she said. But why on earth should she want to sell her chairs?

No reason at all, except that he might be willing to give her a pretty nice price.

And how much would he give? They were definitely not for sale, but just out of curiosity, just for fun, you know, how much would he give?

Thirty-five pounds.

How much?

Thirty-five pounds.

Dear me, thirty-five pounds. Well, well, that was very interesting. She'd always thought they were valuable. They were very old. They were very comfortable too. She couldn't possibly do without them, not possibly. No, they were not for sale but thank you very much all the same.

They weren't really so very old, Mr. Boggis told her, and they wouldn't be at all easy to sell, but it just happened that he had a client who rather liked that sort of thing. Maybe he could go up another two pounds—call it thirty-seven. How about that?

They bargained for half an hour, and of course in the end Mr. Boggis got the chairs and agreed to pay her something less than a twentieth of their value.

That evening, driving back to London in his old station wagon with the two fabulous chairs tucked away snugly in the back, Mr. Boggis had suddenly been struck by what seemed to him to be a most remarkable idea.

Look here, he said. If there is good stuff in one farmhouse, then why not in others? Why shouldn't he search for it? Why shouldn't he comb the countryside? He could do it on Sundays. In that way, it wouldn't interfere with his work at all. He never knew what to do with his Sundays.

So Mr. Boggis bought maps, large-scale maps of all the counties around London, and with a fine pen he divided each of them up into a series of squares. Each of these squares covered an actual area of five miles by five, which was about as much territory, he estimated, as he could cope with on a single Sunday, were he to comb it thoroughly. He didn't want the towns and the villages. It was the comparatively isolated places, the large farmhouses and the rather dilapidated country mansions, that he was looking for; and in this way, if he did one square each Sunday, fifty-two squares a year, he would gradually cover every farm and every country house in the home counties.

But obviously there was a bit more to it than that. Country folk are a suspicious lot. So are the impoverished rich. You can't go about ringing their bells and expecting them to show you around their houses just for the asking, because they won't do it. That way you would never get beyond the front door. How then was he to gain admittance? Perhaps it would be best if he didn't let them know he was a dealer at all. He could be the telephone man, the plumber, the gas inspector. He could even be a clergyman . . .

From this point on, the whole scheme began to take on a more practical aspect. Mr. Boggis ordered a large quantity of superior cards on which the following legend was engraved:

THE REVEREND
CYRIL WINNINGTON BOGGIS

President of the Society	*In association with*
for the Preservation of	*The Victoria and*
Rare Furniture	*Albert Museum*

From now on, every Sunday, he was going to be a nice old parson spending his holiday travelling around on a labour of love for the "Society," compiling an inventory of the treasures that lay hidden in the country homes of England. And who in the world was going to kick him out when they heard that one?

Nobody.

And then, once he was inside, if he happened to spot something he really wanted, well—he knew a hundred different ways of dealing with that.

Rather to Mr. Boggis's surprise, the scheme worked. In fact, the friendliness with which he was received in one house after another through the countryside was, in the beginning, quite embarrassing, even to him. A slice of cold pie, a glass of port, a cup of tea, a basket of plums, even a full sit-down Sunday dinner with the family, such things were constantly being pressed upon him. Sooner or later, of course, there had been some bad moments and a number of unpleasant incidents, but then nine years is more than four hundred Sundays, and that adds up to a great quantity of houses visited. All in all, it had been an interesting, exciting, and lucrative business.

And now it was another Sunday and Mr. Boggis was operating in the country of Buckinghamshire, in one of the most northerly squares on his map, about ten miles from Oxford, and as he drove down the hill and headed for his first house, the dilapidated Queen Anne, he began to get the feeling that this was going to be one of his lucky days.

He parked the car about a hundred yards from the gates and got out to walk the rest of the way. He never liked people to see his car until after a deal was completed. A dear old clergyman and a large station wagon somehow never seemed quite right together. Also the short walk gave him time to examine the property closely from the outside and to assume the mood most likely to be suitable for the occasion.

Mr. Boggis strode briskly up the drive. He was a small fat-legged man with a belly. The face was round and rosy, quite perfect for the part, and the two large brown eyes that bulged out at you from this rosy face gave an impression of gentle imbecility. He was dressed in a black suit with the usual parson's dog-collar round his neck, and on his head a soft black hat. He carried an old oak walking stick which lent him, in his opinion, a rather rustic easygoing air.

He approached the front door and rang the bell. He heard the sound of footsteps in the hall and the door opened and suddenly there stood before him, or rather above him, a gigantic woman dressed in riding breeches. Even through the smoke of her cigarette he could smell the powerful odour of stables and horse manure that clung about her.

"Yes?" she asked, looking at him suspiciously. "What is it you want?"

Mr. Boggis, who half expected her to whinny any moment, raised his hat, made a little bow, and handed her his card. "I do apologize for bothering you," he said, and then he waited, watching her face as she read the message.

"I don't understand," she said, handing back the card. "What is it you want?"

Mr. Boggis explained about the Society for the Preservation of Rare Furniture.

"This wouldn't by any chance be something to do with the Socialist Party?" she asked, staring at him fiercely from under a pair of pale bushy brows.

From then on, it was easy. A Tory in riding breeches, male or female, was always a sitting duck for Mr. Boggis. He spent two minutes delivering an impassioned eulogy on the extreme Right Wing of the Conservative Party, then two more denouncing the Socialists.

As a clincher, he made particular reference to the bill that the Socialists had once introduced for the abolition of bloodsports in the country, and went on to inform his listener that his idea of heaven—"though you better not tell the bishop, my dear"—was a place where one could hunt the fox, the stag, and the hare with large packs of tireless hounds from morn till night every day of the week, including Sundays.

Watching her as he spoke, he could see the magic beginning to do its work. The woman was grinning now, showing Mr. Boggis a set of enormous, slightly yellow teeth. "Madam," he cried, "I beg of you, *please* don't get me started on Socialism." At that point, she let out a great guffaw of laughter, raised an enormous red hand, and slapped him so hard on the shoulder that he nearly went over.

"Come in!" she shouted. "I don't know what the hell you want, but come on in!"

Unfortunately, and rather surprisingly, there was nothing of any value in the whole house, and Mr. Boggis, who never wasted time on barren territory, soon made his excuses and took his leave. The whole visit had taken less than fifteen minutes, and that, he told himself as he climbed back into his car and started off for the next place, was exactly as it should be.

From now on, it was all farmhouses, and the nearest was about half a mile up the road. It was a large half-timbered brick building of considerable age, and there was a magnificent pear tree still in blossom covering almost the whole of the south wall.

Mr. Boggis knocked on the door. He waited, but no one came. He knocked again, but still there was no answer, so he wandered around the back to look for the farmer among the cowsheds. There was no one there either. He guessed that they must all still be in church, so he began peering in the windows to see if he could spot anything interesting. There was nothing in the dining room. Nothing in the library either. He tried the next window, the living room, and there, right under his nose, in the little alcove that the window made, he saw a beautiful thing, a semicircular cardtable in mahogany, richly veneered, and in the style of Hepplewhite, built around 1780.

"Ah-ha," he said aloud, pressing his face hard against the glass. "Well done, Boggis."

But that was not all. There was a chair there as well, a single chair, and if he were not mistaken it was of an even finer quality than the table. Another Hepplewhite, wasn't it? And oh, what a beauty! The lattices on the back were finely carved with the honeysuckle, the husk, and the paterae, the caning on the seat was original, the legs were very gracefully turned and the two back ones had that peculiar outward splay that meant so much. It was an exquisite chair. "Before this day is done," Mr. Boggis said softly, "I shall have the pleasure of sitting down upon that lovely seat." He never bought a chair without doing this. It was a favourite test of his, and it was always an intriguing sight to see him lowering himself delicately into the seat, waiting for the "give," expertly gauging the precise but infinitesimal degree of shrinkage that the years had caused in the mortice and dovetail joints.

But there was no hurry, he told himself. He would return here later. He had the whole afternoon before him.

The next farm was situated some way back in the fields, and in order to keep his car out of sight, Mr. Boggis had to leave it on the road and walk about six hundred yards along a straight track that led directly into the back yard of the farmhouse. This place, he noticed as he approached, was a good deal smaller than the last, and he didn't hold out much hope for it. It looked rambling and dirty, and some of the sheds were clearly in bad repair.

There were three men standing in a close group in a corner of the yard, and one of them had two large black greyhounds with him, on leashes. When the men caught sight of Mr. Boggis walking forward in his black suit and parson's collar, they stopped talking and seemed suddenly to stiffen and freeze, becoming absolutely still, motionless, three faces turned towards him, watching him suspiciously as he approached.

The oldest of the three was a stumpy man with a wide frog-mouth and small shifty eyes, and although Mr. Boggis didn't know it, his name was Rummins and he was the owner of the farm.

The tall youth beside him, who appeared to have something wrong with one eye, was Bert, the son of Rummins.

The shortish flat-faced man with a narrow corrugated brow and immensely broad shoulders was Claud. Claud had dropped in on Rummins in the hope of getting a piece of pork or ham out of him from the pig that had been killed the day before. Claud knew about the killing—the noise of it had carried far across the fields—and he also knew that a man should have a government permit to do that sort of thing, and that Rummins didn't have one.

"Good afternoon," Mr. Boggis said. "Isn't it a lovely day?"

None of the three men moved. At that moment they were all thinking precisely the same thing—that somehow or other this clergyman, who was certainly not the local fellow, had been sent to poke his nose into their business and to report what he found to the government.

"What beautiful dogs," Mr. Boggis said. "I must say I've never been greyhound-racing myself, but they tell me it's a fascinating sport."

Again the silence, and Mr. Boggis glanced quickly from Rummins to Bert, then to Claud, then back again to Rummins, and he noticed that each of them had the same peculiar expression on his face, something between a jeer and a challenge, with a contemptuous curl to the mouth and a sneer around the nose.

"Might I enquire if you are the owner?" Mr. Boggis asked, undaunted, addressing himself to Rummins.

"What is it you want?"

"I do apologize for troubling you, especially on a Sunday."

Mr. Boggis offered his card and Rummins took it and held it up close to his face. The other two didn't move, but their eyes swivelled over to one side, trying to see.

"And what exactly might you be wanting?" Rummins asked.

For the second time that morning, Mr. Boggis explained at some length the aims and ideals of the Society for the Preservation of Rare Furniture.

"We don't have any," Rummins told him when it was over. "You're wasting your time."

"Now, just a minute, sir," Mr. Boggis said, raising a finger. "The last man who said that to me was an old farmer down in Sussex, and when he finally let me into his house, d'you know what I found? A dirty-looking old chair in the corner of the kitchen, and it turned out to be worth *four hundred pounds*! I showed him how to sell it, and he bought himself a new tractor with the money."

"What on earth are you talking about?" Claud said. "There ain't no chair in the world worth four hundred pound."

"Excuse me," Mr. Boggis answered primly, "but there are plenty of chairs in England worth more than twice that figure. And you know where they are? They're tucked away in the farms and cottages all over the country, with the owners using them as steps and ladders and standing on them with hobnailed boots to reach a pot of jam out of the top cupboard or to hang a picture. This is the truth I'm telling you, my friends."

Rummins shifted uneasily on his feet. "You mean to say all you want to do is go inside and stand there in the middle of the room and look around?"

"Exactly," Mr. Boggis said. He was at last beginning to sense what the trouble might be. "I don't want to pry into your cupboards or into your larder. I just want to look at the furniture to see if you happen to have any treasures here, and then I can write about them in our Society magazine."

"You know what I think?" Rummins said, fixing him with his small wicked eyes. "I think you're after buying the stuff yourself. Why else would you be going to all this trouble?"

"Oh, dear me. I only wish I had the money. Of course, if I saw something that I took a great fancy to, and it wasn't beyond my means, I might be tempted to make an offer. But alas, that rarely happens."

"Well," Rummins said, "I don't suppose there's any harm in your taking a look around if that's all you want." He led the way across the yard to the back door of the farmhouse, and Mr. Boggis followed him; so did the son Bert, and Claud with his two dogs. They went through the kitchen, where the only furniture was a cheap deal table with a dead chicken lying on it, and they emerged into a fairly large, exceedingly filthy living room.

And there it was! Mr. Boggis saw it at once, and he stopped dead in his tracks and gave a little shrill gasp of shock. Then he stood there for five, ten, fifteen seconds at least, staring like an idiot, unable to believe, not daring to believe what he saw before him. It *couldn't* be true, not possibly! But the longer he stared, the more true it began to seem. After all, there it was standing against the wall right in front of him, as real and as solid as the house itself. And who in the world could possibly make a mistake about a thing like that? Admittedly it was painted white, but that made not the slightest difference. Some idiot had done that. The paint could easily be stripped off. But good God! Just look at it! And in a place like this!

At this point, Mr. Boggis became aware of the three men, Rummins, Bert, and Claud, standing together in a group over by the fireplace, watching him intently. They had seen him stop and gasp and stare, and they must have seen his face turning red, or maybe it was white, but in any event they had seen enough to spoil the whole goddamn business if he didn't do something about it quick. In a flash, Mr. Boggis clapped one hand over his heart, staggered to the nearest chair, and collapsed into it, breathing heavily.

"What's the matter with you?" Claud asked.

"It's nothing," he gasped. "I'll be all right in a minute. Please—a glass of water. It's my heart."

Bert fetched him the water, handed it to him, and stayed close beside him, staring down at him with a fatuous leer on his face.

"I thought maybe you were looking at something," Rummins said. The wide frog-mouth widened a fraction further into a crafty grin, showing the stubs of several broken teeth.

"No, no," Mr. Boggis said. "Oh dear me, no. It's just my heart. I'm so sorry. It happens every now and then. But it goes away quite quickly. I'll be all right in a couple of minutes."

He *must* have time to think, he told himself. More important still, he must have time to compose himself thoroughly before he said another word. Take it gently, Boggis. And whatever you do, keep calm. These people may be ignorant, but they are not stupid. They are suspicious and wary and sly. And if it is really true—no it *can't* be, it *can't* be true . . .

He was holding one hand up over his eyes in a gesture of pain, and now, very carefully, secretly, he made a little crack between two of the fingers and peeked through.

Sure enough, the thing was still there, and on this occasion he took a good long look at it. Yes—he had been right the first time! There wasn't the slightest doubt about it! It was really unbelievable!

What he saw was a piece of furniture that any expert would have given almost anything to acquire. To a layman, it might not have appeared particularly impressive, especially when covered over as it was with dirty white paint, but to Mr. Boggis it was a dealer's dream. He knew, as does every other dealer in Europe and America, that among the most celebrated and coveted examples of eighteenth-century English furniture in existence are the three famous pieces known as "The Chippendale Commodes." He knew their history backwards—that the first was "discovered" in 1920, in a house at Moreton-in-Marsh, and was sold at Sotheby's the same year; that the other two turned up in the same auction rooms a year later, both coming out of Raynham Hall, Norfolk. They all fetched enormous prices. He couldn't quite remember the exact figure for the first one, or even the second, but he knew for certain that the last one to be sold had fetched thirty-nine hundred guineas. And that was in 1921! Today the same piece would surely be worth ten thousand pounds. Some man, Mr. Boggis couldn't remember his name, had made a study of these commodes fairly recently and had proved that all three must have come from the same workshop, for the veneers were all from the same log, and the same set of templates had been used in the construction of each. No invoices had been found for any of them, but all the experts were agreed that these three commodes could have been executed only by Thomas Chippendale himself, with his own hands, at the most exalted period in his career.

And here, Mr. Boggis kept telling himself as he peered cautiously through the crack in his fingers, here was the fourth Chippendale Commode! And *he* had found it! He would be rich! He would also be famous! Each of the other three was known throughout the furniture world by a special name—The Chastleton Commode, The First Raynham Commode, The Second Raynham Commode. This one would go down in history as The Boggis Commode! Just imagine the faces of the boys up there in London when they got a look at it tomorrow morning! And the luscious offers coming in from the big fellows over in the West End—Frank Partridge, Mallet, Jetley, and the rest of them! There would be a picture of it in *The Times*, and it would say, "The very fine Chippendale Commode which was recently discovered by Mr. Cyril

Boggis, a London dealer . . ." Dear God, what a stir he was going to make!

This one here, Mr. Boggis thought, was almost exactly similar to the Second Raynham Commode. (All three, the Chastleton and the two Raynhams, differed from one another in a number of small ways.) It was a most impressive handsome affair, built in the French rococo style of Chippendale's Directoire period, a kind of large fat chest of drawers set upon four carved and fluted legs that raised it about a foot from the ground. There were six drawers in all, two long ones in the middle and two shorter ones on either side. The serpentine front was magnificently ornamented along the top and sides and bottom, and also vertically between each set of drawers, with intricate carvings of festoons and scrolls and clusters. The brass handles, although partly obscured by white paint, appeared to be superb. It was, of course, a rather "heavy" piece, but the design had been executed with such elegance and grace that the heaviness was in no way offensive.

"How're you feeling now?" Mr. Boggis heard someone saying.

"Thank you, thank you, I'm much better already. It passes quickly. My doctor says it's nothing to worry about really so long as I rest for a few minutes whenever it happens. Ah yes," he said, raising himself slowly to his feet. "That's better. I'm all right now."

A trifle unsteadily, he began to move around the room examining the furniture, one piece at a time, commenting upon it briefly. He could see at once that apart from the commode it was a very poor lot.

"Nice oak table," he said. "But I'm afraid it's not old enough to be of any interest. Good comfortable chairs, but quite modern, yes, quite modern. Now this cupboard, well, it's rather attractive, but again, not valuable. This chest of drawers"—he walked casually past the Chippendale Commode and gave it a little contemptuous flip with his fingers—"worth a few pounds, I dare say, but no more. A rather crude reproduction, I'm afraid. Probably made in Victorian times. Did you paint it white?"

"Yes," Rummins said, "Bert did it."

"A very wise move. It's considerably less offensive in white."

"That's a strong piece of furniture," Rummins said. "Some nice carving on it too."

"Machine-carved," Mr. Boggis answered superbly, bending down to examine the exquisite craftsmanship. "You can tell it a mile off. But still, I suppose it's quite pretty in its way. It has its points."

He began to saunter off, then he checked himself and turned slowly back again. He placed the tip of one finger against the point of his chin, laid his head over to one side, and frowned as though deep in thought.

"You know what?" he said, looking at the commode, speaking so casually that his voice kept trailing off. "I've just remembered . . . I've been wanting a set of legs something like that for a long time. I've got a rather curious table in my own little home, one of those low things that people put in front of the sofa, sort of a coffee-table, and last Michaelmas, when I moved house, the foolish movers damaged the legs in the most shocking way. I'm very fond of that table. I always keep my big Bible on it, and all my sermon notes."

He paused, stroking his chin with the finger. "Now I was just thinking. These legs on your chest of drawers might be very suitable. Yes, they might indeed. They could easily be cut off and fixed on to my table."

He looked around and saw the three men standing absolutely still, watching him suspiciously, three pairs of eyes, all different but equally mistrusting, small pig-eyes for Rummins, large slow eyes for Claud, and two odd eyes for Bert, one of them very queer and boiled and misty pale, with a little black dot in the centre, like a fish eye on a plate.

Mr. Boggis smiled and shook his head. "Come, come, what on earth am I saying? I'm talking as though I owned the piece myself. I do apologize."

"What you mean to say is you'd like to buy it," Rummins said.

"Well . . ." Mr. Boggis glanced back at the commode, frowning. "I'm not sure. I might . . . and then again . . . on second thoughts . . . no . . . I think it might be a bit too much trouble. It's not worth it. I'd better leave it."

"How much were you thinking of offering?" Rummins asked.

"Not much, I'm afraid. You see, this is not a genuine antique. It's merely a reproduction."

"I'm not so sure about that," Rummins told him. "It's been in *here* over twenty years, and before that it was up at the Manor House. I bought it there myself at auction when the old Squire died. You can't tell me that thing's new."

"It's not exactly new, but it's certainly not more than about sixty years old."

"It's more than that," Rummins said. "Bert, where's that bit of paper you once found at the back of one of them drawers? That old bill."

The boy looked vacantly at his father.

Mr. Boggis opened his mouth, then quickly shut it again without uttering a sound. He was beginning literally to shake with excitement, and to calm himself he walked over to the window and stared out at a plump brown hen pecking around for stray grains of corn in the yard.

"It was in the back of that drawer underneath all them rabbit-snares," Rummins was saying. "Go on and fetch it out and show it to the parson."

When Bert went forward to the commode, Mr. Boggis turned round again. He couldn't stand not watching him. He saw him pull out one of the big middle drawers, and he noticed the beautiful way in which the drawer slid open. He saw Bert's hand dipping inside and rummaging around among a lot of wires and strings.

"You mean this?" Bert lifted out a piece of folded yellowing paper and carried it over to the father, who unfolded it and held it up close to his face.

"You can't tell me this writing ain't bloody old," Rummins said, and he held the paper out to Mr. Boggis, whose whole arm was shaking as he took it. It was brittle and it cracked slightly between his fingers. The writing was in a long sloping copperplate hand:

Edward Montagu, Esq.   Dr.

To Thos. Chippendale

A large mahogany Commode Table of exceeding fine wood, very rich carvd, set upon fluted legs, two very neat shapd long drawers in the middle part and two ditto on each side, with rich chasd Brass Handles and Ornaments, the whole completely finished in the most exquisite taste   £87

Mr. Boggis was holding on to himself tight and fighting to suppress the excitement that was spinning round inside him and making him dizzy. Oh God, it was wonderful! With the invoice, the value had climbed even higher. What in heaven's name would it fetch now? Twelve thousand pounds? Fourteen? Maybe fifteen or even twenty? Who knows?

Oh, boy!

He tossed the paper contemptuously on to the table and said quietly, "It's exactly what I told you, a Victorian reproduction. This is simply the invoice that the seller—the man who made it and passed it off as an antique—gave to his client. I've seen lots of them. You'll notice that he doesn't say he made it himself. That would give the game away."

"Say what you like," Rummins announced, "but that's an old piece of paper."

"Of course it is, my dear friend. It's Victorian, late Victorian. About eighteen ninety. Sixty or seventy years old. I've seen hundreds of them. That was a time when masses of cabinet-makers did nothing else but apply themselves to faking the fine furniture of the century before."

"Listen, Parson," Rummins said, pointing at him with a thick dirty finger, "I'm not saying as how you may not know a fair bit about this furniture business, but what I *am* saying is this: How on earth can you be so mighty sure it's a fake when you haven't even seen what it looks like underneath all that paint?"

"Come here," Mr. Boggis said. "Come over here and I'll show you." He stood beside the commode and waited for them to gather round. "Now, anyone got a knife?"

Claud produced a horn-handled pocket knife, and Mr. Boggis took it and opened the smallest blade. Then, working with apparent casualness but actually with extreme care, he began chipping off the white paint from a small area on the top of the commode. The paint flaked away cleanly from the old hard varnish underneath, and when he had cleared away about three square inches, he stepped back and said, "Now, take a look at that!"

It was beautiful—a warm little patch of mahogany, glowing like a topaz, rich and dark with the true colour of its two hundred years.

"What's wrong with it?" Rummins asked.

"It's processed! Anyone can see that!"

"How can you see it, Mister? You tell us."

"Well, I must say that's a trifle difficult to explain. It's chiefly a matter of experience. My experience tells me that without the slightest doubt this wood has been processed with lime. That's what they use for mahogany, to give it that dark aged colour. For oak, they use potash salts, and for walnut it's nitric acid, but for mahogany it's always lime."

The three men moved a little closer to peer at the wood. There was a slight stirring of interest among them now. It was always intriguing to hear about some new form of crookery or deception.

"Look closely at the grain. You see that touch of orange in among the dark red-brown. That's the sign of lime."

They leaned forward, their noses close to the wood, first Rummins, then Claud, then Bert.

"And then there's the patina," Mr. Boggis continued.

"The what?"

He explained to them the meaning of this word as applied to furniture.

"My dear friends, you've no idea the trouble these rascals will go to to imitate the hard beautiful bronze-like appearance of genuine patina. It's terrible, really terrible, and it makes me quite sick to speak of it!" He was spitting each word sharply off the tip of the tongue and making a sour mouth to show his extreme distaste. The men waited, hoping for more secrets.

"The time and trouble that some mortals will go to in order to deceive the innocent!" Mr. Boggis cried. "It's perfectly disgusting! D'you know what they did here, my friends? I can recognize it clearly. I can almost *see* them doing it, the long, complicated ritual of rubbing the wood with linseed oil, coating it over with french polish that has been cunningly coloured, brushing it down with pumice-stone and oil, bees-waxing it with a wax that contains dirt and dust, and finally giving it the heat treatment to crack the polish so that it looks like two-hundred-year-old varnish! It really upsets me to contemplate such knavery!"

The three men continued to gaze at the little patch of dark wood.

"Feel it!" Mr. Boggis ordered. "Put your fingers on it! There, how does it feel, warm or cold?"

"Feels cold," Rummins said.

"Exactly, my friend! It happens to be a fact that faked patina is always cold to the touch. Real patina has a curiously warm feel to it."

"This feels normal," Rummins said, ready to argue.

"No, sir, it's cold. But of course it takes an experienced and sensitive fingertip to pass a positive judgement. You couldn't really be expected to judge this any more than I could be expected to judge the quality of your barley. Everything in life, my dear sir, is experience."

The men were staring at this queer moon-faced clergyman with the bulging eyes, not quite so suspiciously now because he did seem to know a bit about his subject. But they were still a long way from trusting him.

Mr. Boggis bent down and pointed to one of the metal drawer-handles on the commode. "This is another place where the fakers go to work," he said. "Old brass normally has a colour and character all of its own. Did you know that?"

They stared at him, hoping for still more secrets.

"But the trouble is that they've become exceedingly skilled at matching it. In fact it's almost impossible to tell the difference between 'genuine old' and 'faked old.' I don't mind admitting that it has me guessing. So there's not really any point in our scraping the paint off these handles. We wouldn't be any the wiser."

"How can you possibly make new brass look like old?" Claud said. "Brass doesn't rust, you know."

"You are quite right, my friend. But these scoundrels have their own secret methods."

"Such as what?" Claud asked. Any information of this nature was valuable, in his opinion. One never knew when it might come in handy.

"All they have to do," Mr. Boggis said, "is to place these handles overnight in a box of mahogany shavings saturated in sal ammoniac. The sal ammoniac turns the metal green, but if you rub off the green, you will find underneath it a fine soft silvery-warm lustre, a lustre identical to that which comes with very old brass. Oh, it is so bestial, the things they do! With iron they have another trick."

"What do they do with iron?" Claud asked, fascinated.

"Iron's easy," Mr. Boggis said. "Iron locks and plates and hinges are simply buried in common salt and they come out all rusted and pitted in no time."

"All right," Rummins said. "So you admit you can't tell about the handles. For all you know, they may be hundreds and hundreds of years old. Correct?"

"Ah," Mr. Boggis whispered, fixing Rummins with two big bulging brown eyes. "That's where you're wrong. Watch this."

From his jacket pocket, he took out a small screwdriver. At the same time, although none of them saw him do it, he also took out a little brass screw which he kept well hidden in the palm of his hand. Then he selected one of the screws in the commode—there were four to each handle—and began carefully scraping all traces of white paint from its head. When he had done this, he started slowly to unscrew it.

"If this is a genuine old brass screw from the eighteenth century," he was saying, "the spiral will be slightly uneven and you'll be able to see quite easily that it has been hand-cut with a file. But if this brasswork is faked from more recent times, Victorian or later, then obviously the screw will be of the same period. It will be a mass-produced, machine-made article. Anyone can recognize a machine-made screw. Well, we shall see."

It was not difficult, as he put his hands over the old screw and drew it out, for Mr. Boggis to substitute the new one hidden in his palm. This was another little trick of his, and through the years it had proved a most rewarding one. The pockets of his clergyman's jacket were always stocked with a quantity of cheap brass screws of various sizes.

"There you are," he said, handing the modern screw to Rummins. "Take a look at that. Notice the exact evenness of the spiral? See it? Of course you do. It's just a cheap common little screw you yourself could buy today in any ironmonger's in the country."

The screw was handed round from the one to the other, each examining it carefully. Even Rummins was impressed now.

Mr. Boggis put the screwdriver back in his pocket together with the fine hand-cut screw that he'd taken from the commode, and then he turned and walked slowly past the three men towards the door.

"My dear friends," he said, pausing at the entrance to the kitchen, "it was so good of you to let me peep inside your little home—so kind. I do hope I haven't been a terrible old bore."

Rummins glanced up from examining the screw. "You didn't tell us what you were going to offer," he said.

"Ah," Mr. Boggis said. "That's quite right. I didn't did I? Well, to tell you the honest truth, I think it's all a bit too much trouble. I think I'll leave it."

"How much would you give?"

"You mean that you really wish to part with it?"

"I didn't say I wished to part with it. I asked you how much."

Mr. Boggis looked across at the commode, and he laid his head first to one side, then to the other, and he frowned, and pushed out his lips, and shrugged his shoulders, and gave a little scornful wave of the hand as though to say the thing was hardly worth thinking about really, was it?

"Shall we say . . . ten pounds. I think that would be fair."

"Ten pounds!" Rummins cried. "Don't be so ridiculous, Parson, *please*!"

"It's worth more'n that for firewood!" Claud said, disgusted.

"Look here at the bill!" Rummins went on, stabbing that precious document so fiercely with his dirty forefinger that Mr. Boggis became alarmed. "It tells you exactly what it cost! Eighty-seven pounds! And that's when it was new. Now it's antique it's worth double!"

"If you'll pardon me, no, sir, it's not. It's a second-hand reproduction. But I'll tell you what, my friend—I'm being rather reckless, I can't help it—I'll go up as high as fifteen pounds. How's that?"

"Make it fifty," Rummins said.

A delicious little quiver like needles ran all the way down the back of Mr. Boggis's legs and then under the soles of his feet. He had it now. It was his. No question about that. But the habit of buying cheap, as cheap as it was humanly possible to buy, acquired by years of necessity and practice, was too strong in him now to permit him to give in so easily.

"My dear man," he whispered softly, "I only *want* the legs. Possibly I could find some use for the drawers later on, but the rest of it, the carcass itself, as your friend so rightly said, it's firewood, that's all."

"Make it thirty-five," Rummins said.

"I *couldn't* sir, I *couldn't*! It's not worth it. And I simply mustn't allow myself to haggle like this about a price. It's all wrong. I'll make you one final offer, and then I must go. Twenty pounds."

"I'll take it," Rummins snapped. "It's yours."

"Oh dear," Mr. Boggis said, clasping his hands. "There I go again. I should never have started this in the first place."

"You can't back out now, Parson. A deal's a deal."

"Yes, yes, I know."

"How're you going to take it?"

"Well, let me see. Perhaps if I were to drive my car up into the yard, you gentlemen would be kind enough to help me load it?"

"In a car? This thing'll never go in a car! You'll need a truck for this!"

"I don't think so. Anyway, we'll see. My car's on the road. I'll be back in a jiffy. We'll manage it somehow, I'm sure."

Mr. Boggis walked out into the yard and through the gate and then down the long track that led across the field towards the road. He found himself giggling quite uncontrollably, and there was a feeling inside him as though hundreds and hundreds of tiny bubbles were rising up from his stomach and bursting merrily in the top of his head, like sparkling water. All the buttercups in the field were suddenly turning into golden sovereigns, glistening in the sunlight. The ground was littered with them, and he swung off the track on to the grass so that he could walk among them and tread on them and hear the little metallic tinkle they made as he kicked them around with his toes. He was finding it difficult to stop himself from breaking into a run. But clergymen never run; they walk slowly. Walk slowly, Boggis. Keep calm, Boggis. There's no hurry now. The commode is yours! Yours for twenty pounds, and it's worth fifteen or twenty thousand! The Boggis Commode! In ten minutes it'll be loaded into your car—it'll go in easily—and you'll be driving back to London and singing all the way! Mr. Boggis driving the Boggis Commode home in the Boggis car. Historic occasion. What *wouldn't* a newspaperman give to get a picture of that! Should he arrange it? Perhaps he should. Wait and see. Oh, glorious day! Oh, lovely sunny summer day! Oh, glory be!

Back in the farmhouse, Rummins was saying, "Fancy that old bastard giving twenty pound for a load of junk like this."

"You did very nicely, Mr. Rummins," Claud told him. "You think he'll pay you?"

"We don't put it in the car till he do."

"And what if it won't go in the car?" Claud asked. "You know what I think, Mr. Rummins? You want my honest opinion? I think the bloody thing's too big to go in the car. And then what happens? Then he's going to say to hell with it and just drive off without it and you'll never see him again. Nor the money either. He didn't seem all that keen on having it, you know."

Rummins paused to consider this new and rather alarming prospect.

"How can a thing like that possibly go in a car?" Claud went on relentlessly. "A parson never has a big car anyway. You ever seen a parson with a big car, Mr. Rummins?"

"Can't say I have."

"Exactly! And now listen to me. I've got an idea. He told us, didn't he, that it was only the legs he was wanting. Right? So all we've got to do is to cut 'em off quick right here on the spot before he comes back, then it'll be sure to go in the car. All we're doing is saving him the trouble of cutting them off himself when he gets home. How about it, Mr. Rummins?" Claud's flat bovine face glimmered with a mawkish pride.

"It's not such a bad idea at that," Rummins said, looking at the commode. "In fact it's a bloody good idea. Come on then, we'll have to hurry. You and Bert carry it out into the yard. I'll get the saw. Take the drawers out first."

Within a couple of minutes, Claud and Bert had carried the commode outside and had laid it upside down in the yard amidst the chicken droppings and cow dung and mud. In the distance, halfway across the field, they could see a small black figure striding along the path towards the road. They paused to watch. There was something rather comical about the way in which this figure was conducting itself. Every now and again it would break into a trot, then it did a kind of hop, skip, and jump, and once it seemed as though the sound of a cheerful song came rippling faintly to them from across the meadow.

"I reckon he's balmy," Claud said, and Bert grinned darkly, rolling his misty eye slowly round in its socket.

Rummins came waddling over from the shed, squat and frog-like, carrying a long saw. Claud took the saw away from him and went to work.

"Cut 'em close," Rummins said. "Don't forget he's going to use 'em on another table."

The mahogany was hard and very dry, and as Claud worked, a fine red dust sprayed out from the edge of the saw and fell softly to the ground. One by one, the legs came off, and when they were all severed, Bert stooped down and arranged them carefully in a row.

Claud stepped back to survey the results of his labour. There was a longish pause.

"Just let me ask you one question, Mr. Rummins," he said slowly. "Even now, could *you* put that enormous thing into the back of a car?"

"Not unless it was a van."

"Correct!" Claud cried. "And parsons don't have vans, you know. All they've got usually is piddling little Morris Eights or Austin Sevens."

"The legs is all he wants," Rummins said. "If the rest of it won't go in, then he can leave it. He can't complain. He's got the legs."

"Now you know better'n that, Mr. Rummins," Claud said patiently. "You know damn well he's going to start knocking the price if he don't get every single bit of this into the car. A parson's just as cunning as the rest of 'em when it comes to money, don't you make any mistake about that. Especially this old boy. So why don't we give him his firewood now and be done with it. Where d'you keep the axe?"

"I reckon that's fair enough," Rummins said. "Bert, go fetch the axe."

Bert went into the shed and fetched a tall woodcutter's axe and gave it to Claud. Claud spat on the palms of his hands and rubbed them together. Then, with a long-armed high-swinging action, he began fiercely attacking the legless carcass of the commode.

It was hard work, and it took several minutes before he had the whole thing more or less smashed to pieces.

"I'll tell you one thing," he said, straightening up, wiping his brow. "That was a bloody good carpenter put this job together and I don't care what the parson says."

"We're just in time!" Rummins called out. "Here he comes!"

I'm going to tell you about a funny thing that happened to my mother and me yesterday evening. I am twelve years old and I'm a girl. My mother is thirty-four but I am nearly as tall as her already.

Yesterday afternoon, my mother took me up to London to see the dentist. He found one hole. It was in a back tooth and he filled it without hurting me too much. After that, we went to a café. I had a banana split and my mother had a cup of coffee. By the time we got up to leave, it was about six o'clock.

When we came out of the café it had started to rain. "We must get a taxi," my mother said. We were wearing ordinary hats and coats, and it was raining quite hard.

"Why don't we go back into the café and wait for it to stop?" I said. I wanted another of those banana splits. They were gorgeous.

"It isn't going to stop," my mother said. "We must get home."

We stood on the pavement in the rain, looking for a taxi. Lots of them came by but they all had passengers inside them. "I wish we had a car with a chauffeur," my mother said.

Just then a man came up to us. He was a small man and he was pretty old, probably seventy or more. He raised his hat politely and said to my mother, "Excuse me, I do hope you will excuse me . . ." He had a fine white moustache and bushy white eyebrows and a wrinkly pink face. He was sheltering under an umbrella which he held high over his head.

"Yes?" my mother said, very cool and distant.

"I wonder if I could ask a small favour of you," he said. "It is only a very small favour."

I saw my mother looking at him suspiciously. She is a suspicious person, my mother. She is especially suspicious of two things— strange men and boiled eggs. When she cuts the top off a boiled egg, she pokes around inside it with her spoon as though expecting to find a mouse or something. With strange men, she has a golden rule which says, "The nicer the man seems to be, the more suspicious you must become." This little old man was particularly nice. He was polite. He was well spoken. He was well dressed. He was a real gentleman. The reason I knew he was a gentleman was because of his shoes. "You can always spot a gentleman by the shoes he wears," was another of my mother's favourite sayings. This man had beautiful brown shoes.

"The truth of the matter is," the little man was saying, "I've got myself into a bit of a scrape. I need some help. Not much I assure you. It's almost nothing, in fact, but I do need it. You see, madam, old people like me often become terribly forgetful . . ."

My mother's chin was up and she was staring down at him along the full length of her nose. It was a fearsome thing, this frosty-nosed stare of my mother's. Most people go to pieces completely when she gives it to them. I once saw my own headmistress begin to stammer and simper like an idiot when my mother gave her a really foul frosty-noser. But the little man on the pavement with the umbrella over his head didn't bat an eyelid. He gave a gentle smile and said, "I beg you to believe, madam, that I am not in the habit of stopping ladies in the street and telling them my troubles."

"I should hope not," my mother said.

I felt quite embarrassed by my mother's sharpness. I wanted to say to her, "Oh, Mummy, for heaven's sake, he's a very very old man, and he's sweet and polite, and he's in some sort of trouble, so don't be so beastly to him." But I didn't say anything.

The little man shifted his umbrella from one hand to the other. "I've never forgotten it before," he said.

"You've never forgotten what?" my mother asked sternly.

"My wallet," he said. "I must have left it in my other jacket. Isn't that the silliest thing to do?"

"Are you asking me to give you money?" my mother said.

"Oh, good gracious me, no!" he cried. "Heaven forbid I should ever do that!"

"Then what *are* you asking?" my mother said. "Do hurry up. We're getting soaked to the skin here."

"I know you are," he said. "And that is why I'm offering you this umbrella of mine to protect you, and to keep forever, if . . . if only . . ."

"If only what?" my mother said.

"If only you would give me in return a pound for my taxi fare just to get me home."

My mother was still suspicious. "If you had no money in the first place," she said, "then how did you get here?"

"I walked," he answered. "Every day I go for a lovely long walk and then I summon a taxi to take me home. I do it every day of the year."

"Why don't you walk home now?" my mother asked.

"Oh, I wish I could," he said. "I do wish I could. But I don't think I could manage it on these silly old legs of mine. I've gone too far already."

My mother stood there chewing her lower lip. She was beginning to melt a bit, I could see that. And the idea of getting an umbrella to shelter under must have tempted her a good deal.

"It's a lovely umbrella," the little man said.

"So I've noticed," my mother said.

"It's silk," he said.

"I can see that."

"Then why don't you take it, madam," he said. "It cost me over twenty pounds, I promise you. But that's of no importance so long as I can get home and rest these old legs of mine."

I saw my mother's hand feeling for the clasp of her purse. She saw me watching her. I was giving her one of my *own* frosty-nosed looks this time and she knew exactly what I was telling her. Now listen, Mummy, I was telling her, you simply *mustn't* take advantage of a tired old man in this way. It's a rotten thing to do. My mother paused and looked back at me. Then she said to the little man, "I don't think it's quite right that I should take an umbrella from you worth twenty pounds. I think I'd better just *give* you the taxi fare and be done with it."

"No, no no!" he cried. "It's out of the question! I wouldn't dream of it! Not in a million years! I would never accept money from you like that! Take the umbrella, dear lady, and keep the rain off your shoulders!"

My mother gave me a triumphant sideways look. There you are, she was telling me. You're wrong. He *wants* me to have it.

She fished into her purse and took out a pound note. She held it out to the little man. He took it and handed her the umbrella. He pocketed the pound, raised his hat, gave a quick bow from the waist, and said, "Thank you, madam, thank you." Then he was gone.

"Come under here and keep dry, darling," my mother said. "Aren't we lucky. I've never had a silk umbrella before. I couldn't afford it."

"Why were you so horrid to him in the beginning?" I asked.

"I wanted to satisfy myself he wasn't a trickster," she said. "And I did. He was a gentleman. I'm very pleased I was able to help him."

"Yes, Mummy," I said.

"A *real* gentleman," she went on. "Wealthy, too, otherwise he wouldn't have had a silk umbrella. I shouldn't be surprised if he isn't a titled person. Sir Harry Goldsworthy or something like that."

"Yes, Mummy."

"This will be a good lesson to you," she went on. "Never rush things. Always take your time when you are summing someone up. Then you'll never make mistakes."

"There he goes," I said. "Look."

"Where?"

"Over there. He's crossing the street. Goodness, Mummy, what a hurry he's in."

We watched the little man as he dodged nimbly in and out of the traffic. When he reached the other side of the street, he turned left, walking very fast.

"He doesn't look very tired to me, does he to you, Mummy?"

My mother didn't answer.

"He doesn't look as though he's trying to get a taxi, either," I said.

My mother was standing very still and stiff, staring across the street at the little man. We could see him clearly. He was in a terrific hurry. He was bustling along the pavement, sidestepping the other pedestrians and swinging his arms like a soldier on the march.

"He's up to something," my mother said, stony-faced.

"But what?"

"I don't know," my mother snapped. "But I'm going to find out. Come with me." She took my arm and we crossed the street together. Then we turned left.

"Can you see him?" my mother asked.

"Yes. There he is. He's turning right down the next street."

We came to the corner and turned right. The little man was about twenty yards ahead of us. He was scuttling along like a rabbit and we had to walk very fast to keep up with him. The rain was pelting down harder than ever now and I could see it dripping from the brim of his hat on to his shoulders. But we were snug and dry under our lovely big silk umbrella.

"What is he up to?" my mother said.

"What if he turns round and sees us?" I asked.

"I don't care if he does," my mother said. "He lied to us. He said he was too tired to walk any further and he's practically running us off our feet! He's a barefaced liar! He's a crook!"

"You mean he's *not* a titled gentleman?" I asked.

"Be quiet," she said.

At the next crossing, the little man turned right again.

Then he turned left.

Then right.

"I'm not giving up now," my mother said.

"He's disappeared!" I cried. "Where's he gone?"

"He went in that door!" my mother said. "I saw him! Into that house! Great heavens, it's a pub!"

It was a pub. In big letters right across the front it said THE RED LION.

"You're not going in are you, Mummy?"

"No," she said. "We'll watch from outside."

There was a big plate-glass window along the front of the pub, and although it was a bit steamy on the inside, we could see through it very well if we went close.

We stood huddled together outside the pub window. I was clutching my mother's arm. The big raindrops were making a loud noise on our umbrella. "There he is," I said. "Over there."

The room we were looking into was full of people and cigarette smoke, and our little man was in the middle of it all. He was now without his hat and coat, and he was edging his way through the crowd towards the bar. When he reached it, he placed both hands on the bar itself and spoke to the barman. I saw his lips moving as he gave his order. The barman turned away from him for a few seconds and came back with a smallish tumbler filled to the brim with light brown liquid. The little man placed a pound note on the counter.

"That's my pound!" my mother hissed. "By golly, he's got a nerve!"

"What's in the glass?" I asked.

"Whisky," my mother said. "Neat whisky."

The barman didn't give him any change from the pound.

"That must be a treble whisky," my mummy said.

"What's a treble?" I asked.

"Three times the normal measure," she answered.

The little man picked up the glass and put it to his lips. He tilted it gently. Then he tilted it higher . . . and higher . . . and higher . . . and very soon all the whisky had disappeared down his throat in one long pour.

"That's a jolly expensive drink," I said.

"It's ridiculous!" my mummy said. "Fancy paying a pound for something to swallow in one go!"

"It cost him more than a pound," I said. "It cost him a twenty-pound silk umbrella."

"So it did," my mother said. "He must be mad."

The little man was standing by the bar with the empty glass in his hand. He was smiling now, and a sort of golden glow of pleasure was spreading over his round pink face. I saw his tongue come out to lick the white moustache, as though searching for one last drop of that precious whisky.

Slowly, he turned away from the bar and edged his way back through the crowd to where his hat and coat were hanging. He put on his hat. He put on his coat. Then, in a manner so superbly cool and casual that you hardly noticed anything at all, he lifted from the coatrack one of the many wet umbrellas hanging there, and off he went.

"Did you see that!" my mother shrieked. "Did you see what he did!"

"Ssshh!" I whispered. "He's coming out!"

We lowered our umbrella to hide our faces, and peered out from under it.

Out he came. But he never looked in our direction. He opened his new umbrella over his head and scurried off down the road the way he had come.

"So that's his little game!" my mother said.

"Neat," I said. "Super."

We followed him back to the main street where we had first met him, and we watched him as he proceeded, with no trouble at all, to exchange his new umbrella for another pound note. This time it was with a tall thin fellow who didn't even have a coat or hat. And as soon as the transaction was completed, our little man trotted off down the street and was lost in the crowd. But this time he went in the opposite direction.

"You see how clever he is!" my mother said. "He never goes to the same pub twice!"

"He could go on doing this all night," I said.

"Yes," my mother said. "Of course. But I'll bet he prays like mad for rainy days."

KATINA ────────────────────────────

*Some brief notes about the last days of RAF
fighters in the first Greek campaign.*

Peter saw her first.

She was sitting on a stone, quite still, with her hands resting on her lap. She was staring vacantly ahead, seeing nothing, and all around, up and down the little street, people were running backward and forward with buckets of water, emptying them through the windows of the burning houses.

Across the street on the cobblestones, there was a dead boy. Someone had moved his body close in to the side so that it would not be in the way.

A little further down an old man was working on a pile of stones and rubble. One by one he was carrying the stones away and dumping them to the side. Sometimes he would bend down and peer into the ruins, repeating a name over and over again.

All around there was shouting and running and fires and buckets of water and dust. And the girl sat quietly on the stone, staring ahead, not moving. There was blood running down the left side of her face. It ran down from her forehead and dropped from her chin on to the dirty print dress she was wearing.

Peter saw her and said, "Look at that little girl."

We went up to her and Fin put his hand on her shoulder, bending down to examine the cut. "Looks like a piece of shrapnel," he said. "She ought to see the Doc."

Peter and I made a chair with our hands and Fin lifted her up on to it. We started back through the streets and out towards the aerodrome, the two of us walking a little awkwardly, bending down, facing our burden. I could feel Peter's fingers clasping tightly in mine and I could feel the buttocks of the little girl resting lightly on my wrists. I was on the left side and the blood was dripping down from her face on to the arm of my flying suit, running down the waterproof cloth on to the back of my hand. The girl never moved or said anything.

Fin said, "She's bleeding rather fast. We'd better walk a bit quicker."

I couldn't see much of her face because of the blood, but I could tell that she was lovely. She had high cheekbones and large round eyes, pale blue like an autumn sky, and her hair was short and fair. I guessed she was about nine years old.

This was in Greece in early April 1941, at Paramythia. Our fighter squadron was stationed on a muddy field near the village. We were in a deep valley and all around us were the mountains. The freezing winter had passed, and now, almost before anyone knew it, spring had come. It had come quietly and swiftly, melting the ice on the lakes and brushing the snow off the mountain tops;

and all over the airfield we could see the pale green shoots of grass pushing up through the mud, making a carpet for our landings. In our valley there were warm winds and wild flowers.

The Germans, who had pushed in through Yugoslavia a few days before, were now operating in force, and that afternoon they had come over very high with about thirty-five Dorniers and bombed the village. Peter and Fin and I were off duty for a while, and the three of us had gone down to see if there was anything we could do in the way of rescue work. We had spent a few hours digging around in the ruins and helping to put out fires, and we were on our way back when we saw the girl.

Now, as we approached the landing field, we could see the Hurricanes circling around coming in to land, and there was the Doc standing out in front of the dispersal tent, just as he should have been, waiting to see if anyone had been hurt. We walked towards him, carrying the child, and Fin, who was a few yards in front, said,

"Doc, you lazy old devil, here's a job for you."

The Doc was young and kind and morose except when he got drunk. When he got drunk he sang very well.

"Take her into the sick bay," he said. Peter and I carried her in and put her down on a chair. Then we left her and wandered over to the dispersal tent to see how the boys had got along.

It was beginning to get dark. There was a sunset behind the ridge over in the west, and there was a full moon, a bombers' moon, climbing up into the sky. The moon shone upon the shoulders of the tents and made them white; small white pyramids, standing up straight, clustering in little orderly groups around the edges of the aerodrome. They had a scared-sheep look about them the way they clustered themselves together, and they had a human look about them the way they stood up close to one another, and it seemed almost as though they knew that there was going to be trouble, as though someone had warned them that they might be forgotten and left behind. Even as I looked, I thought I saw them move. I thought I saw them huddle just a fraction nearer together.

And then, silently, without a sound, the mountains crept a little closer into our valley.

For the next two days there was much flying. There was the getting up at dawn, there was the flying, the fighting and the sleeping; and there was the retreat of the army. That was about all there was or all there was time for. But on the third day the clouds dropped down over the mountains and slid into the valley. And it rained. So we sat around in the mess-tent drinking beer and resinato, while the rain made a noise like a sewing machine on the roof. Then lunch. For the first time in days the whole squadron was present. Fifteen pilots at a long table with benches on either side and Monkey, the CO sitting at the head.

We were still in the middle of our fried corned beef when the flap of the tent opened and in came the Doc with an enormous dripping raincoat over his head. And with him, under the coat, was the little girl. She had a bandage round her head.

The Doc said, "Hello. I've brought a guest." We looked around and suddenly, automatically, we all stood up.

The Doc was taking off his raincoat and the little girl was standing there with her hands hanging loose by her sides looking at the men, and the men were all looking at her. With her fair hair and pale skin she looked less like a Greek than anyone I've ever seen. She was frightened by the fifteen scruffy-looking foreigners who had suddenly stood up when she came in, and for a moment she half-turned as if she were going to run away out into the rain.

Monkey said, "Hello. Hello there. Come and sit down."

"Talk Greek," the Doc said. "She doesn't understand."

Fin and Peter and I looked at one another and Fin said, "Good God, it's our little girl. Nice work, Doc."

She recognized Fin and walked round to where he was standing. He took her by the hand and sat her down on the bench, and everyone else sat down too. We gave her some fried corned beef and she ate it slowly, looking down at her plate while she ate. Monkey said, "Get Pericles."

Pericles was the Greek interpreter attached to the squadron. He was a wonderful man we'd picked up at Yanina, where he had been the local school teacher. He had been out of work ever since the war started. "The children do not come to school," he said. "They are up in the mountains and fight. I cannot teach sums to the stones."

Pericles came in. He was old, with a beard, a long pointed nose and sad grey eyes. You couldn't see his mouth, but his beard had a way of smiling when he talked.

"Ask her her name," said Monkey.

He said something to her in Greek. She looked up and said, "Katina." That was all she said.

"Look, Pericles," Peter said, "ask her what she was doing sitting by that heap of ruins in the village."

Fin said, "For God's sake leave her alone."

"Ask her, Pericles," said Peter.

"What should I ask?" said Pericles, frowning.

Peter said, "What she was doing sitting on that heap of stuff in the village when we found her."

Pericles sat down on the bench beside her and he talked to her again. He spoke gently and you could see that his beard was smiling a little as he spoke, helping her. She listened and it seemed a long time before she answered. When she spoke, it was only a few words, and the old man translated: "She says that her family were under the stones."

Outside the rain was coming down harder than ever. It beat upon the roof of the mess tent so that the canvas shivered as the water bounced upon it. I got up and walked over and lifted the flap of the tent. The mountains were invisible behind the rain, but I knew they were around us on every side. I had a feeling that they were laughing at us, laughing at the smallness of our numbers and at the hopeless courage of the pilots. I felt that it was the mountains, not us, who were the clever ones. Had not the hills that very morning turned and looked northward towards Tepelene where they had seen a thousand German aircraft gathered under the shadow of Olympus? Was it not true that the snow on the top of Dodona had melted away in a day, sending little rivers of water running down across our landing field? Had not Kataphidi buried his head in a cloud so that our pilots might be tempted to fly through the whiteness and crash against his rugged shoulders?

And as I stood there looking at the rain through the tent flap, I knew for certain that the mountains had turned against us. I could feel it in my stomach.

I went back into the tent and there was Fin, sitting beside Katina, trying to teach her English words. I don't know whether he made much progress, but I do know that once he made her laugh and that was a wonderful thing for him to have done. I remember the sudden sound of her high laughter and how we all looked up and saw her face; how we saw how different it was to what it had been before. No one but Fin could have done it. He was so gay himself that it was difficult to be serious in his presence. He was gay and tall and black-haired, and he was sitting there on the bench, leaning forward, whispering and smiling, teaching Katina to speak English and teaching her how to laugh.

The next day the skies cleared and once again we saw the mountains. We did a patrol over the troops which were already retreating slowly towards Thermopylae, and we met some Messerschmitts and Ju-87s dive-bombing the soldiers. I think we got a few of them, but they got Sandy. I saw him going down. I sat quite still for thirty seconds and watched his plane spiralling gently downward. I sat and waited for the parachute. I remember switching over my radio and saying quietly, "Sandy, you must jump now. You must jump; you're getting near the ground." But there was no parachute.

When we landed and taxied in there was Katina, standing outside the dispersal tent with the Doc; a tiny shrimp of a girl in a dirty print dress, standing there watching the machines as they came in to land. To Fin, as he walked in, she said, "Tha girisis xana."

Fin said, "What does it mean, Pericles?"

"It just means 'you are back again,'" and he smiled.

The child had counted the aircraft on her fingers as they took off, and now she noticed that there was one missing. We were standing around taking off our parachutes and she was trying to ask us about it, when suddenly someone said, "Look out. Here they come." They came through a gap in the hills, a mass of thin, black silhouettes, coming down upon the aerodrome.

There was a scramble for the slit trenches and I remember seeing Fin catch Katina round the waist and carry her off with us, and I remember seeing her fight like a tiger the whole way to the trenches.

As soon as we got into the trench and Fin had let her go, she jumped out and ran over on to the airfield. Down came the Messerschmitts with their guns blazing, swooping so low that you could see the noses of the pilots sticking out under their goggles. Their bullets threw up spurts of dust all around and I saw one of our Hurricanes burst into flames. I saw Katina standing right in the middle of the field, standing firmly with her legs astride and her back to us, looking up at the Germans as they dived past. I have never seen anything smaller and more angry and more fierce in my life. She seemed to be shouting at them, but the noise was great and one could hear nothing at all except the engines and the guns of the aeroplanes.

Then it was over. It was over as quickly as it had begun, and no one said very much except Fin, who said, "I wouldn't have done that, ever; not even if I was crazy."

That evening Monkey got out the squadron records and added Katina's name to the list of members, and the equipment officer was ordered to provide a tent for her. So, on the eleventh of April 1941, she became a member of the squadron.

In two days she knew the first name or nickname of every pilot and Fin had already taught her to say "Any luck?" and "Nice work."

But that was a time of much activity, and when I try to think of it hour by hour, the whole period becomes hazy in my mind. Mostly, I remember, it was escorting the Blenheims to Valona, and if it wasn't that, it was a ground-strafe of Italian trucks on the Albanian border or an SOS from the Northumberland Regiment saying they were having the hell bombed out of them by half the aircraft in Europe.

None of that can I remember. I can remember nothing of that time clearly, save for two things. The one was Katina and how she was with us all the time; how she was everywhere and how wherever she went the people were pleased to see her. The other thing that I remember was when the Bull came into the mess tent one evening after a lone patrol. The Bull was an enormous man with massive, slightly hunched shoulders and his chest was like the top of an oak table. Before the war he had done many things, most of them things which one could not do unless one conceded beforehand that there was no difference between life and death. He was quiet and casual and when he came into a room or into a tent, he always looked as though he had made a mistake and hadn't really meant to come in at all. It was getting dark and we were sitting round in the tent playing shove-halfpenny when the Bull came in. We knew that he had just landed.

He glanced around a little apologetically, then he said, "Hello," and wandered over to the bar and began to get out a bottle of beer.

Someone said, "See anything, Bull?"

The Bull said, "Yes," and went on fiddling with the bottle of beer.

I suppose we were all very interested in our game of shove-half-penny because no one said anything else for about five minutes. Then Peter said, "What did you see, Bull?"

The Bull was leaning against the bar, alternately sipping his beer and trying to make a hooting noise by blowing down the neck of the empty bottle.

Peter said, "What did you see?"

The Bull put down the bottle and looked up. "Five S-79s," he said.

I remember hearing him say it, but I remember also that our game was exciting and that Fin had one more shove to win. We all watched him miss it and Peter said, "Fin, I think you're going to lose." And Fin said, "Go to hell."

We finished the game, then I looked up and saw the Bull still leaning against the bar making noises with his beer bottle.

He said, "This sounds like the old *Mauretania* coming into New York harbour," and he started blowing into the bottle again.

"What happened with the S-79s?" I said.

He stopped his blowing and put down the bottle.

"I shot them down."

Everyone heard it. At that moment eleven pilots in that tent stopped what they were doing and eleven heads flicked around and looked at the Bull. He took another drink of his beer and said quietly, "At one time I counted eighteen parachutes in the air together."

A few days later he went on patrol and did not come back. Shortly afterwards Monkey got a message from Athens. It said that the squadron was to move down to Elevsis and from there do a defence of Athens itself and also cover the troops retreating through the Thermopylae Pass.

Katina was to go with the trucks and we told the Doc he was to see that she arrived safely. It would take them a day to make the journey. We flew over the mountains towards the south, fourteen of us, and at two-thirty we landed at Elevsis. It was a lovely aerodrome with runways and hangars; and best of all, Athens was only twenty-five minutes away by car.

That evening, as it was getting dark, I stood outside my tent. I stood with my hands in my pockets watching the sun go down and thinking of the work which we were to do. The more that I thought of it, the more impossible I knew it to be. I looked up, and once again I saw the mountains. They were closer to us here, crowding in upon us on all sides, standing shoulder to shoulder, tall and naked, with their heads in the clouds, surrounding us everywhere save in the south, where lay Piraeus and the open sea. I knew that each night, when it was very dark, when we were all tired and sleeping in our tents, those mountains would move forward, creeping a little closer, making no noise, until at last on the appointed day they would tumble forward with one great rush and push us into the sea.

Fin emerged from his tent.

"Have you seen the mountains?" I said.

"They're full of gods. They aren't any good," he answered.

"I wish they'd stand still," I said.

Fin looked up at the great crags of Parnes and Pentelikon.

"They're full of gods," he said. "Sometimes, in the middle of the night, when there is a moon, you can see the gods sitting on the summits. There was one on Kataphidi when we were at Paramythia. He was huge, like a house but without any shape and quite black."

"You saw him?"

"Of course I saw him."

"When?" I said. "When did you see him, Fin?"

Fin said, "Let's go into Athens. Let's go and look at the women in Athens."

The next day the trucks carrying the ground staff and the equipment rumbled on to the aerodrome, and there was Katina sitting in the front seat of the leading vehicle with the Doc beside her. She waved to us as she jumped down, and she came running towards us, laughing and calling our names in a curious Greek way. She still had on the same dirty print dress and she still had a bandage round her forehead; but the sun was shining in her hair.

We showed her the tent which we had prepared for her and we showed her the small cotton nightdress which Fin had obtained in some mysterious way the night before in Athens. It was white with a lot of little blue birds embroidered on the front and we all thought that it was very beautiful. Katina wanted to put it on at once and it took a long time to persuade her that it was meant only for sleeping in. Six times Fin had to perform a complicated act which consisted of pretending to put on the nightdress, then jumping on to the bed and falling fast asleep. In the end she nodded vigorously and understood.

For the next two days nothing happened, except that the remnants of another squadron came down from the north and joined us. They brought six Hurricanes, so that altogether we had about twenty machines.

Then we waited.

On the third day German reconnaissance aircraft appeared, circling high over Piraeus, and we chased after them but never got up in time to catch them. This was understandable, because our radar was of a very special type. It is obsolete now, and I doubt whether it will ever be used again. All over the country, in all the villages, up on the mountains and out on the islands, there were Greeks, all of whom were connected to our small operations room by field telephone.

We had no operations officer, so we took it in turns to be on duty for the day. My turn came on the fourth day, and I remember clearly what happened.

At six-thirty in the morning the phone buzzed.

"This is A-7," said a very Greek voice. "This is A-7. There are noises overhead."

I looked at the map. There was a little ring with "A-7" written inside it just beside Yanina. I put a cross on the celluloid which covered the map and wrote "Noises" beside it, as well as the time: "0631 hours."

Three minutes later the phone went again.

"This is A-4. This is A-4. There are many noises above me," said an old quavering voice, "but I cannot see because there are thick clouds."

I looked at the map. A-4 was Mt. Karava. I made another cross on the celluloid and wrote "Many noises—0634," and then I drew a line between Yanina and Karava. It pointed towards Athens, so I signalled the "readiness" crew to scramble, and they took off and circled the city. Later they saw a Ju-88 on reconnaissance high above them, but they never caught it. It was in such a way that one worked the radar.

That evening when I came off duty I could not help thinking of the old Greek, sitting all alone in a hut up at A-4; sitting on the slope of Karava looking up into the whiteness and listening all day and all night for noises in the sky. I imagined the eagerness with which he seized the telephone when he heard something, and the joy he must have felt when the voice at the other end repeated his message and thanked him. I thought of his clothes and wondered if they were warm enough and I thought, for some reason, of his boots, which almost certainly had no soles left upon them and were stuffed with tree bark and paper.

That was April seventeenth. It was the evening when Monkey said, "They say the Germans are at Lamia, which means that we're within range of their fighters. Tomorrow the fun should start."

It did. At dawn the bombers came over, with the fighters circling around overhead, watching the bombers, waiting to pounce, but doing nothing unless someone interfered with the bombers.

I think we got eight Hurricanes into the air just before they arrived. It was not my turn to go up, so with Katina standing by my side I watched the battle from the ground. The child never said a word. Now and again she moved her head as she followed the little specks of silver dancing high above in the sky. I saw a plane coming down in a trail of black smoke and I looked at Katina. The hatred which was on the face of the child was the fierce burning hatred of an old woman who has hatred in her heart; it was an old woman's hatred and it was strange to see it.

In that battle we lost a sergeant called Donald.

At noon Monkey got another message from Athens. It said that morale was bad in the capital and that every available Hurricane was to fly in formation low over the city in order to show the inhabitants how strong we were and how many aircraft we had. Eighteen of us took off. We flew in tight formation up and down the main streets just above the roofs of the houses. I could see the people looking up, shielding their eyes from the sun, looking at us as we flew over, and in one street I saw an old woman who never looked up at all. None of them waved, and I knew then that they were resigned to their fate. None of them waved, and I knew, although I could not see their faces, that they were not even glad as we flew past.

Then we headed out towards Thermopylae, but on the way we circled the Acropolis twice. It was the first time I had seen it so close.

I saw a little hill—a mound almost, it seemed—and on the top of it I saw the white columns. There were a great number of them, grouped together in perfect order, not crowding one another, white in the sunshine, and I wondered, as I looked at them, how anyone could have put so much on top of so small a hill in such an elegant way.

Then we flew up the great Thermopylae Pass and I saw long lines of vehicles moving slowly southwards towards the sea. I saw occasional puffs of white smoke where a shell landed in the valley and I saw a direct hit on the road which made a gap in the line of trucks. But we saw no enemy aircraft.

When we landed Monkey said, "Refuel quickly and get in the air again; I think they're waiting to catch us on the ground."

But it was no use. They came down out of the sky five minutes after we had landed. I remember I was in the pilots' room in Number Two Hangar, talking to Fin and to a big tall man with rumpled hair called Paddy. We heard the bullets on the corrugated iron roof of the hangar, then we heard explosions and the three of us dived under the little wooden table in the middle of the room. But the table upset. Paddy set it up again and crawled underneath. "There's something about being under a table," he said. "I don't feel safe unless I'm under a table."

Fin said, "I never feel safe." He was sitting on the floor watching the bullets making holes in the corrugated iron wall of the room. There was a great clatter as the bullets hit the tin.

Then we became brave and got up and peeped outside the door. There were many Messerschmitt 109s circling the aerodrome, and one by one they straightened out and dived past the hangers, spraying the ground with their guns. But they did something else. They slid back their cockpit hoods and as they came past they threw out small bombs which exploded when they hit the ground and fiercely flung quantities of large lead balls in every direction. Those were the explosions which we had heard, and it was a great noise that the lead balls made as they hit the hangar.

Then I saw the men, the ground crews, standing up in their slit trenches firing at the Messerschmitts with rifles, reloading and firing as fast as they could, cursing and shouting as they shot, aiming ludicrously, hopelessly, aiming at an aeroplane with just a rifle. At Elevsis there were no other defences.

Suddenly the Messerschmitts all turned and headed for home, all except one, which glided down and made a smooth belly landing on the aerodrome.

Then there was chaos. The Greeks around us raised a shout and jumped on to the fire tender and headed out towards the crashed German aeroplane. At the same time more Greeks streamed out from every corner of the field, shouting and yelling and crying for the blood of the pilot. It was a mob intent upon vengeance and one could not blame them; but there were other considerations. We wanted the pilot for questioning, and we wanted him alive.

Monkey, who was standing on the tarmac, shouted to us, and Fin and Paddy and I raced with him towards the station wagon which was standing fifty yards away. Monkey was inside like a flash, started the engine and drove off just as the three of us jumped on the running board. The fire tender with the Greeks on it was not fast and it still had two hundred yards to go, and the other people had a long way to run. Monkey drove quickly and we beat them by about fifty yards.

We jumped up and ran over to the Messerschmitt, and there, sitting in the cockpit, was a fair-haired boy with pink cheeks and blue eyes. I have never seen anyone whose face showed so much fear.

He said to Monkey in English, "I am hit in the leg."

We pulled him out of the cockpit and got him into the car, while the Greeks stood around watching. The bullet had shattered the bone in his shin.

We drove him back and as we handed him over to the Doc, I saw Katina standing close, looking at the face of the German. This kid of nine was standing there looking at the German and she could not speak; she could not even move. She clutched the skirt of her dress in her hands and stared at the man's face. "There is a mistake somewhere," she seemed to be saying. "There must be a mistake. This one has pink cheeks and fair hair and blue eyes. This cannot possibly be one of them. This is an ordinary boy." She watched him as they put him on a stretcher and carried him off, then she turned and ran across the grass to her tent.

In the evening at supper I ate my fried sardines, but I could not eat the bread or the cheese. For three days I had been conscious of my stomach, of a hollow feeling such as one gets just before an operation or while waiting to have a tooth out in the dentist's house. I had had it all day for three days, from the moment I woke up to the time I fell asleep. Peter was sitting opposite me and I asked him about it.

"I've had it for a week," he said. "It's good for the bowels. It loosens them."

"German aircraft are like liver pills," said Fin from the bottom of the table. "They are very good for you, aren't they, Doc?"

The Doc said, "Maybe you've had an overdose."

"I have," said Fin, "I've had an overdose of German liver pills. I didn't read the instructions on the bottle. Take two before retiring."

Peter said, "I would love to retire."

After supper three of us walked down to the hangars with Monkey, who said, "I'm worried about this ground-strafing. They never attack the hangars because they know that we never put anything inside them. Tonight I think we'll collect four of the aircraft and put them into Number Two Hangar."

That was a good idea. Normally the Hurricanes were dispersed all over the edge of the aerodrome, but they were picked off one by one, because it was impossible to be in the air the whole time. The four of us took a machine each and taxied it into Number Two Hangar, and then we pulled the great sliding doors together and locked them.

The next morning, before the sun had risen from behind the mountains, a flock of Ju-87s came over and blew Number Two Hangar right off the face of the earth. Their bombing was good and they did not even hit the hangars on either side of it.

That afternoon they got Peter. He went off towards a village called Khalkis, which was being bombed by Ju-88s, and no one ever saw him again. Gay, laughing Peter, whose mother lived on a farm in Kent and who used to write to him in long, pale-blue envelopes which he carried about in his pockets.

I had always shared a tent with Peter, ever since I came to the squadron, and that evening after I had gone to bed he came back to that tent. You need not believe me; I do not expect you to, but I am telling you what happened.

I always went to bed first, because there is not room in one of those tents for two people to be turning around at the same time. Peter usually came in two or three minutes afterwards. That evening I went to bed and I lay thinking that tonight he would not be coming. I wondered whether his body lay tangled in the wreckage of his aircraft on the side of some bleak mountain or whether it was at the bottom of the sea, and I hoped only that he had had a decent funeral.

Suddenly I heard a movement. The flap of the tent opened and it shut again. But there were no footsteps. Then I heard him sit down on his bed. It was a noise that I had heard every night for weeks past and always it had been the same. It was just a thump and a creaking of the wooden legs of the camp bed. One after the other the flying boots were pulled off and dropped upon the ground, and as always one of them took three times as long to get off as the other. After that there was the gentle rustle of a blanket being pulled back and then the creakings of the rickety bed as it took the weight of a man's body.

They were sounds I had heard every night, the same sounds in the same order, and now I sat up in bed and said, "Peter." It was dark in the tent. My voice sounded very loud.

"Hello, Peter. That was tough luck you had today." But there was no answer.

I did not feel uneasy or frightened, but I remember at the time touching the tip of my nose with my finger to make sure that I was there; then because I was very tired, I went to sleep.

In the morning I looked at the bed and saw it had been slept in. But I did not show it to anyone, not even to Fin. I put the blankets back in place myself and patted the pillow.

It was on that day, the twentieth of April 1941, that we fought the Battle of Athens. It was perhaps the last of the great dogfighting air battles that will ever be fought, because nowadays the planes fly always in great formation of wings and squadrons, and attack is carried out methodically and scientifically upon the orders of the leader. Nowadays one does not dogfight at all over the sky except upon very rare occasions. But the Battle of Athens was a long and beautiful dogfight in which fifteen Hurricanes fought for half an hour with between one hundred and fifty and two hundred German bombers and fighters.

The bombers started coming over early in the afternoon. It was a lovely spring day and for the first time the sun had in it a trace of real summer warmth. The sky was blue, save for a few wispy clouds here and there and the mountains stood out black and clear against the blue of the sky.

Pentelikon no longer hid his head in the clouds. He stood over us, grim and forbidding, watching every move and knowing that each thing we did was of little purpose. Men were foolish and were made only so that they should die, while mountains and rivers went on forever and did not notice the passing of time. Had not Pentelikon himself many years ago looked down upon Thermopylae and seen a handful of Spartans defending the pass against the invaders; seen them fight until there was not one man left alive among them? Had he not seen the Persians cut to pieces by Leonidas at Marathon, and had he not looked down upon Salamis and upon the sea when Themistocles and the Athenians drove the enemy from their shores, causing them to lose more than two hundred sails? All these things and many more he had seen, and now he looked down upon us, we were as nothing in his eyes. Almost there was a look of scorn upon the face of the mountain, and I thought for a moment that I could hear the laughter of the gods. They knew so well that we were not enough and that in the end we must lose.

The bombers came over just after lunch, and at once we saw that there were a great number of them. We looked up and saw that the sky was full of little silver specks and the sunlight danced and sparkled upon a hundred different pairs of wings.

There were fifteen Hurricanes in all and they fought like a storm in the sky. It is not easy to remember much about such a battle, but I remember looking up and seeing in the sky a mass of small black dots. I remember thinking to myself that those could not be aeroplanes; they simply could not be aeroplanes, because there were not so many aeroplanes in the world.

Then they were on us, and I remember that I applied a little flap so that I should be able to turn in tighter circles; then I remember only one or two small incidents which photographed themselves upon my mind. There were the spurts of flame from the guns of a Messerschmitt as he attacked from the frontal quarter of my starboard side. There was the German whose parachute was on fire as it opened. There was the German who flew up beside me and made rude signs at me with his fingers. There was the Hurricane which collided with a Messerschmitt. There was the aeroplane which collided with a man who was descending in a parachute, and which went into a crazy frightful spin towards the earth with the man and the parachute dangling from its port wing. There were the two bombers which collided while swerving to avoid a fighter, and I remember distinctly seeing a man being thrown clear out of the smoke and debris of the collision, hanging in mid-air with his arms outstretched and his legs apart. I tell you there was nothing that did not happen in that battle. There was the moment when I saw a single Hurricane doing tight turns around the summit of

Mt. Parnes with nine Messerschmitts on its tail and then I remember that suddenly the skies seemed to clear. There was no longer any aircraft in sight. The battle was over. I turned around and headed back towards Elevsis, and as I went I looked down and saw Athens and Piraeus and the rim of the sea as it curved around the gulf and travelled southward towards the Mediterranean. I saw the port of Piraeus where the bombs had fallen and I saw the smoke and fire rising above the docks. I saw the narrow coastal plain, and on it I saw tiny bonfires, thin columns of black smoke curling upward and drifting away to the east. They were the fires of aircraft which had been shot down, and I hoped only that none of them were Hurricanes.

Just then I ran straight into a Junkers 88; a straggler, the last bomber returning from the raid. He was in trouble and there was black smoke streaming from one of his engines. Although I shot at him, I don't think that it made any difference. He was coming down anyway. We were over the sea and I could tell that he wouldn't make the land. He didn't. He came down smoothly on his belly in the blue Gulf of Piraeus, two miles from the shore. I followed him and circled, waiting to make sure that the crew got out safely into their dinghy.

Slowly the machine began to sink, dipping its nose under the water and lifting its tail into the air. But there was no sign of the crew. Suddenly, without any warning, the rear gun started to fire. They opened up with their rear gun and the bullets made small jagged holes in my starboard wing. I swerved away and I remember shouting at them. I slid back the hood of the cockpit and shouted,

"You lousy brave bastards. I hope you drown." The bomber sank soon backwards.

When I got back they were all standing around outside the hangars counting the score, and Katina was sitting on a box with tears rolling down her cheeks. But she was not crying, and Fin was kneeling down beside her, talking to her in English, quietly and gently, forgetting that she could not understand.

We lost one third of our Hurricanes in that battle, but the Germans lost more.

The Doc was dressing someone who had been burnt and he looked up and said, "You should have heard the Greeks on the aerodrome cheering as the bombers fell out of the sky."

As we stood around talking, a truck drove up and a Greek got out and said that he had some pieces of body inside. "This is the watch," he said, "that was on the arm." It was a silver wristwatch with a luminous dial, and on the back there were some initials. We did not look inside the truck.

Now we had, I think, nine Hurricanes left.

That evening a very senior RAF officer came out from Athens and said, "Tomorrow at dawn you will all fly to Megara. It is about ten miles down the coast. There is a small field there on which you can land. The Army is working on it throughout the night. They have two big rollers there and they are rolling it smooth. The moment you land you must hide your aircraft in the olive grove which is on the south side of the field. The ground staff are going further south to Argos and you can join them later, but you may be able to operate from Megara for a day or two."

Fin said, "Where's Katina? Doc, you must find Katina and see that she gets to Argos safely."

The Doc said, "I will," and we knew that we could trust him.

At dawn the next morning, when it was still dark, we took off and flew to the little field at Megara, ten miles away. We landed and hid our Hurricanes in the olive grove and broke off branches of the trees and put them over the aircraft. Then we sat down on the slope of a small hill and waited for orders.

As the sun rose up over the mountains we looked across the field and saw a mass of Greek villagers coming down from the village of Megara, coming down towards our field. There were many hundreds of them, women and children mostly, and they all came down towards our field, hurrying as they came.

Fin said, "What the hell," and we sat up on our little hill and watched, wondering what they were going to do.

They dispersed all around the edge of the field and gathered armfuls of heather and bracken. They carried it out on to the field, and forming themselves into long lines, they began to scatter the heather and the bracken over the grass. They were camouflaging our landing field. The rollers, when they had rolled out the ground and made it flat for landing, had left marks which were easily visible from above, and so the Greeks came out of their village, every man, woman and child, and began to put matters right. To this day I do not know who told them to do it. They stretched in a long line across the field, walking forward slowly and scattering the heather, and Fin and I went out and walked among them.

They were old women and old men mostly, very small and very sad-looking, with dark, deeply wrinkled faces and they worked slowly scattering the heather. As we walked by, they would stop their work and smile, saying something in Greek which we could not understand. One of the children gave Fin a small pink flower and he did not know what to do with it, but walked around carrying it in his hand.

Then we went back to the slope of the hill and waited. Soon the field telephone buzzed. It was the very senior officer speaking. He said that someone must fly back to Elevsis at once and collect important messages and money. He said also that all of us must leave our little field at Megara and go to Argos that evening. The others said that they would wait until I came back with the money so that we could all fly to Argos together.

At the same time, someone had told the two Army men who were still rolling our field, to destroy their rollers so that the Germans would not get them. I remember, as I was getting into my Hurricane, seeing the two huge rollers charging towards each other across the field and I remember seeing the Army men jump aside just before they collided. There was a great crash and I saw all the Greeks who were scattering heather stop in their work and look up. For a moment they stood rock still, looking at the rollers. Then one of them started to run. It was an old woman and she started to run back to the village as fast as she could, shouting something as she went, and instantly every man, woman and child in the field seemed to take fright and ran after her. I wanted to get out and run beside them and explain to them; to say I was sorry but that there was nothing else we could do. I wanted to tell them that we would not forget them and that one day we would come back. But it was no use. Bewildered and frightened, they ran back to their homes, and they did not stop running until they were out of sight, not even the old men.

I took off and flew to Elevsis. I landed on a dead aerodrome. There was not a soul to be seen. I parked my Hurricane, and as I walked over to the hangars the bombers came over once again. I hid in a ditch until they had finished their work, then got up and walked over to the small operations room. The telephone was still on the table, so for some reason I picked up the receiver and said, "Hello."

A rather German voice at the other end answered.

I said, "Can you hear me?" and the voice said:

"Yes, yes, I can hear you."

"All right," I said, "listen carefully."

"Yes, continue please."

"This is the RAF speaking. And one day we will come back, do you understand. One day we will come back."

Then I tore the telephone from its socket and threw it through the glass of the closed window. When I went outside there was a small man in civilian clothes standing near the door. He had a revolver in one hand and a small bag in the other.

"Do you want anything?" he said in quite good English.

I said, "Yes, I want important messages and papers which I am to carry back to Argos."

"Here you are," he said, as he handed me the bag. "And good luck."

I flew back to Megara. There were two Greek destroyers standing offshore, burning and sinking. I circled our field and the others taxied out, took off and we all flew off towards Argos.

The landing ground at Argos was just a kind of small field. It was surrounded by thick olive groves into which we taxied our aircraft for hiding. I don't know how long the field was, but it was not easy to land upon it. You had to come in low hanging on the prop, and the moment you touched down you had to start putting on brake, jerking it on and jerking it off again the moment she started to nose over. But only one man overshot and crashed.

The ground staff had arrived already and as we got out of our aircraft Katina came running up with a basket of black olives, offering them to us and pointing to our stomachs, indicating that we must eat.

Fin bent down and ruffled her hair with his hand. He said, "Katina, one day we must go into town and buy you a new dress." She smiled at him but did not understand and we all started to eat black olives.

Then I looked around and saw that the wood was full of aircraft. Around every corner there was an aeroplane hidden in the trees, and when we asked about it we learned that the Greeks had brought the whole of their air force down to Argos and parked them in that little wood. They were peculiar ancient models, not one of them less than five years old, and I don't know how many dozen there were there.

That night we slept under the trees. We wrapped Katina up in a large flying suit and gave her a flying helmet for a pillow, and after she had gone to sleep we sat around eating black olives and drinking resinato out of an enormous cask. But we were very tired, and soon we fell asleep.

All the next day we saw the truckloads of troops moving down the road towards the sea, and as often as we could we took off and flew above them.

The Germans kept coming over and bombing the road nearby, but they had not yet spotted our airfield.

Later in the day we were told that every available Hurricane was to take off at six P.M. to protect an important shipping move, and the nine machines, which were all that were now left, were refuelled and got ready. At three minutes to six we began to taxi out of the olive grove on to the field.

The first two machines took off, but just as they left the ground something black swept down out of the sky and shot them both down in flames. I looked around and saw at least fifty Messerschmitt 110s circling our field, and even as I looked some of them turned and came down upon the remaining seven Hurricanes which were waiting to take off.

There was no time to do anything. Each one of our aircraft was hit in that first swoop, although funnily enough only one of the pilots was hurt. It was impossible now to take off, so we jumped out of our aircraft, hauled the wounded pilot out of his cockpit and ran with him back to the slit trenches, to the wonderful big, deep zigzagging slit trenches which had been dug by the Greeks.

The Messerschmitts took their time. There was no opposition either from the ground or from the air, except that Fin was firing his revolver.

It is not a pleasant thing to be ground-strafed especially if they have cannon in their wings; and unless one has a deep slit trench in which to lie, there is no future in it. For some reason, perhaps because they thought it was a good joke, the German pilots went for the slit trenches before they bothered about the aircraft. The first ten minutes was spent rushing madly around the corners of the trenches so as not to be caught in a trench which ran parallel with the line of flight of the attacking aircraft. It was a hectic, dreadful ten minutes, with everyone shouting "Here comes another," and scrambling and rushing to get around the corner into the other section of the trench.

Then the Germans went for the Hurricanes and at the same time for the mass of old Greek aircraft parked all around the olive grove, and one by one, methodically and systematically, they set them on fire. The noise was terrific, and everywhere—in the trees, on the rocks and on the grass—the bullets splattered.

I remember peeping cautiously over the top of our trench and seeing a small white flower growing just a few inches away from my nose. It was pure white and it had three petals. I remember looking past it and seeing three of the Germans diving on my own Hurricane which was parked on the other side of the field and I remember shouting at them, although I do not know what I said.

Then suddenly I saw Katina. She was running out from the far corner of the aerodrome, running right out into the middle of this mass of blazing guns and burning aircraft, running as fast as she could. Once she stumbled, but she scrambled to her feet again and went on running. Then she stopped and stood looking up, raising her fists at the planes as they flew past.

Now as she stood there, I remember seeing one of the Messerschmitts turning and coming in low straight towards her and I remember thinking that she was so small that she could not be hit. I remember seeing the spurts of flame from his guns as he came, and I remember seeing the child, for a split second, standing quite still, facing the machine. I remember that the wind was blowing in her hair.

Then she was down.

The next moment I shall never forget. On every side, as if by magic, men appeared out of the ground. They swarmed out of their trenches and like a crazy mob poured on to the aerodrome, running towards the tiny little bundle, which lay motionless in the middle of the field. They ran fast, crouching as they went, and I remember jumping up out of my slit trench and joining with them. I remember thinking of nothing at all and watching the boots of the man in front of me, noticing that he was a little bow-legged and that his blue trousers were much too long.

I remember seeing Fin arrive first, followed closely by a sergeant called Wishful, and I remember seeing the two of them pick up Katina and start running with her back towards the trenches. I saw her leg, which was just a lot of blood and bones, and I saw her chest where the blood was spurting out on to her white print dress; I saw, for a moment, her face, which was white as the snow on top of Olympus.

I ran beside Fin, and as he ran, he kept saying, "The lousy bastards, the lousy, bloody bastards"; and then as we got to our trench I remember looking round and finding that there was no longer any noise or shooting. The Germans had gone.

Fin said, "Where's the Doc?" and suddenly there he was, standing beside us, looking at Katina—looking at her face.

The Doc gently touched her wrist and without looking up he said, "She is not alive."

They put her down under a little tree, and when I turned away I saw on all sides the fires of countless burning aircraft. I saw my own Hurricane burning near by and I stood staring hopelessly into the flames as they danced around the engine and licked against the metal of the wings.

I stood staring into the flames, and as I stared the fire became a deeper red and I saw beyond it not a tangled mass of smoking wreckage, but the flames of a hotter and intenser fire which now burned and smouldered in the hearts of the people of Greece.

Still I stared, and as I stared I saw in the centre of the fire, whence the red flames sprang, a bright, white heat, shining bright and without any colour.

As I stared, the brightness diffused and became soft and yellow like sunlight, and through it, beyond it, I saw a young child standing in the middle of a field with the sunlight shining in her hair. For a moment she stood looking up into the sky, which was clear and blue and without any clouds; then she turned and looked towards me, and as she turned I saw that the front of her white print dress was stained deep red, the colour of blood.

Then there was no longer any fire or any flames and I saw before me only the glowing twisted wreckage of a burned-out plane. I must have been standing there for quite a long time.

THE WAY UP TO HEAVEN

All her life, Mrs. Foster had had an almost pathological fear of missing a train, a plane, a boat, or even a theatre curtain. In other respects, she was not a particularly nervous woman, but the mere thought of being late on occasions like these would throw her into such a state of nerves that she would begin to twitch. It was nothing much—just a tiny vellicating muscle in the corner of the left eye, like a secret wink—but the annoying thing was that it refused to disappear until an hour or so after the train or plane or whatever it was had been safely caught.

It was really extraordinary how in certain people a simple apprehension about a thing like catching a train can grow into a serious obsession. At least half an hour before it was time to leave the house for the station, Mrs. Foster would step out of the elevator all ready to go, with hat and coat and gloves, and then, being quite unable to sit down, she would flutter and fidget about from room to room until her husband, who must have been well aware of her state, finally emerged from his privacy and suggested in a cool dry voice that perhaps they had better get going now, had they not?

Mr. Foster may possibly have had a right to be irritated by this foolishness of his wife's, but he could have had no excuse for increasing her misery by keeping her waiting unnecessarily. Mind you, it is by no means certain that this is what he did, yet whenever they were to go somewhere, his timing was so accurate—just a minute or two late, you understand—and his manner so bland that it was hard to believe he wasn't purposely inflicting a nasty private little torture of his own on the unhappy lady. And one thing he must have known—that she would never dare to call out and tell him to hurry. He had disciplined her too well for that. He must also have known that if he was prepared to wait even beyond the last moment of safety, he could drive her nearly into hysterics. On one or two special occasions in the later years of their married life, it seemed almost as though he had *wanted* to miss the train simply in order to intensify the poor woman's suffering.

Assuming (though one cannot be sure) that the husband was guilty, what made his attitude doubly unreasonable was the fact that, with the exception of this one small irrepressible foible, Mrs. Foster was and always had been a good and loving wife. For over thirty years, she had served him loyally and well. There was no doubt about this. Even she, a very modest woman, was aware of it, and although she had for years refused to let herself believe that Mr. Foster would ever consciously torment her, there had been times recently when she had caught herself beginning to wonder.

Mr. Eugene Foster, who was nearly seventy years old, lived with his wife in a large six-storey house in New York City, on East Sixty-second Street, and they had four servants. It was a gloomy place, and few people came to visit them. But on this particular morning in January, the house had come alive and there was a great deal of bustling about. One maid was distributing bundles of dust sheets to every room, while another was draping them over the furniture. The butler was bringing down suitcases and putting them in the hall. The cook kept popping up from the kitchen to have a word with the butler, and Mrs. Foster herself, in an old-fashioned fur coat and with a black hat on the top of her head, was flying from room to room and pretending to supervise these operations. Actually, she was thinking of nothing at all except that she was going to miss her plane if her husband didn't come out of his study soon and get ready.

"What time is it, Walker?" she said to the butler as she passed him.

"It's ten minutes past nine, madam."

"And has the car come?"

"Yes, madam, it's waiting. I'm just going to put the luggage in now."

"It takes an hour to get to Idlewild," she said. "My plane leaves at eleven. I have to be there half an hour beforehand for the formalities. I shall be late. I just *know* I'm going to be late."

"I think you have plenty of time, madam," the butler said kindly. "I warned Mr. Foster that you must leave at nine-fifteen. There's still another five minutes."

"Yes, Walker, I know, I know. But get the luggage in quickly, will you please?"

She began walking up and down the hall, and whenever the butler came by, she asked him the time. This, she kept telling herself, was the *one* plane she must not miss. It had taken months to persuade her husband to allow her to go. If she missed it, he might easily decide that she should cancel the whole thing. And the trouble was that he insisted on coming to the airport to see her off.

"Dear God," she said aloud, "I'm going to miss it. I know, I know, I *know* I'm going to miss it." The little muscle beside the left eye was twitching madly now. The eyes themselves were very close to tears.

"What time is it, Walker?"

"It's eighteen minutes past, madam."

"Now I really *will* miss it!" she cried. "Oh, I wish he would come!"

This was an important journey for Mrs. Foster. She was going all alone to Paris to visit her daughter, her only child, who was married to a Frenchman. Mrs. Foster didn't care much for the Frenchman, but she was fond of her daughter, and, more than that, she had developed a great yearning to set eyes on her three grandchildren. She knew them only from the many photographs that she had received and that she kept putting up all over the house. They were beautiful, these children. She doted on them, and each time a new picture arrived she would carry it away and sit with it for a long time, staring at it lovingly and searching the small faces for signs of that old satisfying blood likeness that meant so much. And now, lately, she had come more and more to feel that she did not really wish to live out her days in a place where she could not be near these children, and have them visit her, and take them for walks, and buy them presents, and watch them grow. She knew, of course, that it was wrong and in a way disloyal to have thoughts like these while her husband was still alive. She knew also that although he was no longer active in his many enterprises, he would never consent to leave New York and live in Paris. It was a miracle that he had ever agreed to let her fly over there alone for six weeks to visit them. But, oh, how she wished she could live there always, and be close to them!

"Walker, what time is it?"

"Twenty-two minutes past, madam."

As he spoke, a door opened and Mr. Foster came into the hall. He stood for a moment, looking intently at his wife, and she looked back at him—at this diminutive but still quite dapper old man with the huge bearded face that bore such an astonishing resemblance to those old photographs of Andrew Carnegie.

"Well," he said, "I suppose perhaps we'd better get going fairly soon if you want to catch that plane."

"*Yes*, dear—*yes*! Everything's ready. The car's waiting."

"That's good," he said. With his head over to one side, he was watching her closely. He had a peculiar way of cocking the head and then moving it in a series of small, rapid jerks. Because of this and because he was clasping his hands up high in front of him, near the chest, he was somehow like a squirrel standing there—a quick clever old squirrel from the park.

"Here's Walker with your coat, dear. Put it on."

"I'll be with you in a moment," he said. "I'm just going to wash my hands."

She waited for him, and the tall butler stood beside her, holding the coat and the hat.

"Walker, will I miss it?"

"No, madam," the butler said. "I think you'll make it all right."

Then Mr. Foster appeared again, and the butler helped him on with his coat. Mrs. Foster hurried outside and got into the hired Cadillac. Her husband came after her, but he walked down the steps of the house slowly, pausing halfway to observe the sky and to sniff the cold morning air.

"It looks a bit foggy," he said as he sat down beside her in the car. "And it's always worse out there at the airport. I shouldn't be surprised if the flight's cancelled already."

"Don't say that, dear—*please*."

They didn't speak again until the car had crossed over the river to Long Island.

"I arranged everything with the servants," Mr. Foster said. "They're all going off today. I gave them half-pay for six weeks and told Walker I'd send him a telegram when we wanted them back."

"Yes," she said. "He told me."

"I'll move into the club tonight. It'll be a nice change staying at the club."

"Yes, dear. I'll write to you."

"I'll call in at the house occasionally to see that everything's all right and to pick up the mail."

"But don't you really think Walker should stay there all the time to look after things?" she asked meekly.

"Nonsense. It's quite unnecessary. And anyway, I'd have to pay him full wages."

"Oh yes," she said. "Of course."

"What's more, you never know what people get up to when they're left alone in a house," Mr. Foster announced, and with that he took out a cigar and, after snipping off the end with a silver cutter, lit it with a gold lighter.

She sat still in the car with her hands clasped together tight under the rug.

"Will you write to me?" she asked.

"I'll see," he said. "But I doubt it. You know I don't hold with letter-writing unless there's something specific to say."

"Yes, dear, I know. So don't you bother."

They drove on, along Queen's Boulevard, and as they approached the flat marshland on which Idlewild is built, the fog began to thicken and the car had to slow down.

"Oh dear!" cried Mrs. Foster. "I'm *sure* I'm going to miss it now! What time is it?"

"Stop fussing," the old man said. "It doesn't matter anyway. It's bound to be cancelled now. They never fly in this sort of weather. I don't know why you bothered to come out."

She couldn't be sure, but it seemed to her that there was suddenly a new note in his voice, and she turned to look at him. It was difficult to observe any change in his expression under all that hair. The mouth was what counted. She wished, as she had so often before, that she could see the mouth clearly. The eyes never showed anything except when he was in a rage.

"Of course," he went on, "if by any chance it *does* go, then I agree with you—you'll be certain to miss it now. Why don't you resign yourself to that?"

She turned away and peered through the window at the fog. It seemed to be getting thicker as they went along, and now she could only just make out the edge of the road and the margin of grassland beyond it. She knew that her husband was still look-ing at her. She glanced at him again, and this time she noticed with a kind of horror that he was staring intently at the little place in the corner of her left eye where she could feel the muscle twitching.

"Won't you?" he said.

"Won't I what?"

"Be sure to miss it now if it goes. We can't drive fast in this muck."

He didn't speak to her any more after that. The car crawled on and on. The driver had a yellow lamp directed on to the edge of the road, and this helped him to keep going. Other lights, some white and some yellow, kept coming out of the fog towards them, and there was an especially bright one that followed close behind them all the time.

Suddenly, the driver stopped the car.

"There!" Mr. Foster cried. "We're stuck. I knew it."

"No, sir," the driver said, turning round. "We made it. This is the airport."

Without a word, Mrs. Foster jumped out and hurried through the main entrance into the building. There was a mass of people in-side, mostly disconsolate passengers standing around the ticket counters. She pushed her way through and spoke to the clerk.

"Yes," he said. "Your flight is temporarily postponed. But please don't go away. We're expecting this weather to clear any moment."

She went back to her husband who was still sitting in the car and told him the news. "But don't you wait, dear," she said. "There's no sense in that."

"I won't," he answered. "So long as the driver can get me back. Can you get me back, driver?"

"I think so," the man said.

"Is the luggage out?"

"Yes, sir."

"Good-bye, dear," Mrs. Foster said, leaning into the car and giving her husband a small kiss on the coarse grey fur of his cheek.

"Good-bye," he answered. "Have a good trip."

The car drove off, and Mrs. Foster was left alone.

The rest of the day was a sort of nightmare for her. She sat for hour after hour on a bench, as close to the airline counter as possible, and every thirty minutes or so she would get up and ask the clerk if the situation had changed. She always received the same reply—that she must continue to wait, because the fog might blow away at any moment. It wasn't until after six in the evening that the loudspeakers finally announced that the flight had been postponed until eleven o'clock the next morning.

Mrs. Foster didn't quite know what to do when she heard this news. She stayed sitting on her bench for at least another half-hour, wondering, in a tired, hazy sort of way, where she might go to spend the night. She hated to leave the airport. She didn't wish to see her husband. She was terrified that in one way or another he would eventually manage to prevent her from getting to France. She would have liked to remain just where she was, sitting on the bench the whole night through. That would be the safest. But she was already exhausted, and it didn't take her long to realize that this was a ridiculous thing for an elderly lady to do. So in the end she went to a phone and called the house.

Her husband, who was on the point of leaving for the club, answered it himself. She told him the news, and asked whether the servants were still there.

"They've all gone," he said.

"In that case, dear, I'll just get myself a room somewhere for the night. And don't you bother yourself about it at all."

"That would be foolish," he said. "You've got a large house here at your disposal. Use it."

"But, dear, it's *empty*."

"Then I'll stay with you myself."

"There's no food in the house. There's nothing."

"Then eat before you come in. Don't be so stupid, woman. Everything you do, you seem to want to make a fuss about it."

"Yes," she said. "I'm sorry. I'll get myself a sandwich here, and then I'll come on in."

Outside, the fog had cleared a little, but it was still a long, slow drive in the taxi, and she didn't arrive back at the house on Sixty-second Street until fairly late.

Her husband emerged from his study when he heard her coming in. "Well," he said, standing by the study door, "how was Paris?"

"We leave at eleven in the morning," she answered. "It's definite."

"You mean if the fog clears."

"It's clearing now. There's a wind coming up."

"You look tired," he said. "You must have had an anxious day."

"It wasn't very comfortable. I think I'll go straight to bed."

"I've ordered a car for the morning," he said. "Nine o'clock."

"Oh, thank you, dear. And I certainly hope you're not going to bother to come all the way out again to see me off."

"No," he said slowly. "I don't think I will. But there's no reason why you shouldn't drop me at the club on your way."

She looked at him, and at that moment he seemed to be standing a long way off from her, beyond some borderline. He was suddenly so small and far away that she couldn't be sure what he was doing, or what he was thinking, or even what he was.

"The club is downtown," she said. "It isn't on the way to the airport."

"But you'll have plenty of time, my dear. Don't you want to drop me at the club?"

"Oh, yes—of course."

"That's good. Then I'll see you in the morning at nine."

She went up to her bedroom on the second floor, and she was so exhausted from her day that she fell asleep soon after she lay down.

Next morning, Mrs. Foster was up early, and by eight-thirty she was downstairs and ready to leave.

Shortly after nine, her husband appeared. "Did you make any coffee?" he asked.

"No, dear. I thought you'd get a nice breakfast at the club. The car is here. It's been waiting. I'm all ready to go."

They were standing in the hall—they always seemed to be meeting in the hall nowadays—she with her hat and coat and purse, he in a curiously cut Edwardian jacket with high lapels.

"Your luggage?"

"It's at the airport."

"Ah yes," he said. "Of course. And if you're going to take me to the club first, I suppose we'd better get going fairly soon, hadn't we?"

"Yes!" she cried. "Oh, yes—*please*!"

"I'm just going to get a few cigars. I'll be right with you. You get in the car."

She turned and went out to where the chauffeur was standing, and he opened the car door for her as she approached.

"What time is it?" she asked him.

"About nine-fifteen."

Mr. Foster came out five minutes later, and watching him as he walked slowly down the steps, she noticed that his legs were like goat's legs in those narrow stovepipe trousers that he wore. As on the day before, he paused halfway down to sniff the air and to examine the sky. The weather was still not quite clear, but there was a wisp of sun coming through the mist.

"Perhaps you'll be lucky this time," he said as he settled himself beside her in the car.

"Hurry, please," she said to the chauffeur. "Don't bother about the rug. I'll arrange the rug. Please get going. I'm late."

The man went back to his seat behind the wheel and started the engine.

"*Just* a moment!" Mr. Foster said suddenly. "Hold it a moment, chauffeur, will you?"

"What is it, dear?" She saw him searching the pockets of his overcoat.

"I had a little present I wanted you to take to Ellen," he said. "Now, where on earth is it? I'm sure I had it in my hand as I came down."

"I never saw you carrying anything. What sort of present?"

"A little box wrapped up in white paper. I forgot to give it to you yesterday. I don't want to forget it today."

"A little box!" Mrs. Foster cried. "I never saw any little box!" She began hunting frantically in the back of the car.

Her husband continued searching through the pockets of his coat. Then he unbuttoned the coat and felt around in his jacket. "Confound it," he said, "I must've left it in my bedroom. I won't be a moment."

"Oh, *please*!" she cried. "We haven't got time! *Please* leave it! You can mail it. It's only one of those silly combs anyway. You're always giving her combs."

"And what's wrong with combs, may I ask?" he said, furious that she should have forgotten herself for once.

"Nothing, dear, I'm sure. But . . ."

"Stay here!" he commanded. "I'm going to get it."

"Be quick, dear! Oh, *please* be quick!"

She sat still, waiting and waiting.

"Chauffeur, what time is it?"

The man had a wristwatch, which he consulted. "I make it nearly nine-thirty."

"Can we get to the airport in an hour?"

"Just about."

At this point, Mrs. Foster suddenly spotted a corner of something white wedged down in the crack of the seat on the side where her husband had been sitting. She reached over and pulled out a small paper-wrapped box, and at the same time she couldn't help noticing that it was wedged down firm and deep, as though with the help of a pushing hand.

"Here it is!" she cried. "I've found it! Oh dear, and now he'll be up there for ever searching for it! Chauffeur, quickly—run in and call him down, will you please?"

The chauffeur, a man with a small rebellious Irish mouth, didn't care very much for any of this, but he climbed out of the car and went up the steps to the front door of the house. Then he turned and came back. "Door's locked," he announced. "You got a key?"

"Yes—wait a minute." She began hunting madly in her purse. The little face was screwed up tight with anxiety, the lips pushed outward like a spout.

"Here it is! No—I'll go myself. It'll be quicker. I know where he'll be."

She hurried out of the car and up the steps to the front door, holding the key in one hand. She slid the key into the keyhole and was about to turn it—and then she stopped. Her head came up, and she stood there absolutely motionless, her whole body arrested right in the middle of all this hurry to turn the key and get into the house, and she waited—five, six, seven, eight, nine, ten seconds, she waited. The way she was standing there, with her head in the air and the body so tense, it seemed as though she were listening for the repetition of some sound that she had heard a moment before from a place far away inside the house.

Yes—quite obviously she was listening. Her whole attitude was a *listening* one. She appeared actually to be moving one of her ears closer and closer to the door. Now it was right up against the door, and for still another few seconds she remained in that position, head up, ear to door, hand on key, about to enter but not entering, trying instead, or so it seemed, to hear and to analyse these sounds that were coming faintly from this place deep within the house.

Then, all at once, she sprang to life again. She withdrew the key from the door and came running back down the steps.

"It's too late!" she cried to the chauffeur. "I can't wait for him, I simply can't. I'll miss the plane. Hurry now, driver, hurry! To the airport!"

The chauffeur, had he been watching her closely, might have noticed that her face had turned absolutely white and that the whole expression had suddenly altered. There was no longer that rather soft and silly look. A peculiar hardness had settled itself upon the features. The little mouth, usually so flabby, was now tight and thin, the eyes were bright, and the voice, when she spoke, carried a new note of authority.

"Hurry, driver, hurry!"

"Isn't your husband travelling with you?" the man asked, astonished.

"Certainly not! I was only going to drop him at the club. It won't matter. He'll understand. He'll get a cab. Don't sit there talking, man. *Get going*! I've got a plane to catch for Paris!"

With Mrs. Foster urging him from the back seat, the man drove fast all the way, and she caught her plane with a few minutes to spare. Soon she was high up over the Atlantic, reclining comfortably in her aeroplane chair, listening to the hum of the motors, heading for Paris at last. The new mood was still with her. She felt remarkably strong and, in a queer sort of way, wonderful. She was a trifle breathless with it all, but this was more from pure astonishment at what she had done than anything else, and as the plane flew further and further away from New York and East Sixty-second Street, a great sense of calmness began to settle upon her. By the time she reached Paris, she was just as strong and cool and calm as she could wish.

She met her grandchildren, and they were even more beautiful in the flesh than in their photographs. They were like angels, she told herself, so beautiful they were. And every day she took them for walks, and fed them cakes, and bought them presents, and told them charming stories.

Once a week, on Tuesdays, she wrote a letter to her husband—a nice, chatty letter—full of news and gossip, which always ended with the words "Now be sure to take your meals regularly, dear, although this is something I'm afraid you may not be doing when I'm not with you."

When the six weeks were up, everybody was sad that she had to return to America, to her husband. Everybody, that is, except her. Surprisingly, she didn't seem to mind as much as one might have expected, and when she kissed them all good-bye, there was something in her manner and in the things she said that appeared to hint at the possibility of a return in the not too distant future.

However, like the faithful wife she was, she did not overstay her time. Exactly six weeks after she had arrived, she sent a cable to her husband and caught the plane back to New York.

Arriving at Idlewild, Mrs. Foster was interested to observe that there was no car to meet her. It is possible that she might even have been a little amused. But she was extremely calm and did not over-tip the porter who helped her into a taxi with her baggage.

New York was colder than Paris, and there were lumps of dirty snow lying in the gutters of the streets. The taxi drew up before the house on Sixty-second Street, and Mrs. Foster persuaded the driver to carry her two large cases to the top of the steps. Then she paid him off and rang the bell. She waited, but there was no answer. Just to make sure, she rang again, and she could hear it tinkling shrilly far away in the pantry, at the back of the house. But still no one came.

So she took out her own key and opened the door herself.

The first thing she saw as she entered was a great pile of mail lying on the floor where it had fallen after being slipped through the letter box. The place was dark and cold. A dust sheet was still draped over the grandfather clock. In spite of the cold, the atmosphere was peculiarly oppressive, and there was a faint and curious odour in the air that she had never smelled before.

She walked quickly across the hall and disappeared for a moment around the corner to the left, at the back. There was something deliberate and purposeful about this action; she had the air of a woman who is off to investigate a rumour or to confirm a suspicion. And when she returned a few seconds later, there was a little glimmer of satisfaction on her face.

She paused in the centre of the hall, as though wondering what to do next. Then, suddenly, she turned and went across into her husband's study. On the desk she found his address book, and after hunting through it for a while she picked up the phone and dialled a number.

"Hello," she said. "Listen—this is Nine East Sixty-second Street . . . Yes, that's right. Could you send someone round as soon as possible, do you think? Yes, it seems to be stuck between the second and third floors. At least, that's where the indicator's pointing . . . Right away? Oh, that's very kind of you. You see, my legs aren't any too good for walking up a lot of stairs. Thank you so much. Good-bye."

She replaced the receiver and sat there at her husband's desk, patiently waiting for the man who would be coming soon to repair the lift.

"It worries me to death, Albert, it really does," Mrs. Taylor said.

She kept her eyes fixed on the baby who was now lying absolutely motionless in the crook of her left arm.

"I just know there's something wrong."

The skin on the baby's face had a pearly translucent quality and was stretched very tightly over the bones.

"Try again," Albert Taylor said.

"It won't do any good."

"You have to keep trying, Mabel," he said.

She lifted the bottle out of the saucepan of hot water and shook a few drops of milk on to the inside of her wrist, testing for temperature.

"Come on," she whispered. "Come on, my baby. Wake up and take a bit more of this."

There was a small lamp on the table close by that made a soft yellow glow all around her.

"Please," she said. "Take just a weeny bit more."

The husband watched her over the top of his magazine. She was half dead with exhaustion, he could see that, and the pale oval face, usually so grave and serene, had taken on a kind of pinched and desperate look. But even so, the drop of her head as she gazed down at the child was curiously beautiful.

"You see," she murmured. "It's no good. She won't have it."

She held the bottle up to the light, squinting at the calibrations.

"One ounce again. That's all she's taken. No—it isn't even that. It's only three-quarters. It's not enough to keep body and soul together, Albert, it really isn't. It worries me to death."

"I know," he said.

"If only they could *find out* what was wrong."

"There's nothing wrong, Mabel. It's just a matter of time."

"Of course there's something wrong."

"Dr. Robinson says no."

"Look," she said, standing up. "You can't tell me it's natural for a six-week-old child to weigh less, less by more than *two whole pounds* than she did when she was born! Just look at those legs! They're nothing but skin and bone!"

The tiny baby lay limply on her arm, not moving.

"Dr. Robinson said you was to stop worrying, Mabel. So did that other one."

"Ha!" she said. "Isn't that wonderful! I'm to stop worrying!"

"Now, Mabel."

"What does he want me to do? Treat it as some sort of a joke?"

"He didn't say that."

"I hate doctors! I hate them all!" she cried, and she swung away from him and walked quickly out of the room towards the stairs, carrying the baby with her.

Albert Taylor stayed where he was and let her go.

In a little while he heard her moving about in the bedroom directly over his head, quick nervous footsteps going tap tap tap on the linoleum above. Soon the footsteps would stop, and then he would have to get up and follow her, and when he went into the bedroom he would find her sitting beside the cot as usual, staring at the child and crying softly to herself and refusing to move.

"She's starving, Albert," she would say.

"Of course she's not starving."

"She *is* starving. I know she is. And Albert?"

"Yes?"

"I believe you know it too, but you won't admit it. Isn't that right?"

Every night now it was like this.

Last week they had taken the child back to the hospital, and the doctor had examined it carefully and told them that there was nothing the matter.

"It took us nine years to get this baby, Doctor," Mabel had said. "I think it would kill me if anything should happen to her."

That was six days ago and since then it had lost another five ounces.

But worrying about it wasn't going to help anybody, Albert Taylor told himself. One simply had to trust the doctor on a thing like this. He picked up the magazine that was still lying on his lap and glanced idly down the list of contents to see what it had to offer this week:

Royal Jelly

All his life Albert Taylor had been fascinated by anything that had to do with bees. As a small boy he often used to catch them in his bare hands and go running with them into the house to show to his mother, and sometimes he would put them on his face and let them crawl about over his cheeks and neck, and the astonishing thing about it all was that he never got stung. On the contrary, the bees seemed to enjoy being with him. They never tried to fly away, and to get rid of them he would have to brush them off gently with his fingers. Even then they would frequently return and settle again on his arm or hand or knee, any place where the skin was bare.

His father, who was a bricklayer, said there must be some witch's stench about the boy, something noxious that came oozing out through the pores of the skin, and that no good would ever come of it, hypnotizing insects like that. But the mother said it was a gift given him by God, and even went so far as to compare him with St. Francis and the birds.

As he grew older, Albert Taylor's fascination with bees developed into an obsession, and by the time he was twelve he had built his first hive. The following summer he had captured his first swarm. Two years later, at the age of fourteen, he had no less than five hives standing neatly in a row against the fence in his father's small back yard, and already—apart from the normal task of producing honey—he was practising the delicate and complicated business of rearing his own queens, grafting larvae into artificial cell cups, and all the rest of it.

He never had to use smoke when there was work to do inside a hive, and he never wore gloves on his hands or a net over his head. Clearly there was some strange sympathy between this boy and the bees, and down in the village, in the shops and pubs, they began to speak about him with a certain kind of respect, and people started coming up to the house to buy his honey.

When he was eighteen, he had rented one acre of rough pasture alongside a cherry orchard down the valley about a mile from the village, and there he had set out to establish his own business. Now, eleven years later, he was still in the same spot, but he had six acres of ground instead of one, two hundred and forty well-stocked hives, and a small house he'd built mainly with his own hands. He had married at the age of twenty and that, apart from the fact that it had taken them over nine years to get a child, had also been a success. In fact, everything had gone pretty well for Albert until this strange little baby girl came along and started frightening them out of their wits by refusing to eat properly and losing weight every day.

He looked up from the magazine and began thinking about his daughter.

That evening, for instance, when she had opened her eyes at the beginning of the feed, he had gazed into them and seen something that frightened him to death—a kind of misty vacant stare, as though the eyes themselves were not connected to the brain at all but were just lying loose in their sockets like a couple of small grey marbles.

Did those doctors really know what they were talking about?

He reached for an ashtray and started slowly picking the ashes out from the bowl of his pipe with a matchstick.

One could always take her along to another hospital, somewhere in Oxford perhaps. He might suggest that to Mabel when he went upstairs.

He could still hear her moving around in the bedroom, but she must have taken off her shoes now and put on slippers because the noise was very faint.

He switched his attention back to the magazine and went on with his reading. He finished the article called "Experiences in the Control of Nosema," then turned over the page and began reading the next one, "The Latest on Royal Jelly." He doubted very much whether there would be anything in this that he didn't know already:

What is this wonderful substance called royal jelly?

He reached for the tin of tobacco on the table beside him and began filling his pipe, still reading.

Royal jelly is a glandular secretion produced by the nurse bees to feed the larvae immediately they have hatched from the egg. The pharyngeal glands of bees produce this substance in much the same way as the mammary glands of vertebrates produce milk. The fact is of great biological interest because no other insects in the world are known to have evolved such a process.

All old stuff, he told himself, but for want of anything better to do, he continued to read.

Royal jelly is fed in concentrated form to all bee larvae for the first three days after hatching from the egg; but beyond that point, for all those who are destined to become drones or workers, this precious food is greatly diluted with honey and pollen. On the other hand, the larvae which are destined to become queens are fed throughout the whole of their larval period on a concentrated diet of pure royal jelly. Hence the name.

Above him, up in the bedroom, the noise of the footsteps had stopped altogether. The house was quiet. He struck a match and put it to his pipe.

Royal jelly must be a substance of tremendous nourishing power, for on this diet alone, the honey-bee larva increases in weight fifteen hundred times in five days.

That was probably about right, he thought, although for some reason it had never occurred to him to consider larval growth in terms of weight before.

This is as if a seven-and-a-half-pound baby should increase in that time to five tons.

Albert Taylor stopped and read that sentence again. He read it a third time.

This is as if a seven-and-a-half-pound baby . . .

"Mabel!" he cried, jumping up from his chair. "Mabel! Come here!"

He went out into the hall and stood at the foot of the stairs calling for her to come down.

There was no answer.

He ran up the stairs and switched on the light on the landing. The bedroom door was closed. He crossed the landing and opened it and stood in the doorway looking into the dark room. "Mabel," he said. "Come downstairs a moment, will you please? I've just had a bit of an idea. It's about the baby."

The light from the landing behind him cast a faint glow over the bed and he could see her dimly now, lying on her stomach with her face buried in the pillow and her arms up over her head. She was crying again.

"Mabel," he said, going over to her, touching her shoulder. "Please come down a moment. This may be important."

"Go away," she said "Leave me alone."

"Don't you want to hear about my idea?"

"Oh, Albert, I'm *tired*," she sobbed. "I'm so tired I don't know what I'm doing anymore. I don't think I can go on. I don't think I can stand it."

There was a pause. Albert Taylor turned away from her and walked slowly over to the cradle where the baby was lying, and peered in. It was too dark for him to see the child's face, but when he bent down close he could hear the sound of breathing, very faint and quick. "What time is the next feed?" he asked.

"Two o'clock, I suppose."

"And the one after that?"

"Six in the morning."

"I'll do them both," he said. "You go to sleep."

She didn't answer.

"You get properly into bed, Mabel, and go straight to sleep, you understand? And stop worrying. I'm taking over completely for the next twelve hours. You'll give yourself a nervous breakdown going on like this."

"Yes," she said. "I know."

"I'm taking the nipper and myself *and* the alarm clock into the spare room this very moment, so you just lie down and relax and forget all about us. Right?" Already he was pushing the cradle out through the door.

"Oh, Albert," she sobbed.

"Don't you worry about a thing. Leave it to me."

"Albert . . ."

"Yes?"

"I love you, Albert."

"I love you too, Mabel. Now go to sleep."

Albert Taylor didn't see his wife again until nearly eleven o'clock the next morning.

"Good *gracious* me!" she cried, rushing down the stairs in dressing gown and slippers. "Albert! Just look at the time! I must have slept twelve hours at least! Is everything all right? What happened?"

He was sitting quietly in his armchair, smoking a pipe and reading the morning paper. The baby was in a sort of carry-cot on the floor at his feet, sleeping.

"Hallo, dear," he said, smiling.

She ran over to the cot and looked in. "Did she take anything, Albert? How many times have you fed her? She was due for another one at ten o'clock, did you know that?"

Albert Taylor folded the newspaper neatly into a square and put it away on the side table. "I fed her at two in the morning," he said, "and she took about half an ounce, no more. I fed her again at six and she did a bit better that time, two ounces . . ."

"*Two ounces*! Oh, Albert, that's marvellous!"

"And we just finished the last feed ten minutes ago. There's the bottle on the mantelpiece. Only one ounce left. She drank three. How's that?" He was grinning proudly, delighted with his achievement.

The woman quickly got down on her knees and peered at the baby.

"Don't she look better?" he asked eagerly. "Don't she look fatter in the face?"

"It may sound silly," the wife said, "but I actually think she does. Oh, Albert, you're a marvel! How did you do it?"

"She's turning the corner," he said. "That's all it is. Just like the doctor prophesied, she's turning the corner."

"I pray to God you're right, Albert."

"Of course I'm right. From now on, you watch her go."

The woman was gazing lovingly at the baby.

"You look a lot better yourself too, Mabel."

"I feel wonderful. I'm sorry about last night."

"Let's keep it this way," he said. "I'll do all the night feeds in future. You do the day ones."

She looked up at him across the cot, frowning. "No," she said. "Oh no, I wouldn't allow you to do that."

"I don't want you to have a breakdown, Mabel."

"I won't, not now I've had some sleep."

"Much better we share it."

"No, Albert. This is my job and I intend to do it. Last night won't happen again."

There was a pause. Albert Taylor took the pipe out of his mouth and examined the grain on the bowl. "All right," he said. "In that case I'll just relieve you of the donkey work, I'll do all the sterilizing and the mixing of the food and getting everything ready. That'll help you a bit, anyway."

She looked at him carefully, wondering what could have come over him all of a sudden.

"You see, Mabel, I've been thinking . . ."

"Yes, dear."

"I've been thinking that up until last night I've never even raised a finger to help you with this baby."

"That isn't true."

"Oh yes it is. So I've decided that from now on I'm going to do *my* share of the work. I'm going to be the feed-mixer and the bottle-sterilizer. Right?"

"It's very sweet of you, dear, but I really don't think it's necessary . . ."

"Come on!" he cried. "Don't change the luck! I done it the last three times and just *look* what happened! When's the next one? Two o'clock, isn't it?"

"Yes."

"It's all mixed," he said. "Everything's all mixed and ready and all you've got to do when the time comes is to go out there to the larder and take it off the shelf and warm it up. That's *some* help, isn't it?"

The woman got up off her knees and went over to him and kissed him on the cheek. "You're such a nice man," she said. "I love you more and more every day I know you."

Later, in the middle of the afternoon, when Albert was outside in the sunshine working among the hives, he heard her calling to him from the house.

"Albert!" she shouted. "Albert, come here!" She was running through the buttercups towards him.

He started forward to meet her, wondering what was wrong.

"Oh, Albert! Guess what!"

"What?"

"I've just finished giving her the two-o'clock feed and she's taken the whole lot!"

"No!"

"Every drop of it! Oh, Albert, I'm so happy! She's going to be all right! She's turned the corner just like you said!" She came up to him and threw her arms around his neck and hugged him, and he clapped her on the back and laughed and said what a marvellous little mother she was.

"Will you come in and watch the next one and see if she does it again, Albert?"

He told her he wouldn't miss it for anything, and she hugged him again, then turned and ran back to the house, skipping over the grass and singing all the way.

Naturally, there was a certain amount of suspense in the air as the time approached for the six-o'clock feed. By five thirty both parents were already seated in the living room waiting for the moment to arrive. The bottle with the milk formula in it was standing in a saucepan of warm water on the mantelpiece. The baby was asleep in its carry-cot on the sofa.

At twenty minutes to six it woke up and started screaming its head off.

"There you are!" Mrs. Taylor cried. "She's asking for the bottle. Pick her up quick, Albert, and hand her to me here. Give me the bottle first."

He gave her the bottle, then placed the baby on the woman's lap. Cautiously, she touched the baby's lips with the end of the nipple. The baby seized the nipple between its gums and began to suck ravenously with a rapid powerful action.

"Oh, Albert, isn't it wonderful?" she said, laughing.

"It's terrific, Mabel."

In seven or eight minutes, the entire contents of the bottle had disappeared down the baby's throat.

"You clever girl," Mrs. Taylor said. "Four ounces again."

Albert Taylor was leaning forward in his chair, peering intently into the baby's face. "You know what?" he said. "She even seems as though she's put on a touch of weight already. What do you think?"

The mother looked down at the child.

"Don't she seem bigger and fatter to you, Mabel, than she was yesterday?"

"Maybe she does, Albert. I'm not sure. Although actually there couldn't be any *real* gain in such a short time as this. The important thing is that she's eating normally."

"She's turned the corner," Albert said. "I don't think you need worry about her any more."

"I certainly won't."

"You want me to go up and fetch the cradle back into our own bedroom, Mabel?"

"Yes, please," she said.

Albert went upstairs and moved the cradle. The woman followed with the baby, and after changing its nappy, she laid it gently down on its bed. Then she covered it with sheet and blanket.

"Doesn't she look lovely, Albert?" she whispered. "Isn't that the most beautiful baby you've ever seen in your *entire* life?"

"Leave her be now, Mabel," he said. "Come on downstairs and cook us a bit of supper. We both deserve it."

After they had finished eating, the parents settled themselves in armchairs in the living room, Albert with his magazine and his pipe, Mrs. Taylor with her knitting. But this was a very different scene from the one of the night before. Suddenly, all tensions had vanished. Mrs. Taylor's handsome oval face was glowing with pleasure, her cheeks were pink, her eyes were sparkling bright, and her mouth was fixed in a little dreamy smile of pure content. Every now and again she would glance up from her knitting and gaze affectionately at her husband. Occasionally, she would stop the clicking of her needles altogether for a few seconds and sit quite still, looking at the ceiling, listening for a cry or a whimper from upstairs. But all was quiet.

"Albert," she said after a while.

"Yes, dear?"

"What was it you were going to tell me last night when you came rushing up to the bedroom? You said you had an idea for the baby."

Albert Taylor lowered the magazine on to his lap and gave her a long sly look.

"Did I?" he said.

"Yes." She waited for him to go on, but he didn't.

"What's the big joke?" she asked. "Why are you grinning like that?"

"It's a joke all right," he said.

"Tell it to me, dear."

"I'm not sure I ought to," he said. "You might call me a liar."

She had seldom seen him looking so pleased with himself as he was now, and she smiled back at him, egging him on.

"I'd just like to see your face when you hear it, Mabel, that's all."

"Albert, what is all this?"

He paused, refusing to be hurried.

"You do think the baby's better, don't you?" he asked.

"Of course I do."

"You agree with me that all of a sudden she's feeding marvellously and looking one-hundred-per-cent different?"

"I do, Albert, yes."

"That's good," he said, the grin widening. "You see, it's me that did it."

"Did what?"

"I cured the baby."

"Yes, dear, I'm sure you did." Mrs. Taylor went right on with her knitting.

"You don't believe me, do you?"

"Of course I believe you, I give you all the credit, every bit of it."

"Then how did I do it?"

"Well," she said, pausing a moment to think. "I suppose it's simply that you're a brilliant feed-mixer. Ever since you started mixing the feeds she's got better and better."

"You mean there's some sort of an art in mixing the feeds?"

"Apparently there is." She was knitting away and smiling quietly to herself, thinking how funny men were.

"I'll tell you a secret," he said. "You're absolutely right. Although, mind you, it isn't so much *how* you mix it that counts. It's what you put in. You realize that, don't you, Mabel?"

Mrs. Taylor stopped knitting and looked up sharply at her husband.

"Albert," she said, "don't tell me you've been putting things into that child's milk?"

He sat there grinning.

"Well, have you or haven't you?"

"It's possible," he said.

"I don't believe it."

He had a strange fierce way of grinning that showed his teeth.

"Albert," she said. "Stop playing with me like this."

"Yes, dear, all right."

"You haven't *really* put anything into her milk, have you? Answer me properly, Albert. This could be serious with such a tiny baby."

"The answer is yes, Mabel."

"*Albert Taylor*! How could you?"

"Now don't get excited," he said. "I'll tell you all about it if you really want me to, but for heaven's sake keep your hair on."

"It was beer!" she cried. "I just know it was beer!"

"Don't be so daft, Mabel, please."

"Then what was it?"

Albert laid his pipe down carefully on the table beside him and leaned back in his chair. "Tell me," he said, "did you ever by any chance happen to hear me mentioning something called royal jelly?"

"I did not."

"It's magic," he said. "Pure magic. And last night I suddenly got the idea that if I was to put some of this into the baby's milk . . ."

"How *dare* you!"

"Now, Mabel, you don't even know what it is yet."

"I don't care what it is," she said. "You can't go putting foreign bodies like that into a tiny baby's milk. You must be mad."

"It's perfectly harmless, Mabel, otherwise I wouldn't have done it. It comes from bees."

"I might have guessed that."

"And it's so precious that practically no one can afford to take it. When they do, it's only one little drop at a time."

"And how much did you give to our baby, might I ask?"

"Ah," he said, "that's the whole point. That's where the difference lies. I reckon that our baby, just in the last four feeds, has already swallowed about fifty times as much royal jelly as anyone else in the world has ever swallowed before. How about that?"

"Albert, stop pulling my leg."

"I swear it," he said proudly.

She sat there staring at him, her brow wrinkled, her mouth slightly open.

"You know what this stuff actually costs, Mabel, if you want to buy it? There's a place in America advertising it for sale at this very moment for something like five hundred dollars a pound jar! *Five hundred dollars*! That's more than gold, you know!"

She hadn't the faintest idea what he was talking about.

"I'll prove it," he said, and he jumped up and went across to the large bookcase where he kept all his literature about bees. On the top shelf, the back numbers of the *American Bee Journal* were neatly stacked alongside those of the *British Bee Journal, Beecraft*, and other magazines. He took down the last issue of the *American Bee Journal* and turned to a page of small classified advertisements at the back.

"Here you are," he said. "Exactly as I told you. 'We sell royal jelly—$480 per lb. jar wholesale.'"

He handed her the magazine so she could read it herself.

"Now do you believe me? This is an actual shop in New York, Mabel. It says so."

"It doesn't say you can go stirring it into the milk of a newborn baby," she said. "I don't know what's come over you, Albert, I really don't."

"It's curing her, isn't it?"

"I'm not so sure about that, now."

"Don't be so damn silly, Mabel. You know it is."

"Then why haven't other people done it with *their* babies?"

"I keep telling you," he said. "It's too expensive. Practically nobody in the world can afford to buy royal jelly just for *eating* except maybe one or two multimillionaires. The people who buy it are the big companies that make women's face creams and things like that. They're using it as a stunt. They mix a tiny pinch of it into a big jar of face cream and it's selling like hot cakes for absolutely enormous prices. They claim it takes out the wrinkles."

"And does it?"

"Now how on earth would I know that, Mabel? Anyway," he said, returning to his chair, "that's not the point. The point is this. It's done so much good to our little baby just in the last few hours that I think we ought to go right on giving it to her. Now don't interrupt, Mabel. Let me finish. I've got two hundred and forty hives out there and if I turn over maybe a hundred of them to making royal jelly, we ought to be able to supply her with all she wants."

"Albert Taylor," the woman said, stretching her eyes wide and staring at him. "Have you gone out of your mind?"

"Just hear me through, will you please?"

"I forbid it," she said, "absolutely. You're not to give my baby another drop of that horrid jelly, you understand?"

"Now, Mabel . . ."

"And quite apart from that, we had a shocking honey crop last year, and if you go fooling around with those hives now, there's no telling what might not happen."

"There's nothing wrong with my hives, Mabel."

"You know very well we had only half the normal crop last year."

"Do me a favour, will you?" he said. "Let me explain some of the marvellous things this stuff does."

"You haven't even told me what it is yet."

"All right, Mabel. I'll do that too. Will you listen? Will you give me a chance to explain it?"

She sighed and picked up her knitting once more. "I suppose you might as well get it off your chest, Albert. Go on and tell me."

He paused, a bit uncertain now how to begin. It wasn't going to be easy to explain something like this to a person with no detailed knowledge of apiculture at all.

"You know, don't you," he said, "that each colony has only one queen?"

"Yes."

"And that this queen lays all the eggs?"

"Yes, dear. That much I know."

"All right. Now the queen can actually lay two different kinds of eggs. You didn't know that, but she can. It's what we call one of the miracles of the hive. She can lay eggs that produce drones, and she can lay eggs that produce workers. Now if that isn't a miracle, Mabel, I don't know what is."

"Yes, Albert, all right."

"The drones are the males. We don't have to worry about them. The workers are all females. So is the queen, of course. But the workers are unsexed females, if you see what I mean. Their organs are completely undeveloped, whereas the queen is tremendously sexy. She can actually lay her own weight in eggs in a single day."

He hesitated, marshalling his thoughts.

"Now what happens is this. The queen crawls around on the comb and lays her eggs in what we call cells. You know all those hundreds of little holes you see in a honeycomb? Well, a brood comb is just about the same except the cells don't have honey in them, they have eggs. She lays one egg to each cell, and in three days each of these eggs hatches out into a tiny grub. We call it a larva.

"Now, as soon as this larva appears, the nurse bees—they're young workers—all crowd round and start feeding it like mad. And you know what they feed it on?"

"Royal jelly," Mabel answered patiently.

"Right!" he cried. "That's exactly what they do feed it on. They get this stuff out of a gland in their heads and they start pumping it into the cell to feed the larva. And what happens then?"

He paused dramatically, blinking at her with his small watery-grey eyes. Then he turned slowly in his chair and reached for the magazine that he had been reading the night before.

"You want to know what happens then?" he asked, wetting his lips.

"I can hardly wait."

"'Royal jelly,'" he read aloud, "'must be a substance of tremendous nourishing power, for on this diet alone, the honey-bee larva increases in weight *fifteen hundred times* in five days!'"

"How much?"

"*Fifteen hundred times*, Mabel. And you know what that means if you put it in terms of a human being? It means," he said, lowering his voice, leaning forward, fixing her with those small pale eyes, "it means that in five days a baby weighing seven and a half pounds to start off with would increase in weight to *five tons*!"

For the second time, Mrs. Taylor stopped knitting.

"Now you mustn't take that too literally, Mabel."

"Who says I mustn't?"

"It's just a scientific way of putting it, that's all."

"Very well, Albert. Go on."

"But that's only half the story," he said. "There's more to come. The really amazing thing about royal jelly, I haven't told you yet. I'm going to show you now how it can transform a plain dull-looking little worker bee with practically no sex organs at all into a great big beautiful fertile queen."

"Are you saying our baby is dull-looking and plain?" she asked sharply.

"Now don't go putting words into my mouth, Mabel, please. Just listen to this. Did you know that the queen bee and the worker bee, although they are completely different when they grow up, are both hatched out of exactly the same kind of egg?"

"I don't believe that," she said.

"It's as true as I'm sitting here, Mabel, honest it is. Any time the bees want a queen to hatch out of the egg instead of a worker, they can do it."

"How?"

"Ah," he said, shaking a thick forefinger in her direction. "That's just what I'm coming to. That's the secret of the whole thing. Now—what do *you* think it is, Mabel, that makes this miracle happen?"

"Royal jelly," she answered. "You already told me."

"Royal jelly it is!" he cried, clapping his hands and bouncing up on his seat. His big round face was glowing with excitement now, and two vivid patches of scarlet had appeared high up on each cheek.

"Here's how it works. I'll put it very simply for you. The bees want a new queen. So they build an extra-large cell, a queen cell we call it, and they get the old queen to lay one of her eggs in there. The other one thousand nine hundred and ninety-nine eggs she lays in ordinary worker cells. Now. As soon as these eggs hatch into larvae, the nurse bees rally round and start pumping in the royal jelly. All of them get it, workers as well as queen. But here's the vital thing, Mabel, so listen carefully. Here's where the difference comes. The worker larvae only receive this special marvellous food for the *first three days* of their larval life. After that they have a complete change of diet. What really happens is they get weaned, except that it's not like an ordinary weaning because it's so sudden. After the third day they're put straight away on to more or less routine bees' food—a mixture of honey and pollen—and then about two weeks later they emerge from the cells as workers.

"But not so the larva in the queen cell! This one gets royal jelly *all the way through its larval life*. The nurse bees simply pour it into the cell, so much so in fact that the little larva is literally floating in it. And that's what makes it into a queen!"

"You can't prove it," she said.

"Don't talk so damn silly, Mabel, please. Thousands of people have proved it time and time again, famous scientists in every country in the world. All you have to do is take a larva out of a worker cell and put it in a queen cell—that's what we call graft-

Royal Jelly

ing—and just so long as the nurse bees keep it well supplied with royal jelly, then presto!—it'll grow up into a queen! And what makes it more marvellous still is the absolutely enormous difference between a queen and a worker when they grow up. The abdomen is a different shape. The sting is different. The legs are different. The . . ."

"In what way are the legs different?" she asked, testing him.

"The legs? Well, the workers have little pollen baskets on their legs for carrying the pollen. The queen has none. Now here's another thing. The queen has fully developed sex organs. The workers don't. And most amazing of all, Mabel, the queen lives for an average of four to six years. The worker hardly lives that many months. And all this difference simply because one of them got royal jelly and the other didn't!"

"It's pretty hard to believe," she said, "that a food can do all that."

"Of course it's hard to believe. It's another of the miracles of the hive. In fact it's the biggest ruddy miracle of them all. It's such a hell of a big miracle that it's baffled the greatest men of science for hundreds of years. Wait a moment. Stay here. Don't move."

Again he jumped up and went over to the bookcase and started rummaging among the books and magazines.

"I'm going to find you a few of the reports. Here we are. Here's one of them. Listen to this." He started reading aloud from a copy of the *American Bee Journal*:

"'Living in Toronto at the head of a fine research laboratory given to him by the people of Canada in recognition of his truly great contribution to humanity in the discovery of insulin, Dr. Frederick

A. Banting became curious about royal jelly. He requested his staff to do a basic fractional analysis . . .' "

He paused.

"Well, there's no need to read it all, but here's what happened. Dr. Banting and his people took some royal jelly from queen cells that contained two-day-old larvae, and then they started analysing it. And what d'you think they found?

"They found," he said, "that royal jelly contained phenols, sterols, glycerils, dextrose, *and*—now here it comes—and eighty to eighty-five per cent *unidentified* acids!"

He stood beside the bookcase with the magazine in his hand, smiling a funny little furtive smile of triumph, and his wife watched him, bewildered.

He was not a tall man; he had a thick plump pulpy-looking body that was built close to the ground on abbreviated legs. The legs were slightly bowed. The head was huge and round, covered with bristly short-cut hair, and the greater part of the face—now that he had given up shaving altogether—was hidden by a brownish-yellow fuzz about an inch long. In one way and another, he was rather grotesque to look at, there was no denying that.

"Eighty to eighty-five per cent," he said, "unidentified acids. Isn't that fantastic?" He turned back to the bookshelf and began hunting through the other magazines.

"What does it mean, unidentified acids?"

"That's the whole point! No one knows! Not even Banting could find out. You've heard of Banting?"

"No."

"He just happens to be about the most famous living doctor in the world today, that's all."

Looking at him now as he buzzed around in front of the bookcase with his bristly head and his hairy face and his plump pulpy body, she couldn't help thinking that somehow, in some curious way, there was a touch of the bee about this man. She had often seen women grow to look like the horses that they rode, and she had noticed that people who bred birds or bull terriers or pomeranians frequently resembled in some small but startling manner the creature of their choice. But up until now it had never occurred to her that her husband might look like a bee. It shocked her a bit.

"And did Banting ever try to eat it," she asked, "this royal jelly?"

"Of course he didn't eat it, Mabel. He didn't have enough for that. It's too precious."

"You know something?" she said, staring at him but smiling a little all the same. "You're getting to look just a teeny bit like a bee yourself, did you know that?"

He turned and looked at her.

"I suppose it's the beard mostly," she said. "I do wish you'd stop wearing it. Even the colour is sort of bee-ish, don't you think?"

"What the hell are you talking about, Mabel?"

"Albert," she said. "Your language."

"Do you want to hear any more of this or don't you?"

"Yes, dear, I'm sorry. I was only joking. Do go on."

He turned away again and pulled another magazine out of the bookcase and began leafing through the pages. "Now just listen to this, Mabel. 'In 1939, Heyl experimented with twenty-one-day-old rats, injecting them with royal jelly in varying amounts. As a result, he found a precocious follicular development of the ovaries directly in proportion to the quantity of royal jelly injected.'"

"There!" she cried. "I knew it!"

"Knew what?"

"I knew something terrible would happen."

"Nonsense. There's nothing wrong with that. Now here's another, Mabel. 'Still and Burdett found that a male rat which hitherto had been unable to breed, upon receiving a minute daily dose of royal jelly, became a father many times over.'"

"Albert," she cried, "this stuff is *much* too strong to give to a baby! I don't like it at all."

"Nonsense, Mabel."

"Then why do they only try it out on rats, tell me that? Why don't some of these famous scientists take it themselves? They're too clever, that's why. Do you think Dr. Banting is going to risk finishing up with precious ovaries? Not him."

"But they *have* given it to people, Mabel. Here's a whole article about it. Listen." He turned the page and again began reading from the magazine. "'In Mexico, in 1953, a group of enlightened physicians began prescribing minute doses of royal jelly for such things as cerebral neuritis, arthritis, diabetes, autointoxication from tobacco, impotence in men, asthma, croup, and gout . . . There are stacks of signed testimonials . . . A celebrated stockbroker in Mexico City contracted a particularly stubborn case of psoriasis. He became physically unattractive. His clients began to forsake him. His business began to suffer. In desperation he turned to royal jelly—one drop with every meal—and presto! he was cured in a fortnight. A waiter in the Café Jena, also in Mexico City, reported that his father, after taking minute doses of this wonder substance in capsule form, sired a healthy boy child at the age of ninety. A bullfight promoter in Acapulco, finding himself landed with a rather lethargic-looking bull, injected it with one gramme of royal jelly (an excessive dose) just before it entered the arena. Thereupon, the beast became so swift and savage that it promptly dispatched two picadors, three horses, and a matador, and finally . . .'"

"Listen!" Mrs. Taylor said, interrupting him. "I think the baby's crying." Albert glanced up from his reading. Sure enough, a lusty yelling noise was coming from the bedroom above.

"She must be hungry," he said.

His wife looked at the clock. "Good gracious me!" she cried, jumping up. "It's past her time again already! You mix the feed, Albert, quickly, while I bring her down! But hurry! I don't want to keep her waiting."

In half a minute, Mrs. Taylor was back, carrying the screaming infant in her arms. She was flustered now, still quite unaccustomed to the ghastly nonstop racket that a healthy baby makes when it wants its food. "Do be quick, Albert!" she called, settling herself in the armchair and arranging the child on her lap. "Please hurry!"

Albert entered from the kitchen and handed her the bottle of warm milk. "It's just right," he said. "You don't have to test it."

She hitched the baby's head a little higher in the crook of her arm, then pushed the rubber teat straight into the wide-open yelling mouth. The baby grabbed the teat and began to suck. The yelling stopped. Mrs. Taylor relaxed.

"Oh, Albert, isn't she lovely?"

"She's terrific, Mabel—thanks to royal jelly."

"Now, dear, I don't want to hear another word about that nasty stuff. It frightens me to death."

"You're making a big mistake," he said.

"We'll see about that."

The baby went on sucking the bottle.

"I do believe she's going to finish the whole lot again, Albert."

"I'm sure she is," he said.

And a few minutes later, the milk was all gone.

"Oh, what a good girl you are!" Mrs. Taylor cried, as very gently she started to withdraw the nipple. The baby sensed what she was doing and sucked harder, trying to hold on. The woman gave a quick little tug, and *plop*, out it came.

"Waa! Waa! Waa! Waa! Waa!" the baby yelled.

"Nasty old wind," Mrs. Taylor said, hoisting the child on to her shoulder and patting its back.

It belched twice in quick succession.

"There you are, my darling, you'll be all right now."

For a few seconds, the yelling stopped. Then it started again.

"Keep belching her," Albert said. "She's drunk it too quick."

His wife lifted the baby back on to her shoulder. She rubbed its spine. She changed it from one shoulder to the other. She laid it on its stomach on her lap. She sat it up on her knee. But it didn't belch again, and the yelling became louder and more insistent every minute.

"Good for the lungs," Albert Taylor said, grinning. "That's the way they exercise their lungs, Mabel, did you know that?"

"There, there, there," the wife said, kissing it all over the face. "There, there, there."

They waited another five minutes, but not for one moment did the screaming stop.

"Change the nappy," Albert said. "It's got a wet nappy, that's all it is." He fetched a clean one from the kitchen, and Mrs. Taylor took the old one off and put the new one on.

This made no difference at all.

"Waa! Waa! Waa! Waa! Waa!" the baby yelled.

"You didn't stick the safety pin through the skin, did you, Mabel?"

"Of course I didn't," she said, feeling under the nappy with her fingers to make sure.

The parents sat opposite one another in their armchairs, smiling nervously, watching the baby on the mother's lap, waiting for it to tire and stop screaming.

"You know what?" Albert Taylor said at last.

"What?"

"I'll bet she's still hungry. I'll bet all she wants is another swig at that bottle. How about me fetching her an extra lot?"

"I don't think we ought to do that, Albert."

"It'll do her good," he said, getting up from his chair. "I'm going to warm her up a second helping."

He went into the kitchen, and was away several minutes. When he returned he was holding a bottle brimful of milk.

"I made her a double," he announced. "Eight ounces. Just in case."

"Albert! Are you mad? Don't you know it's just as bad to over-feed as it is to underfeed?"

"You don't have to give her the lot, Mabel. You can stop any time you like. Go on," he said, standing over her. "Give her a drink."

Mrs. Taylor began to tease the baby's upper lip with the end of the nipple. The tiny mouth closed like a trap over the rubber teat and suddenly there was silence in the room. The baby's whole body relaxed and a look of absolute bliss came over its face as it started to drink.

"There you are, Mabel! What did I tell you?"

The woman didn't answer.

"She's ravenous, that's what she is. Just look at her suck."

Mrs. Taylor was watching the level of the milk in the bottle. It was dropping fast, and before long three or four ounces out of the eight had disappeared.

"There," she said. "That'll do."

"You can't pull it away now, Mabel."

"Yes, dear. I must."

"Go on, woman. Give her the rest and stop fussing."

"But *Albert* . . ."

"She's famished, can't you see that? Go on, my beauty," he said. "You finish that bottle."

"I don't like it, Albert," the wife said, but she didn't pull the bottle away.

"She's making up for lost time, Mabel, that's all she's doing."

Five minutes later the bottle was empty. Slowly, Mrs. Taylor withdrew the nipple, and this time there was no protest from the baby, no sound at all. It lay peacefully on the mother's lap, the eyes glazed with contentment, the mouth half-open, the lips smeared with milk.

"Twelve whole ounces, Mabel!" Albert Taylor said. "Three times the normal amount! Isn't that amazing!"

The woman was staring down at the baby. And now the old anxious tight-lipped look of the frightened mother was slowly returning to her face.

"What's the matter with *you*?" Albert asked. "You're not worried by that, are you? You can't expect her to get back to normal on a lousy four ounces, don't be ridiculous."

"Come here, Albert," she said.

"What?"

"I said come here."

He went over and stood beside her.

"Take a good look and tell me if you see anything different."

He peered closely at the baby. "She seems bigger, Mabel, if that's what you mean. Bigger and fatter."

"Hold her," she ordered. "Go on, pick her up."

He reached out and lifted the baby up off the mother's lap. "Good God!" he cried. "She weighs a ton!"

"Exactly."

"Now isn't that marvellous!" he cried, beaming. "I'll bet she must be back to normal already!"

"It frightens me, Albert. It's too quick."

"Nonsense, woman."

"It's that disgusting jelly that's done it," she said. "I hate the stuff."

"There's nothing disgusting about royal jelly," he answered, indignant.

"Don't be a fool, Albert! You think it's *normal* for a child to start putting on weight at this speed?"

"You're never satisfied!" he cried. "You're scared stiff when she's losing and now you're absolutely terrified because she's gaining! What's the matter with you, Mabel?"

The woman got up from her chair with the baby in her arms and started towards the door. "All I can say is," she said, "It's lucky I'm here to see you don't give her any more of it, that's all I can say." She went out, and Albert watched her through the open door as she crossed the hall to the foot of the stairs and started to ascend, and when she reached the third or fourth step she suddenly stopped and stood quite still for several seconds as though remembering something. Then she turned and came down again rather quickly and re-entered the room.

"Albert," she said.

"Yes?"

"I assume there wasn't any royal jelly in this last feed we've just given her?"

"I don't see why you should assume that, Mabel."

"Albert!"

"What's wrong?" he asked, soft and innocent.

"How *dare* you!" she cried.

Albert Taylor's great bearded face took on a pained and puzzled look. "I think you ought to be very glad she's got another big dose of it inside her," he said. "Honest I do. And this *is* a very big dose, Mabel, believe you me."

The woman was standing just inside the doorway clasping the sleeping baby in her arms and staring at her husband with huge eyes. She stood very erect, her body absolutely still with fury, her face paler, more tight-lipped than ever.

"You mark my words," Albert was saying, "you're going to have a nipper there soon that'll win first prize in any baby show in the *entire* country. Hey, why don't you weigh her now and see what she is? You want me to get the scales, Mabel, so you can weigh her?"

The woman walked straight over to the large table in the centre of the room and laid the baby down and quickly started taking off its clothes. "Yes!" she snapped. "Get the scales!" Off came the little nightgown, then the undervest.

Then she unpinned the nappy and she drew it away and the baby lay naked on the table.

"But Mabel!" Albert cried. "It's a miracle! She's fat as a puppy!"

Indeed, the amount of flesh the child had put on since the day before was astounding. The small sunken chest with the rib bones showing all over it was now plump and round as a barrel, and the belly was bulging high in the air. Curiously, though, the arms and legs did not seem to have grown in proportion. Still short and skinny, they looked like little sticks protruding from a ball of fat.

"Look!" Albert said. "She's even beginning to get a bit of fuzz on the tummy to keep her warm!" He put out a hand and was about to

ROALD DAHL

run the tips of his fingers over the powdering of silky yellowy-brown hairs that had suddenly appeared on the baby's stomach.

"*Don't you touch her!*" the woman cried. She turned and faced him, her eyes blazing, and she looked suddenly like some kind of little fighting bird with her neck arched over towards him as though she were about to fly at his face and peck his eyes out.

"Now wait a minute," he said, retreating.

"You must be mad!" she cried.

"Now wait just one minute, Mabel, will you please, because if you're still thinking this stuff is dangerous . . . That *is* what you're thinking, isn't it? All right, then. Listen carefully. I shall now proceed to *prove* to you once and for all, Mabel, that royal jelly is absolutely harmless to human beings, even in enormous doses. For example—why do you think we had only half the usual honey crop last summer? Tell me that."

His retreat, walking backwards, had taken him three or four yards away from her, where he seemed to feel more comfortable.

"The reason we had only half the usual crop last summer," he said slowly, lowering his voice, "was because I turned one hundred of my hives over to the production of royal jelly."

"You *what*?"

"Ah," he whispered. "I thought that might surprise you a bit. And I've been making it ever since right under your very nose." His small eyes were glinting at her, and a slow sly smile was creeping around the corners of his mouth.

"You'll never guess the reason, either," he said. "I've been afraid to mention it up to now because I thought it might . . . well . . . sort of embarrass you."

208

There was a slight pause. He had his hands clasped high in front of him, level with his chest, and he was rubbing one palm against the other, making a soft scraping noise.

"You remember that bit I read you out of the magazine? That bit about the rat? Let me see now, how does it go? 'Still and Burdett found that a male rat which hitherto had been unable to breed . . .'" He hesitated, the grin widening, showing his teeth.

"You get the message, Mabel?"

She stood quite still, facing him.

"The very first time I ever read that sentence, Mabel, I jumped straight out of my chair and I said to myself if it'll work with a lousy rat, I said, then there's no reason on earth why it shouldn't work with Albert Taylor."

He paused again, craning his head forward and turning one ear slightly in his wife's direction, waiting for her to say something. But she didn't.

"And here's another thing," he went on. "It made me feel so absolutely marvellous, Mabel, and so sort of completely different to what I was before that I went right on taking it even after you'd announced the joyful tidings. *Buckets* of it I must have swallowed during the last twelve months."

The big heavy haunted-looking eyes of the woman were moving intently over the man's face and neck. There was no skin showing at all on the neck, not even at the sides below the ears. The whole of it, to a point where it disappeared into the collar of the shirt, was covered all the way around with those shortish silky hairs, yellowy black.

"Mind you," he said, turning away from her, gazing lovingly now at the baby, "it's going to work far better on a tiny infant than on a fully developed man like me. You've only got to look at her to see that, don't you agree?"

The woman's eyes travelled slowly downward and settled on the baby. The baby was lying naked on the table, fat and white and co-matose, like some gigantic grub that was approaching the end of its larval life and would soon emerge into the world complete with mandibles and wings.

"Why don't you cover her up, Mabel?" he said. "We don't want our little queen to catch a cold."

It was snowing when I woke up.

I could tell that it was snowing because there was a kind of brightness in the room and it was quiet outside with no footstep-noises coming up from the street and no tyre-noises but only the engines of the cars. I looked up and I saw George over by the window in his green dressing gown, bending over the paraffin stove, making the coffee.

"Snowing," I said.

"It's cold," George answered. "It's really cold."

I got out of bed and fetched the morning paper from outside the door. It was cold all right and I ran back quickly and jumped into bed and lay still for a while under the bedclothes, holding my hands tight between my legs for warmth.

"No letters?" George said.

"No. No letters."

"Doesn't look as if the old man's going to cough up."

"Maybe he thinks four hundred and fifty is enough for one month," I said.

"He's never been to New York. He doesn't know the cost of living here."

"You shouldn't have spent it all in one week."

George stood up and looked at me. "*We* shouldn't have spent it, you mean."

"That's right," I said. "We." I began reading the paper.

The coffee was ready now and George brought the pot over and put it on the table between our beds. "A person can't live without money," he said. "The old man ought to know that." He got back into his bed without taking off his green dressing gown. I went on reading. I finished the racing page and the football page and then I started on Lionel Pantaloon, the great political and society columnist. I always read Pantaloon—same as the other twenty or thirty million other people in the country. He's a habit with me; he's more than a habit; he's part of my morning, like three cups of coffee, or shaving.

"This fellow's got a nerve," I said.

"Who?"

"This Lionel Pantaloon."

"What's he saying now?"

"Same sort of thing he's always saying. Same sort of scandal. Always about the rich. Listen to this: '. . . seen at the Penguin Club . . . banker William S. Womberg with beauteous starlet Theresa Williams . . . three nights running . . . Mrs. Womberg at home with a headache . . . which is something anyone's wife would have if hubby was out squiring Miss Williams of an evening . . .'"

"That fixes Womberg," George said.

"I think it's a shame," I said. "That sort of thing could cause a divorce. How can this Pantaloon get away with stuff like that?"

"He always does, they're all scared of him. But if I was William S. Womberg," George said, "you know what I'd do? I'd go right out and punch this Lionel Pantaloon right on the nose. Why, that's the only way to handle those guys."

"Mr. Womberg couldn't do that."

"Why not?"

"Because he's an old man," I said. "Mr. Womberg is a dignified and respectable old man. He's a very prominent banker in the town. He couldn't possibly . . ."

And then it happened. Suddenly, from nowhere, the idea came. It came to me in the middle of what I was saying to George and I stopped short and I could feel the idea itself kind of flowing into my brain and I kept very quiet and let it come and it kept on coming and almost before I knew what had happened I had it all, the whole plan, the whole brilliant magnificent plan worked out clearly in my head; and right then I knew it was a beauty.

I turned and I saw George staring at me with a look of wonder on his face. "What's wrong?" he said. "What's the matter?"

I kept quite calm. I reached out and got myself some more coffee before I allowed myself to speak.

"George," I said, and I still kept calm. "I have an idea. Now listen very carefully because I have an idea which will make us both very rich. We are broke, are we not?"

"We are."

"And this William S. Womberg," I said, "would you consider that he is angry with Lionel Pantaloon this morning?"

"Angry!" George shouted. "Angry! Why, he'll be madder than hell!"

"Quite so. And do you think that he would like to see Lionel Pantaloon receive a good hard punch on the nose?"

"Damn right he would!"

"And now tell me, is it not possible that Mr. Womberg would be prepared to pay a sum of money to someone who would undertake to perform this nose-punching operation efficiently and discreetly on his behalf?"

George turned and looked at me, and gently, carefully, he put down his coffee cup on the table. A slowly widening smile began to spread across his face. "I get you," he said. "I get the idea."

"That's just a little part of the idea. If you read Pantaloon's column here you will see that there is another person who has been insulted today." I picked up the paper. "There is a Mrs. Ella Gimple, a prominent socialite who has perhaps a million dollars in the bank . . ."

"What does Pantaloon say about her?"

I looked at the paper again. "He hints," I answered, "at how she makes a stack of money out of her own friends by throwing roulette parties and acting as the bank."

"That fixes Gimple," George said. "And Womberg. Gimple and Womberg." He was sitting up straight in bed waiting for me to go on.

"Now," I said, "we have two different people both loathing Lionel Pantaloon's guts this morning, both wanting desperately to go out and punch him on the nose, and neither of them daring to do it. You understand that?"

"Absolutely."

"So much then," I said, "for Lionel Pantaloon. But don't forget that there are others like him. There are dozens of other columnists who spend their time insulting wealthy and important people. There's Harry Weyman, Claude Taylor, Jacob Swinski, Walter Kennedy, and the rest of them."

"That's right," George said. "That's absolutely right."

"I'm telling you, there's nothing that makes the rich so furious as being mocked and insulted in the newspapers."

"Go on," George said. "Go on."

"All right. Now this is the plan." I was getting rather excited myself. I was leaning over the side of the bed, resting one hand on the little table, waving the other about in the air as I spoke. "We will set up immediately an organization and we will call it . . . what shall we call it . . . we will call it . . . let me see . . . we will call it 'Vengeance Is Mine Inc.' . . . How about that?"

"Peculiar name."

"It's biblical. It's good. I like it. 'Vengeance Is Mine Inc.' It sounds fine. And we will have little cards printed which we will send to all our clients reminding them that they have been insulted and mortified in public and offering to punish the offender in consideration of a sum of money. We will buy all the newspapers and read all the columnists and every day we will send out a dozen or more of our cards to prospective clients."

"It's marvellous!" George shouted. "It's terrific!"

"We shall be rich," I told him. "We shall be exceedingly wealthy in no time at all."

"We must start at once!"

I jumped out of bed, fetched a writing-pad and a pencil and ran back to bed again. "Now," I said, pulling my knees under the blankets and propping the writing-pad against them, "the first thing is to decide what we're going to say on the printed cards which we'll be sending to our clients," and I wrote, "VENGEANCE IS MINE INC." as a heading on the top of the sheet of paper. Then, with much care, I composed a finely phrased letter explaining the functions of the organization. It finished up with the following sentence: "*Therefore VENGEANCE IS MINE INC. will undertake, on your behalf and in absolute confidence, to administer suitable punishment to columnist........and in this regard we respectfully submit to you a choice of methods (together with prices) for your consideration.*"

"What do you mean, 'a choice of methods'?" George said.

"We must give them a choice. We must think up a number of things . . . a number of different punishments. Number one will be . . ." and I wrote down, "*1. Punch him on the nose, once, hard.*" "What shall we charge for that?"

"Five hundred dollars," George said instantly.

I wrote it down. "What's the next one?"

"Black his eye," George said.

I wrote it down, "*2. Black his eye . . . $500.*"

"No!" George said. "I disagree with the price. It definitely requires more skill and timing to black an eye nicely than to punch a nose. It is a skilled job. It should be six hundred."

"OK," I said. "Six hundred. And what's the next one?"

"Both together, of course. The old one two." We were in George's territory now. This was right up his street.

"Both together?"

"Absolutely. Punch his nose *and* black his eye. Eleven hundred dollars."

"There should be a reduction for taking the two," I said. "We'll make it a thousand."

"It's dirt cheap," George said. "They'll snap it up."

"What's next?"

We were both silent now, concentrating fiercely. Three deep parallel grooves of skin appeared upon George's rather low sloping forehead. He began to scratch his scalp, slowly but very strongly. I looked away and tried to think of all the terrible things which people had done to other people. Finally, I got one, and with George watching the point of my pencil moving over the paper, I wrote: "*4. Put a rattlesnake (with venom extracted) on the floor of his car, by the pedals, when he parks it.*"

"Jesus Christ!" George whispered. "You want to kill him with fright!"

"Sure," I said.

"And where'd you get a rattlesnake, anyway?"

"Buy it. You can always buy them. How much shall we charge for that one?"

"Fifteen hundred dollars," George said firmly. I wrote it down.

"Now we need one more."

"Here it is," George said. "Kidnap him in a car, take all his clothes away except his underpants and his shoes and socks, then dump him out on Fifth Avenue in the rush hour." He smiled, a broad triumphant smile.

"We can't do that."

"Write it down. And charge two thousand five hundred bucks. You'd do it all right if old Womberg were to offer you that much."

"Yes," I said. "I suppose I would." And I wrote it down. "That's enough now," I added. "That gives them a wide choice."

"And where will we get the cards printed?" George asked.

"George Karnoffsky," I said. "Another George. He's a friend of mine. Runs a small printing shop down on Third Avenue. Does wedding invitations and things like that for all the big stores. He'll do it. I know he will."

"Then what are we waiting for?"

We both leapt out of bed and began to dress. "It's twelve o'clock," I said. "If we hurry we'll catch him before he goes to lunch."

It was still snowing when we went out into the street and the snow was four or five inches thick on the sidewalk, but we covered the fourteen blocks to Karnoffsky's shop at a tremendous pace and we arrived there just as he was putting his coat on to go out.

"Claude!" he shouted. "Hi boy! How you been keeping," and he pumped my hand. He had a fat friendly face and a terrible nose with great wide-open nose-wings which overlapped his cheeks by at least an inch on either side. I greeted him and told him that we had come to discuss some most urgent business. He took off his coat and led us back into the office, then I began to tell him our plans and what we wanted him to do.

When I'd got about quarter way through my story, he started to roar with laughter and it was impossible for me to continue; so I cut it short and handed him the piece of paper with the stuff on it that we wanted him to print. And now, as he read it, his whole body began to shake with laughter and he kept slapping the desk with his hand and coughing and choking and roaring like someone crazy. We sat watching him. We didn't see anything particular to laugh about.

Finally he quietened down and he took out a handkerchief and made a great business about wiping his eyes. "Never laughed so much," he said weakly. "That's a great joke, that is. It's worth a lunch. Come on out and I'll give you lunch."

"Look," I said severely, "this isn't any joke. There is nothing to laugh at. You are witnessing the birth of a new and powerful organization . . ."

"Come on," he said and he began to laugh again. "Come on and have lunch."

"When can you get those cards printed?" I said. My voice was stern and businesslike.

He paused and stared at us. "You mean . . . you really mean . . . you're serious about this thing?"

"Absolutely. You are witnessing the birth . . ."

"All right," he said, "all right," he stood up. "I think you're crazy and you'll get in trouble. Those boys like messing other people about, but they don't much fancy being messed about themselves."

"When can you get them printed, and without any of your workers reading them?"

"For this," he answered gravely, "I will give up my lunch. I will set the type myself. It is the least I can do." He laughed again and the rims of his huge nostrils twitched with pleasure. "How many do you want?"

"A thousand—to start with, and envelopes."

"Come back at two o'clock," he said and I thanked him very much and as we went out we could hear his laughter rumbling down the passage into the back of the shop.

At exactly two o'clock we were back. George Karnoffsky was in his office and the first thing I saw as we went in was the high stack of printed cards on his desk in front of him. They were large cards, about twice the size of ordinary wedding or cocktail invitation-cards. "There you are," he said. "All ready for you." The fool was still laughing.

He handed us each a card and I examined mine carefully. It was a beautiful thing. He had obviously taken much trouble over it. The card itself was thick and stiff with narrow gold edging all the way around, and the letters of the heading were exceedingly elegant. I cannot reproduce it here in all its splendour, but I can at least show you how it read:

VENGEANCE IS MINE INC.

Dear.....................

You have probably seen columnist.....................'s slanderous and unprovoked attack upon your character in today's paper. It is an outrageous insinuation, a deliberate distortion of the truth.

Are you yourself prepared to allow this miserable malice-monger to insult you in this manner?

The whole world knows that it is foreign to the nature of the American people to permit themselves to be insulted either in public or in private without rising up in righteous indignation and demanding—nay, exacting—a just measure of retribution.

On the other hand, it is only natural that a citizen of your standing and reputation will not wish *personally* to become further involved in this sordid petty affair, or indeed to have any *direct* contact whatsoever with this vile person.

How then are you to obtain satisfaction?

The answer is simple, VENGEANCE IS MINE INC. will obtain it for you. We will undertake, on your behalf and in absolute confidence, to administer individual punishment to columnist...................., and in this regard we respectfully submit to you a choice of methods (together with prices) for your consideration:

1. Punch him on the nose, once, hard $500
2. Black his eye $600
3. Punch him on the nose and black his eye $1000
4. Introduce a rattlesnake (with venom extracted) into his
   car, on the floor by his pedals, when he parks it $1500
5. Kidnap him, take all his clothes away except his underpants, his shoes and socks, then dump him out on Fifth
   Ave. in the rush hour $2500

This work executed by a professional.

If you desire to avail yourself of any of these offers, kindly reply to VENGEANCE IS MINE INC. at the address indicated upon the enclosed slip of paper. If it is practicable, you will be notified in advance of the place where the action will occur and of the time, so that you may, if you wish, watch the proceedings in person from a safe and anonymous distance.

No payment need be made until after your order has been satisfactorily executed, when an account will be rendered in the usual manner.

George Karnoffsky had done a beautiful job of printing.

"Claude," he said, "you like?"

"It's marvellous."

"It's the best I could do for you. It's like in the war when I would see soldiers going off perhaps to get killed and all the time I would want to be giving them things and doing things for them." He was beginning to laugh again, so I said, "We'd better be going now. Have you got large envelopes for these cards?"

"Everything is here. And you can pay me when the money starts coming in." That seemed to set him off worse than ever and he collapsed into his chair, giggling like a fool. George and I hurried out of the shop into the street, into the cold snow-falling afternoon.

We almost ran the distance back to our room and on the way up I borrowed a Manhattan telephone directory from the public telephone in the hall. We found "Womberg, William S.," without any trouble and while I read out the address—somewhere up in the East Nineties—George wrote it on one of the envelopes.

"Gimple, Mrs. Ella H.," was also in the book and we addressed an envelope to her as well. "We'll just send to Womberg and Gimple today," I said. "We haven't really got started yet. Tomorrow we'll send a dozen."

"We'd better catch the next post," George said.

"We'll deliver them by hand," I said. "Now, at once. The sooner they get them the better. Tomorrow might be too late. They won't be half so angry tomorrow as they are today. People are apt to cool off through the night. See here," I said, "you go ahead and deliver those two cards right away. While you're doing that I'm going to snoop around the town and try to find out something about the habits of Lionel Pantaloon. See you back here later in the evening . . ."

At about nine o'clock that evening I returned and found George lying on his bed smoking cigarettes and drinking coffee.

"I delivered them both," he said. "Just slipped them through the letter-boxes and rang the bells and beat it up the street. Womberg had a huge house, a huge white house. How did you get on?"

"I went to see a man I know who works in the sports section of the *Daily Mirror*. He told me all."

"What did he tell you?"

"He said Pantaloon's movements are more or less routine. He operates at night, but wherever he goes earlier in the evening, he *always*—and this is the important point—he *always* finishes up at the Penguin Club. He gets there round about midnight and stays until two or two-thirty. That's when his legmen bring him all the dope."

"That's all we want to know," George said happily.

"It's too easy."

"Money for old rope."

There was a full bottle of blended whisky in the cupboard and George fetched it out. For the next two hours we sat upon our beds drinking the whisky and making wonderful and complicated plans for the development of our organization. By eleven o'clock we were employing a staff of fifty, including twelve famous pugilists, and our offices were in Rockefeller Center. Towards midnight we had obtained control over all columnists and were dictating their daily columns to them by telephone from our headquarters, taking care to insult and infuriate at least twenty rich persons in one part of the country or another every day. We were immensely wealthy and George had a British Bentley, I had five Cadillacs. George kept practising telephone talks with Lionel Pantaloon. "That you, Pantaloon?" "Yes, sir." "Well, listen here. I think your column stinks today. It's lousy." "I'm very sorry, sir. I'll try to do better to-morrow." "Damn right you'll do better, Pantaloon. Matter of fact we've been thinking about getting someone else to take over." "But please, please sir, just give me another chance." "OK, Pantaloon, but this is the last. And by the way, the boys are putting a rattle-snake in your car tonight, on behalf of Mr. Hiram C. King, the soap manufacturer. Mr. King will be watching from across the street so don't forget to act scared when you see it." "Yes, sir, of course, sir. I won't forget, sir . . ."

When we finally went to bed and the light was out, I could still hear George giving hell to Pantaloon on the telephone.

The next morning we were both woken up by the church clock on the corner striking nine. George got up and went to the door to get the papers and when he came back he was holding a letter in his hand.

"Open it!" I said.

He opened it and carefully unfolded a single sheet of thin notepaper.

"Read it!" I shouted.

He began to read it aloud, his voice low and serious at first but rising gradually to a high, almost hysterical shout of triumph as the full meaning of the letter was revealed to him. It said:

"Your methods appear curiously unorthodox. At the same time anything you do to that scoundrel has my approval. So go ahead. Start with Item 1, and if you are successful I'll be only too glad to give you an order to work right on through the list. Send the bill to me. William S. Womberg."

I recollect that in the excitement of the moment we did a kind of dance around the room in our pyjamas, praising Mr. Womberg in loud voices and shouting that we were rich. George turned somersaults on his bed and it is possible that I did the same.

"When shall we do it?" he said. "Tonight?"

I paused before replying. I refused to be rushed. The pages of history are filled with the names of great men who have come to grief by permitting themselves to make hasty decisions in the excitement of a moment. I put on my dressing gown, lit a cigarette and began to pace up and down the room. "There is no hurry," I said. "Womberg's order can be dealt with in due course. But first of all we must send out today's cards."

I dressed quickly, we went out to the newsstand across the street, bought one copy of every daily paper there was and returned to our room. The next two hours was spent in reading the columnists' columns, and in the end we had a list of eleven people—eight men and three women—all of whom had been insulted in one way or another by one of the columnists that morning. Things were going well. We were working smoothly. It took us only another half hour to look up the addresses of the insulted ones—two we couldn't find—and to address the envelopes.

In the afternoon we delivered them, and at about six in the evening we got back to our room, tired but triumphant. We made coffee and we fried hamburgers and we had supper in bed.

Then we re-read Womberg's letter aloud to each other many many times.

"What's he doing he's giving us an order for six thousand one hundred dollars," George said. "Items 1 to 5 inclusive."

"It's not a bad beginning. Not bad for the first day. Six thousand a day works out at . . . let me see . . . it's nearly two million dollars a year, not counting Sundays. A million each. It's more than Betty Grable."

"We are very wealthy people," George said. He smiled, a slow and wondrous smile of pure contentment.

"In a day or two we will move to a suite of rooms at the St. Regis."

"I think the Waldorf," George said.

"All right, the Waldorf. And later on we might as well take a house."

"One like Womberg's?"

"All right. One like Womberg's. But first," I said, "we have work to do. Tomorrow we shall deal with Pantaloon. We will catch him as he comes out of the Penguin Club. At two-thirty A.M. we will be waiting for him, and when he comes out into the street you will step forward and punch him once, hard, right upon the point of the nose as per contract."

"It will be a pleasure," George said. "It will be a real pleasure. But how do we get away? Do we run?"

"We shall hire a car for an hour. We have just enough money left for that, and I shall be sitting at the wheel with the engine running, not ten yards away, and the door will be open and when you've punched him you'll just jump back into the car and we'll be gone."

"It is perfect. I shall punch him very hard." George paused. He clenched his right fist and examined his knuckles. Then he smiled again and he said slowly, "This nose of his, is it not possible that it will afterwards be so much blunted that it will no longer poke well into other people's business?"

"It is quite possible," I answered, and with that happy thought in our minds we switched out the lights and went early to sleep.

The next morning I was woken by a shout and I sat up and saw George standing at the foot of my bed in his pyjamas, waving his arms. "Look!" he shouted, "there are four! There are four!" I looked, and indeed there were four letters in his hand.

"Open them. Quickly, open them."

The first one he read aloud: "'*Dear Vengeance Is Mine Inc., That's the best proposition I've had in years. Go right ahead and give Mr. Jacob Swinski the rattlesnake treatment (Item 4). But I'll be glad to pay double if you'll forget to extract the poison from its fangs. Yours Gertrude Porter-Vandervelt. P.S. You'd better insure the snake. That guy's bite carries more poison than the rattler's.*'"

George read the second one aloud: "'*My cheque for $500 is made out and lies before me on my desk. The moment I receive proof that you have punched Lionel Pantaloon hard on the nose, it will be posted to you, I should prefer a fracture, if possible. Yours etc. Wilbur H. Gollogly.*'"

George read the third one aloud: "'*In my present frame of mind and against my better judgement, I am tempted to reply to your card and to request that you deposit that scoundrel Walter Kennedy upon Fifth Avenue*" *dressed only in his underwear. I make the proviso that there shall be snow on the ground at the time and that the temperature shall be sub-zero. H. Gresham.'"*

The fourth one he also read aloud: "'*A good hard sock on the nose for Pantaloon is worth five hundred of mine or anybody else's money. I should like to watch. Yours sincerely, Claudia Calthorpe Hines.*'"

George laid the letters down gently, carefully upon the bed. For a while there was silence. We stared at each other, too astonished, too happy to speak. I began to calculate the value of those four orders in terms of money.

"That's five thousand dollars' worth," I said softly.

Upon George's face there was a huge bright grin. "Claude," he said, "should we not move now to the Waldorf?"

"Soon," I answered, "but at the moment we have no time for moving. We have not even time to send out fresh cards today. We must start to execute the orders we have in hand. We are overwhelmed with work."

"Should we not engage extra staff and enlarge our organization?"

"Later," I said. "Even for that there is no time today. Just think what we have to do. We have to put a rattlesnake in Jacob Swinski's car . . . we have to dump Walter Kennedy on Fifth Avenue in his underpants . . . we have to punch Pantaloon on the nose . . . let me see . . . yes, for three different people we have to punch Pantaloon . . ."

I stopped. I closed my eyes. I sat still. Again I became conscious of a small clear stream of inspiration flowing into the tissues of my brain. "I have it!" I shouted. "I have it! I have it! Three birds with one stone! Three customers with one punch!"

"How?"

"Don't you see? We only need to punch Pantaloon once and each of the three customers ... Womberg, Gollogly and Claudia Hines ... will think it's being done specially for him or her."

"Say it again." I said it again.

"It's brilliant."

"It's common sense. And the same principle will apply to the others. The rattlesnake treatment and the others can wait until we have more orders. Perhaps in a few days we will have ten orders for rattlesnakes in Swinski's car. Then we will do them all in one go."

"It's wonderful."

"This evening then," I said, "we will handle Pantaloon. But first we must hire a car. Also we must send telegrams, one to Womberg, one to Gollogly and one to Claudia Hines, telling them where and when the punching will take place."

We dressed rapidly and went out.

In a dirty silent little garage down on East 9th Street we managed to hire a car, a 1934 Chevrolet, eight dollars for the evening. We then sent three telegrams, each one identical and cunningly worded to conceal its true meaning from inquisitive people: "*Hope to see you outside Penguin Club two-thirty A.M. Regards V.I.Mine.*"

"There is one thing more," I said. "It is essential that you should be disguised. Pantaloon, or the doorman, for example, must not be able to identify you afterwards. You must wear a false moustache."

"What about you?"

"Not necessary. I'll be sitting in the car. They won't see me."

We went to a children's toy shop and we bought for George a magnificent black moustache, a thing with long pointed ends, waxed and stiff and shining, and when he held it up against his face he looked exactly like the Kaiser of Germany. The man in the shop also sold us a tube of glue and he showed us how the moustache should be attached to the upper lip. "Going to have fun with the kids?" he asked, and George said, "Absolutely."

All was now ready, but there was a long time to wait. We had three dollars left between us and with this we bought a sandwich each and went to a movie. Then, at eleven o'clock that evening, we collected our car and in it we began to cruise slowly through the streets of New York waiting for the time to pass.

"You'd better put on your moustache so as you get used to it."

We pulled up under a street lamp and I squeezed some glue on to George's upper lip and fixed on the huge black hairy thing with its pointed ends. Then we drove on. It was cold in the car and outside it was beginning to snow again. I could see a few small snowflakes falling through the beams of the car lights. George kept saying, "How hard shall I hit him?" and I kept answering, "Hit him as hard as you can, and on the nose. It must be on the nose because that is a part of the contract. Everything must be done right. Our clients may be watching."

At two in the morning we drove slowly past the entrance to the Penguin Club in order to survey the situation. "I will park there," I said, "just past the entrance in that patch of dark. But I will leave the door open for you."

We drove on. Then George said, "What does he look like? How do I know it's him?"

"Don't worry," I answered. "I've thought of that," and I took from my pocket a piece of paper and handed it to him. "You take this and fold it up small and give it to the doorman and tell him to see it gets to Pantaloon quickly. Act as though you are scared to death and in an awful hurry. It's a hundred to one that Pantaloon will come out. No columnist could resist that message."

On the paper I had written: "*I am a worker in Soviet Consulate. Come to the door very quickly please I have something to tell but come quickly as I am in danger. I cannot come in to you.*"

"You see," I said, "your moustache will make you look like a Russian. All Russians have big moustaches."

George took the paper and folded it up very small and held it in his fingers. It was nearly half past two in the morning now and we began to drive towards the Penguin Club.

"You all set?" I said.

"Yes."

"We're going in now. Here we come. I'll park just past the entrance . . . here. Hit him hard," I said, and George opened the door and got out of the car. I closed the door behind him but I leant over and kept my hand on the handle so I could open it again quick, and I let down the window so I could watch. I kept the engine ticking over.

I saw George walk swiftly up to the doorman who stood under the red and white canopy which stretched out over the sidewalk. I saw the doorman turn and look down at George and I didn't like the way he did it. He was a tall proud man dressed in a magenta-coloured uniform with gold buttons and gold shoulders and a broad white stripe down each magenta trouser leg. Also he wore white gloves and he stood there looking proudly down at George, frowning, pressing his lips together hard. He was looking at George's moustache and I thought Oh my God we have overdone it. We have over-disguised him. He's going to know it's false and he's going to take one of the long pointed ends in his fingers and he'll give it a tweak and it'll come off. But he didn't. He was distracted by George's acting, for George was acting well. I could see him hopping about, clasping and unclasping his hands, swaying his body and shaking his head, and I could hear him saying, "Plees plees plees you must hurry. It is life and teth. Plees plees take it kvick to Mr. Pantaloon." His Russian accent was not like any accent I had heard before, but all the same there was a quality of real despair in his voice.

Finally, gravely, proudly, the doorman said, "Give me the note." George gave it to him and said, "Tank you, tank you, but say it is urgent," and the doorman disappeared inside. In a few moments he returned and said, "It's being delivered now." George paced nervously up and down. I waited, watching the door. Three or four minutes elapsed. George wrung his hands and said, "Vere is he? Vere is he? Plees to go and see if he is not coming!"

"What's the matter with you?" the doorman said. Now he was looking at George's moustache again.

"It is life and teth! Mr. Pantaloon can help! He must come!"

"Why don't you shut up," the doorman said, but he opened the door again and he poked his head inside and I heard him saying something to someone.

To George he said, "They say he's coming now."

A moment later the door opened and Pantaloon himself, small and dapper, stepped out. He paused by the door, looking quickly from side to side like an inquisitive ferret. The doorman touched his cap and pointed at George. I heard Pantaloon say, "Yes, what did you want?"

George said, "Plees, dis vay a leetle so as novone can hear," and he led Pantaloon along the pavement, away from the doorman and towards the car.

"Come on, now," Pantaloon said. "What is it you want?"

Suddenly George shouted "Look!" and he pointed up the street. Pantaloon turned his head and as he did so George swung his right arm and he hit Pantaloon plumb on the point of the nose. I saw George leaning forward on the punch, all his weight behind it, and the whole of Pantaloon appeared somehow to lift slightly off the ground and to float backwards for two or three feet until the façade of the Penguin Club stopped him. All this happened very quickly, and then George was in the car beside me and we were off and I could hear the doorman blowing a whistle behind us.

"We've done it!" George gasped. He was excited and out of breath. "I hit him good! Did you see how good I hit him!"

It was snowing hard now and I drove fast and made many sudden turnings and I knew no one would catch us in this snowstorm.

"Son of a bitch almost went through the wall I hit him so hard."

"Well done, George," I said. "Nice work, George."

"And did you see him lift? Did you see him lift right up off the ground?"

"Womberg will be pleased," I said.

"And Gollogly, and the Hines woman."

"They'll all be pleased," I said. "Watch the money coming in."

"There's a car behind us!" George shouted. "It's following us! It's right on our tail! Drive like mad!"

"Impossible," I said. "They couldn't have picked us up already. It's just another car going somewhere." I turned sharply to the right.

"He's still with us," George said. "Keep turning. We'll lose him soon."

"How the hell can we lose a police car in a nineteen-thirty-four Chev," I said. "I'm going to stop."

"Keep going!" George shouted. "You're doing fine."

"I'm going to stop," I said. "It'll only make them mad if we go on."

George protested fiercely but I knew it was no good and I pulled in to the side of the road. The other car swerved out and went past us and skidded to a standstill in front of us.

"Quick," George said. "Let's beat it." He had the door open and he was ready to run.

"Don't be a fool," I said. "Stay where you are. You can't get away now."

A voice from outside said, "All right boys, what's the hurry?"

"No hurry," I answered. "We're just going home."

"Yeah?"

"Oh yes, we're just on our way home now."

The man poked his head in through the window on my side, and he looked at me, then at George, then at me again.

"It's a nasty night," George said. "We're just trying to reach home before the streets get all snowed up."

"Well," the man said, "you can take it easy. I just thought I'd like to give you this right away." He dropped a wad of banknotes on to my lap. "I'm Gollogly," he added, "Wilbur H. Gollogly," and he stood out there in the snow grinning at us, stamping his feet and rubbing his hands to keep them warm. "I got your wire and I watched the whole thing from across the street. You did a fine job. I'm paying you boys double. It was worth it. Funniest thing I ever seen. Good-bye boys. Watch your steps. They'll be after you now. Get out of town if I were you. Good-bye." And before we could say anything, he was gone.

When finally we got back to our room I started packing at once.

"You crazy?" George said. "We've only got to wait a few hours and we receive five hundred dollars each from Womberg and the Hines woman. Then we'll have two thousand altogether and we can go anywhere we want."

So we spent the next day waiting in our room and reading the papers, one of which had a whole column on the front page headed, "Brutal Assault on Famous Columnist." But sure enough the late afternoon post brought us two letters and there was five hundred dollars in each.

And right now, at this moment, we are sitting in a Pullman car, drinking Scotch whisky and heading south for a place where there is always sunshine and where the horses are running every day. We are immensely wealthy and George keeps saying that if we put the whole of our two thousand dollars on a horse at ten to one we shall make another twenty thousand and we will be able to retire. "We will have a house at Palm Beach," he says, "and we will entertain upon a lavish scale. Beautiful socialites will loll around the edge of our swimming pool sipping cool drinks, and after a while we will perhaps put another large sum of money upon another horse and we shall become wealthier still. Possibly we will become tired of Palm Beach and then we will move around in a leisurely manner among the playgrounds of the rich. Monte Carlo and places like that. Like the Ali Khan and the Duke of Windsor. We will become prominent members of the international set and film stars will smile at us and head waiters will bow to us and perhaps, in time to come, perhaps we might even get ourselves mentioned in Lionel Pantaloon's column."

"That would be something," I said.

"Wouldn't it just," he answered happily. "Wouldn't that just be something."

There were six of us to dinner that night at Mike Schofield's house in London: Mike and his wife and daughter, and my wife and I, and a man called Richard Pratt.

Richard Pratt was a famous gourmet. He was president of a small society known as the Epicures, and each month he circulated privately to its members a pamphlet on food and wines. He organized dinners where sumptuous dishes and rare wines were served. He refused to smoke for fear of harming his palate, and when discussing a wine, he had a curious, rather droll habit of referring to it as though it were a living being. "A prudent wine," he would say, "rather diffident and evasive, but quite prudent." Or, "A good-humoured wine, benevolent and cheerful—slightly obscene, perhaps, but none the less good-humoured."

I had been to dinner at Mike's twice before when Richard Pratt was there, and on each occasion Mike and his wife had gone out of their way to produce a special meal for the famous gourmet. And this one, clearly, was to be no exception. The moment we entered the dining room, I could see that the table was laid for a feast. The tall candles, the yellow roses, the quantity of shining silver, the three wineglasses to each person, and above all, the faint scent of roasting meat from the kitchen brought the first warm oozings of saliva to my mouth.

As we sat down, I remembered that on both Richard Pratt's previous visits Mike had played a little betting game with him over the claret, challenging him to name its breed and its vintage. Pratt had replied that that should not be too difficult provided it was one of the great years. Mike had then bet him a case of the wine in question that he could not do it. Pratt had accepted, and had won both times. Tonight I felt sure that the little game would be played over again, for Mike was quite willing to lose the bet in order to prove that his wine was good enough to be recognized, and Pratt, for his part, seemed to take a grave, restrained pleasure in displaying his knowledge.

The meal began with a plate of whitebait, fried very crisp in butter, and to go with it there was a Moselle. Mike got up and poured the wine himself, and when he sat down again. I could see that he was watching Richard Pratt. He had set the bottle in front of me so that I could read the label. It said, "Geierslay Ohligsberg, 1945." He leaned over and whispered to me that Geierslay was a tiny village in the Moselle, almost unknown outside Germany. He said that this wine we were drinking was something unusual, that the output of the vineyard was so small that it was almost impossible for a stranger to get any of it. He had visited Geierslay personally the previous summer in order to obtain the few bottles that they had finally allowed him to have.

"I doubt whether anyone else in the country has any of it at the moment," he said. I saw him glance again at Richard Pratt. "Great thing about Moselle," he continued, raising his voice, "it's the perfect wine to serve before a claret. A lot of people serve Rhine wine instead, but that's because they don't know any better. A Rhine wine will kill a delicate claret, you know that? It's barbaric to serve a Rhine before a claret. But a Moselle—ah!—a Moselle is exactly right."

Mike Schofield was an amiable, middle-aged man. But he was a stockbroker. To be precise, he was a jobber in the stock market, and like a number of his kind, he seemed to be somewhat embarrassed, almost ashamed to find that he had made so much money with so slight a talent. In his heart he knew that he was not really much more than a bookmaker—an unctuous, infinitely respectable, secretly unscrupulous bookmaker—and he knew that his friends knew it, too. So he was seeking now to become a man of culture, to cultivate a literary and aesthetic taste, to collect paintings, music, books, and all the rest of it. His little sermon about Rhine wine and Moselle was a part of this thing, this culture that he sought.

"A charming little wine, don't you think?" he said. He was still watching Richard Pratt. I could see him give a rapid furtive glance down the table each time he dropped his head to take a mouthful of whitebait. I could almost *feel* him waiting for the moment when Pratt would take his first sip, and look up from his glass with a smile of pleasure, of astonishment, perhaps even of wonder, and then there would be a discussion and Mike would tell him about the village of Geierslay.

But Richard Pratt did not taste his wine. He was completely engrossed in conversation with Mike's eighteen-year-old daughter, Louise. He was half turned towards her, smiling at her, telling her, so far as I could gather, some story about a chef in a Paris restaurant. As he spoke, he leaned closer and closer to her, seeming in his eagerness almost to impinge upon her, and the poor girl leaned as far as she could away from him nodding politely, rather desperately, and looking not at his face but at the topmost button of his dinner jacket.

We finished our fish, and the maid came round removing the plates. When she came to Pratt, she saw that he had not yet touched his food, so she hesitated, and Pratt noticed her. He waved her away, broke off his conversation, and quickly began to eat, popping the little crisp brown fish quickly into his mouth with rapid jabbing movements of his fork. Then, when he had finished, he reached for his glass, and in two short swallows he tipped the wine down his throat and turned immediately to resume his conversation with Louise Schofield.

Mike saw it all. I was conscious of him sitting there, very still, containing himself, looking at his guest. His round jovial face seemed to loosen slightly and to sag, but he contained himself and was still and said nothing.

Soon the maid came forward with the second course. This was a large roast beef. She placed it on the table in front of Mike who stood up and carved it, cutting the slices very thin, laying them gently on the plates for the maid to take around. When he had served everyone, including himself, he put down the carving knife and leaned forward with both hands on the edge of the table.

"Now," he said, speaking to all of us but looking at Richard Pratt. "Now for the claret. I must go and fetch the claret, if you'll excuse me."

"You go and fetch it, Mike?" I said. "Where is it?"

"In my study, with the cork out—breathing."

"Why the study?"

"Acquiring room temperature, of course. It's been there twenty-four hours."

"But why the study?"

"It's the best place in the house. Richard helped me choose it last time he was here."

At the sound of his name, Pratt looked round.

"That's right, isn't it?" Mike said.

"Yes," Pratt answered, nodding gravely. "That's right."

"On top of the green filing cabinet in my study," Mike said. "That's the place we chose. A good draught-free spot in a room with an even temperature. Excuse me now, will you, while I fetch it."

The thought of another wine to play with had restored his humour, and he hurried out of the door, to return a minute later more slowly, walking softly, holding in both hands a wine basket in which a dark bottle lay. The label was out of sight, facing downwards. "Now!" he cried as he came towards the table. "What about this one, Richard? You'll never name this one!"

Richard Pratt turned slowly and looked up at Mike, then his eyes travelled down to the bottle nestling in its small wicker basket, and he raised his eyebrows; a slight supercilious arching of the brows, and with it a pushing outward of the wet lower lip, suddenly imperious and ugly.

"You'll never get it," Mike said. "Not in a hundred years."

"A claret?" Richard Pratt asked, condescending.

"Of course."

"I assume, then, that it's from one of the smaller vineyards?"

"Maybe it is, Richard. And then again, maybe it isn't."

"But it's a good year? One of the great years?"

"Yes, I guarantee that."

"Then it shouldn't be too difficult," Richard Pratt said, drawling his words, looking exceedingly bored. Except that, to me, there was something strange about his drawling and his boredom: between the eyes a shadow of something evil, and in his bearing an intentness that gave me a faint sense of uneasiness as I watched him.

"This one is really rather difficult," Mike said. "I won't force you to bet on this one."

"Indeed. And why not?" Again the slow arching of the brows, the cool, intent look.

"Because it's difficult."

"That's not very complimentary to me, you know."

"My dear man," Mike said, "I'll bet you with pleasure, if that's what you wish."

"It shouldn't be too hard to name it."

"You mean you want to bet?"

"I'm perfectly willing to bet," Richard Pratt said.

"All right, then, we'll have the usual. A case of the wine itself."

"You don't think I'll be able to name it, do you?"

"As a matter of fact, and with all due respect, I don't," Mike said. He was making some effort to remain polite, but Pratt was not bothering overmuch to conceal his contempt for the whole proceeding. And yet, curiously, his next question seemed to betray a certain interest.

"You like to increase the bet?"

"No, Richard. A case is plenty."

"Would you like to bet fifty cases?"

"That would be silly."

Mike stood very still behind his chair at the head of the table, carefully holding the bottle in its ridiculous wicker basket. There was a trace of whiteness around his nostrils now, and his mouth was shut very tight.

Pratt was lolling back in his chair, looking up at him, the eyebrows raised, the eyes half closed, a little smile touching the corners of his lips. And again I saw, or thought I saw, something distinctly disturbing about the man's face, that shadow of intentness between the eyes, and in the eyes themselves, right in their centres where it was black, a small slow spark of shrewdness, hiding.

"So you don't want to increase the bet?"

"As far as I'm concerned, old man, I don't give a damn," Mike said. "I'll bet you anything you like."

The three women and I sat quietly, watching the two men. Mike's wife was becoming annoyed; her mouth had gone sour and I felt that at any moment she was going to interrupt. Our roast beef lay before us on our plates, slowly steaming.

"So you'll bet me anything I like?"

"That's what I told you. I'll bet you anything you damn well please, if you want to make an issue out of it."

"Even ten thousand pounds?"

"Certainly I will, if that's the way you want it." Mike was more confident now. He knew quite well that he could call any sum Pratt cared to mention.

"So you say I can name the bet?" Pratt asked again.

"That's what I said."

There was a pause while Pratt looked slowly around the table, first at me, then at the three women, each in turn. He appeared to be reminding us that we were witness to the offer.

"Mike!" Mrs. Schofield said. "Mike, why don't we stop this nonsense and eat our food. It's getting cold."

"But it isn't nonsense," Pratt told her evenly. "We're making a little bet."

I noticed the maid standing in the background holding a dish of vegetables, wondering whether to come forward with them or not.

"All right, then," Pratt said. "I'll tell you what I want you to bet."

"Come on, then," Mike said, rather reckless. "I don't give a damn what it is—you're on."

Pratt nodded, and again the little smile moved the corners of his lips, and then, quite slowly, looking at Mike all the time, he said, "I want you to bet me the hand of your daughter in marriage."

Louise Schofield gave a jump. "Hey!" she cried. "No! That's not funny! Look here, Daddy, that's not funny at all."

"No, dear," her mother said. "They're only joking."

"I'm not joking," Richard Pratt said.

"It's ridiculous," Mike said. He was off balance again now.

"You said you'd bet anything I liked."

"I meant money."

"You didn't *say* money."

"That's what I meant."

"Then it's a pity you didn't say it. But anyway, if you wish to go back on your offer, that's quite all right with me."

"It's not a question of going back on my offer, old man. It's a no-bet anyway, because you can't match the stake. You yourself don't happen to have a daughter to put up against mine in case you lose. And if you had, I wouldn't want to marry her."

"I'm glad of that, dear," his wife said.

"I'll put up anything you like," Pratt announced. "My house, for example. How about my house?"

"Which one?" Mike asked, joking now.

"The country one."

"Why not the other one as well?"

"All right then, if you wish it. Both my houses."

At that point I saw Mike pause. He took a step forward and placed the bottle in its basket gently down on the table. He moved the salt cellar to one side, then the pepper, and then he picked up his knife, studied the blade thoughtfully for a moment, and put it down again. His daughter, too, had seen him pause.

"Now, Daddy!" she cried. "Don't be *absurd!* It's *too* silly for words. I refuse to be betted on like this."

"Quite right, dear," her mother said. "Stop it at once, Mike, and sit down and eat your food."

Mike ignored her. He looked over at his daughter and he smiled, a slow, fatherly, protective smile. But in his eyes, suddenly, there glimmered a little triumph. "You know," he said, smiling as he spoke. "You know, Louise, we ought to think about this a bit."

"Now, stop it, Daddy! I refuse even to listen to you! Why, I've never heard anything so ridiculous in my life!"

"No, seriously, my dear. Just wait a moment and hear what I have to say."

"But I don't *want* to hear it."

"Louise! Please! It's like this. Richard, here, has offered us a serious bet. He is the one who wants to make it, not me. And if he loses, he will have to hand over a considerable amount of property. Now, wait a minute, my dear, don't interrupt. The point is this. *He cannot possibly win.*"

"He seems to think he can."

"Now listen to me, because I know what I'm talking about. The expert, when tasting a claret—so long as it is not one of the famous great wines like Lafite or Latour—can only get a certain way towards naming the vineyard. He can, of course, tell you the Bordeaux district from which the wine comes, whether it is from St. Emilion, Pomerol, Graves, or Médoc. But then each district has several communes, little counties, and each county had many, many small vineyards. It is impossible for a man to differentiate between them all by taste and smell alone. I don't mind telling you that this one I've got here is a wine from a small vineyard that is surrounded by many other small vineyards, and he'll never get it. It's impossible."

"You can't be sure of that," his daughter said.

"I'm telling you I can. Though I say it myself, I understand quite a bit about this wine business, you know. And anyway, heavens alive, girl, I'm your father and you don't think I'd let you in for—for something you didn't want, do you? I'm trying to make you some money."

"Mike!" his wife said sharply. "Stop it now, Mike, please!"

Again he ignored her. "If you will take this bet," he said to his daughter, "in ten minutes you will be the owner of two large houses."

"But I don't want two large houses, Daddy."

"Then sell them. Sell them back to him on the spot. I'll arrange all that for you. And then, just think of it, my dear, you'll be rich! You'll be independent for the rest of your life!"

"Oh, Daddy, I don't like it. I think it's silly."

"So do I," the mother said. She jerked her head briskly up and down as she spoke, like a hen. "You ought to be ashamed of yourself, Michael, even suggesting such a thing! Your own daughter, too!"

Mike didn't even look at her. "Take it!" he said eagerly, staring hard at the girl. "Take it, quick! I'll guarantee you won't lose."

"But I don't like it, Daddy."

"Come on, girl. Take it!"

Mike was pushing her hard. He was leaning towards her, fixing her with two hard bright eyes, and it was not easy for the daughter to resist him.

"But what if I lose?"

"I keep telling you, you can't lose. I'll guarantee it."

"Oh, Daddy must I?"

"I'm making you a fortune. So come on now. What do you say, Louise? All right?"

For the last time, she hesitated. Then she gave a helpless little shrug of the shoulders and said, "Oh, all right, then. Just so long as you swear there's no danger of losing."

"Good!" Mike cried. "That's fine! Then it's a bet!"

"Yes," Richard Pratt said, looking at the girl. "It's a bet."

Immediately, Mike picked up the wine, tipped the first thimbleful into his own glass, then skipped excitedly around the table filling up the others. Now everyone was watching Richard Pratt, watching his face as he reached slowly for his glass with his right hand and lifted it to his nose. The man was about fifty years old and he did not have a pleasant face. Somehow, it was all mouth—mouth and lips—the full, wet lips of the professional gourmet, the lower lip hanging downward in the centre, a pendulous, permanently open taster's lip, shaped open to receive the rim of a glass or a morsel of food. Like a keyhole, I thought, watching it; his mouth is like a large wet keyhole.

Slowly he lifted the glass to his nose. The point of the nose entered the glass and moved over the surface of the wine, delicately sniffing. He swirled the wine gently around in the glass to receive the bouquet. His concentration was intense. He had closed his eyes, and now the whole top half of his body, the head and neck and chest, seemed to become a kind of huge sensitive smelling-machine, receiving, filtering, analysing the message from the sniffing nose.

Mike, I noticed, was lounging in his chair, apparently unconcerned, but he was watching every move. Mrs. Schofield, the wife, sat prim and upright at the other end of the table, looking straight ahead, her face tight with disapproval. The daughter, Louise, had shifted her chair away a little, and sidewise, facing the gourmet, and she, like her father, was watching closely.

For at least a minute, the smelling process continued; then, without opening his eyes or moving his head, Pratt lowered the glass to his mouth and tipped in almost half the contents. He paused, his mouth full of wine, getting the first taste; then, he permitted some of it to trickle down his throat and I saw his Adam's apple move as it passed by. But most of it he retained in his mouth. And now, without swallowing again, he drew in through the lips a thin breath of air which mingled with the fumes of the wine in the mouth and passed on down into his lungs. He held the breath, blew it out through his nose, and finally began to roll the wine around under the tongue, and chewed it, actually chewed it with his teeth as though it were bread.

It was a solemn, impressive performance, and I must say he did it well.

"Um," he said, putting down the glass, running a pink tongue over his lips, "Um—yes. A very interesting little wine—gentle and gracious, almost feminine in the aftertaste."

There was an excess of saliva in his mouth, and as he spoke he spat an occasional bright speck of it on the table.

"Now we can start to eliminate," he said. "You will pardon me for doing this carefully, but there is much at stake. Normally I would perhaps take a bit of a chance, leaping forward quickly and landing right in the middle of the vineyard of my choice. But this time—I must move cautiously this time, must I not?" He looked up at Mike and he smiled, a thick-lipped, wet-lipped smile. Mike did not smile back.

"First, then, which district in Bordeaux does this wine come from? That's not too difficult to guess. It is far too light in the body to be from either St. Emilion or Graves. It is obviously a Médoc. There's no doubt about *that*.

"Now—from which commune in Médoc does it come? That also, by elimination, should not be too difficult to decide. Margaux? No. It cannot be Margaux. It has not the violent bouquet of a Margaux. Pauillac? It cannot be Pauillac, either. It is too tender, too gentle and wistful for Pauillac. The wine of Pauillac has a character that is almost imperious in its taste. And also, to me, a Pauillac contains just a little pith, a curious dusty, pithy flavour that the grape acquires from the soil of the district. No, no. This—this is a very gentle wine, demure and bashful in the first taste, emerging shyly but quite graciously in the second. A little arch, perhaps, in the second taste, and a little naughty also, teasing the tongue with a trace, just a trace of tannin. Then, in the aftertaste, delightful—consoling and feminine, with a certain blithely generous quality that one associates only with the wines of the commune of St. Julien. Unmistakably this is a St. Julien."

He leaned back in his chair, held his hands up level with his chest, and placed the fingertips carefully together. He was becoming ridiculously pompous, but I thought that some of it was deliberate, simply to mock his host. I found myself waiting rather tensely for him to go on. The girl Louise was lighting a cigarette. Pratt heard the match strike and he turned on her, flaring suddenly with real anger. "Please!" he said. "Please don't do that! It's a disgusting habit, to smoke at table!"

She looked up at him, still holding the burning match in one hand, the big slow eyes settling on his face, resting there a moment, moving away again, slow and contemptuous. She bent her head and blew out the match, but continued to hold the unlighted cigarette in her fingers.

"I'm sorry, my dear," Pratt said, "but I simply cannot have smoking at table."

She didn't look at him again.

"Now, let me see—where were we?" he said. "Ah, yes. This wine is from Bordeaux, from the commune of St. Julien, in the district of Médoc. So far, so good. But now we come to the more difficult part—the name of the vineyard itself. For in St. Julien there are many vineyards, and as our host so rightly remarked earlier on, there is often not much difference between the wine of one and wine of another. But we shall see."

He paused again, closing his eyes. "I am trying to establish the 'growth,'" he said. "If I can do that, it will be half the battle. Now, let me see. This wine is obviously not from a first-growth vineyard—nor even a second. It is not a great wine. The quality, the—the—what do you call it?—the radiance, the power, is lacking. But a third growth—that it could be. And yet I doubt it. We know it is a good year—our host has said so—and this is probably flattering it a little bit. I must be careful. I must be very careful here."

He picked up his glass and took another small sip.

"Yes," he said, sucking his lips, "I was right. It is a fourth growth. Now I am sure of it. A fourth growth from a very good year—from a great year, in fact. And that's what made it taste for a moment like a third—or even a second-growth wine. Good! That's

251

better! Now we are closing in! What are the fourth-growth vine-yards in the commune of St. Julien?"

Again he paused, took up his glass, and held the rim against that sagging, pendulous lower lip of his. Then I saw the tongue shoot out, pink and narrow, the tip of it dipping into the wine, with-drawing swiftly again—a repulsive sight. When he lowered the glass, his eyes remained closed, the face concentrated, only the lips moving, sliding over each other like two pieces of wet, spongy rub-ber.

"There it is again!" he cried. "Tannin in the middle taste, and the quick astringent squeeze upon the tongue. Yes, yes, of course! Now I have it! The wine comes from one of those small vineyards around Beychevelle. I remember now. The Beychevelle district, and the river and the little harbour that has silted up so the wine ships can no longer use it. Beychevelle . . . could it actually be a Beychevelle itself? No, I don't think so. Not quite. But it is somewhere very close. Château Talbot? Could it be Talbot? Yes, it could. Wait one moment."

He sipped the wine again, and out of the side of my eye I noticed Mike Schofield and how he was leaning further and further forward over the table, his mouth slightly open, his small eyes fixed upon Richard Pratt.

"No. I was wrong. It is not a Talbot. A Talbot comes forward to you just a little quicker than this one; the fruit is nearer the surface. If it is a '34, which I believe it is, then it couldn't be Talbot. Well, well. Let me think. It is not a Beychevelle and it is not a Talbot, and yet—yet it is so close to both of them, so close, that the vineyard must be almost in between. Now, which could that be?"

He hesitated, and we waited, watching his face. Everyone, even Mike's wife, was watching him now. I heard the maid put down the dish of vegetables on the sideboard behind me, gently, so as not to disturb the silence.

"Ah!" he cried. "I have it! Yes, I think I have it!"

For the last time, he sipped the wine. Then, still holding the glass up near his mouth, he turned to Mike and he smiled, a slow, silky smile, and he said, "You know what this is? This is the little Château Branaire-Ducru."

Mike sat tight, not moving.

"And the year, 1934."

We all looked at Mike, waiting for him to turn the bottle around in its basket and show the label.

"Is that your final answer?" Mike said.

"Yes, I think so."

"Well, is it or isn't it?"

"Yes, it is."

"What was the name again?"

"Château Branaire-Ducru. Pretty little vineyard. Lovely old château. Know it quite well. Can't think why I didn't recognize it at once."

"Come on, Daddy," the girl said. "Turn it round and let's have a peek. I want my two houses."

"Just a minute," Mike said. "Wait just a minute." He was sitting very quiet, bewildered-looking, and his face was becoming puffy and pale, as though all the force was draining slowly out of him.

"Michael!" his wife called sharply from the other end of the table. "What's the matter?"

"Keep out of this, Margaret, will you please."

Richard Pratt was looking at Mike, smiling with his mouth, his eyes small and bright. Mike was not looking at anyone.

"Daddy!" the daughter cried, agonized. "But, Daddy, you don't mean to say he guessed it right!"

"Now, stop worrying, my dear," Mike said. "There's nothing to worry about."

I think it was more to get away from his family than anything else that Mike then turned to Richard Pratt and said, "I'll tell you what, Richard. I think you and I better slip off into the next room and have a little chat."

"I don't want a little chat," Pratt said. "All I want is to see the label on that bottle." He knew he was a winner now; he had the bearing, the quiet arrogance of a winner, and I could see that he was prepared to become thoroughly nasty if there was any trouble. "What are you waiting for?" he said to Mike. "Go on and turn it round."

Then this happened: the maid, the tiny, erect figure of the maid in her white-and-black uniform, was standing beside Richard Pratt, holding something out in her hand. "I believe these are yours, sir," she said.

Pratt glanced around, saw the pair of thin horn-rimmed spectacles that she held out to him, and for a moment he hesitated. "Are they? Perhaps they are, I don't know."

"Yes, sir, they're yours." The maid was an elderly woman—nearer seventy than sixty—a faithful family retainer of many years' standing. She put the spectacles down on the table beside him.

Without thanking her, Pratt took them up and slipped them into his top pocket, behind the white handkerchief.

But the maid didn't go away. She remained standing beside and slightly behind Richard Pratt, and there was something so unusual in her manner and in the way she stood there, small, motionless and erect, that I for one found myself watching her with a sudden apprehension. Her old grey face had a frosty, determined look, the lips were compressed, the little chin was out, and the hands were clasped together tight before her. The curious cap on her head and the flash of white down the front of her uniform made her seem like some tiny, ruffled, white-breasted bird.

"You left them in Mr. Schofield's study," she said. Her voice was unnaturally, deliberately polite. "On top of the green filing cabinet in his study, sir, when you happened to go in there by yourself before dinner."

It took a few moments for the full meaning of her words to penetrate, and in the silence that followed I became aware of Mike and how he was slowly drawing himself up in his chair, and the colour coming to his face, and the eyes opening wide, and the curl of the mouth, and the dangerous little patch of whiteness beginning to spread around the area of the nostrils.

"Now, Michael!" his wife said. "Keep calm now, Michael dear! Keep calm!"

When, about eight years ago, old Sir William Turton died and his son Basil inherited *The Turton Press* (as well as the title), I can remember how they started laying bets around Fleet Street as to how long it would be before some nice young woman managed to persuade the little fellow that she must look after him. That is to say, him and his money.

The new Sir Basil Turton was maybe forty years old at the time, a bachelor, a man of mild and simple character who up to then had shown no interest in anything at all except his collection of modern paintings and sculpture. No woman had disturbed him; no scandal or gossip had ever touched his name. But now that he had become the proprietor of quite a large newspaper and magazine empire, it was necessary for him to emerge from the calm of his father's country house and come up to London.

Naturally, the vultures started gathering at once, and I believe that not only Fleet Street but very nearly the whole of the city was looking on eagerly as they scrambled for the body. It was slow motion, of course, deliberate and deadly slow motion, and therefore not so much like vultures as a bunch of agile crabs clawing for a piece of horsemeat underwater.

But to everyone's surprise the little chap proved to be remarkably elusive, and the chase dragged on right through the spring and early summer of that year. I did not know Sir Basil personally, nor did I have any reason to feel friendly towards him, but I couldn't help taking the side of my own sex and found myself cheering loudly every time he managed to get himself off the hook.

Then, round about the beginning of August, apparently at some secret female signal, the girls declared a sort of truce among themselves while they went abroad, and rested, and regrouped, and made fresh plans for the winter kill. This was a mistake because precisely at that moment a dazzling creature called Natalia something or other, whom nobody had heard of before, swept in from the Continent, took Sir Basil firmly by the wrist and led him off in a kind of swoon to the Registry Office at Caxton Hall where she married him before anyone else, least of all the bridegroom, realized what was happening.

You can imagine that the London ladies were indignant, and naturally they started disseminating a vast amount of fruity gossip about the new Lady Turton ("That dirty poacher," they called her). But we don't have to go into that. In fact, for the purposes of this story we can skip the next six years, which brings us right up to the present, to an occasion exactly one week ago today when I myself had the pleasure of meeting her ladyship for the first time. By now, as you must have guessed, she was not only running the whole of *The Turton Press*, but as a result had become a considerable political force in the country. I realize that other women have done this sort of thing before, but what made her particular case unusual was the fact that she was a foreigner and that nobody seemed to know precisely what country she came from—Yugoslavia, Bulgaria, or Russia.

So last Thursday I went to this small dinner party at a friend's in London, and while we were standing around in the drawing room before the meal, sipping good martinis and talking about the atom bomb and Mr. Bevan, the maid popped her head in to announce the last guest.

"Lady Turton," she said.

Nobody stopped talking; we were too well mannered for that. No heads were turned. Only our eyes swung round to the door, waiting for the entrance.

She came in fast—tall and slim in a red-gold dress with sparkles on it—the mouth smiling, the hand outstretched towards her hostess, and my heavens, I must say she was a beauty.

"Mildred, good evening!"

"My dear Lady Turton! How nice!"

I believe we *did* stop talking then, and we turned and stared and stood waiting quite meekly to be introduced, just like she might have been the queen or a famous film star. But she was better looking than either of those. The hair was black, and to go with it she had one of those pale, oval, innocent fifteenth-century Flemish faces, almost exactly a Madonna by Memling or Van Eyck. At least that was the first impression. Later, when my turn came to shake hands, I got a closer look and saw that except for the outline and colouring it wasn't really a Madonna at all—far, far from it.

The nostrils for example were very odd, somehow more open, more flaring than any I had seen before, and excessively arched. This gave the whole nose a kind of open, snorting look that had something of the wild animal about it—the mustang.

And the eyes when I saw them close, were not wide and round the way the Madonna painters used to make them, but long and half-closed, half smiling, half sullen, and slightly vulgar, so that in one way and another they gave her a most delicately dissipated air. What's more they didn't look at you directly. They came to you slowly from over on one side with a curious sliding motion that made me nervous. I tried to see their colour, thought it was pale grey, but couldn't be sure.

Then she was led away across the room to meet other people. I stood watching her. She was clearly conscious of her success and of the way these Londoners were deferring to her. "Here am I," she seemed to be saying, "and I only came over a few years ago, but already I am richer and more powerful than any of you." There was a little prance of triumph in her walk.

A few minutes later we went in to dinner, and to my surprise I found myself seated at her ladyship's right. I presumed that our hostess had done this as a kindness to me, thinking I might pick up some material for the social column I write each day in the evening paper. I settled myself down ready for an interesting meal. But the famous lady took no notice of me at all; she spent her time talking to the man on her left; the host. Until at last, just as I was finishing my ice cream, she suddenly turned, reached over, picked up my place card and read the name. Then, with that queer sliding motion of the eyes she looked into my face. I smiled and made a little bow.

She didn't smile back, but started shooting questions at me, rather personal questions—job, age, family, things like that—in a peculiar lapping voice, and I found myself answering as best I could.

During this inquisition it came out among other things that I was a lover of painting and sculpture.

"Then you should come down to the country some time and see my husband's collection." She said it casually, merely as a form of conversation, but you must realize that in my job I cannot afford to lose an opportunity like this.

"How kind of you, Lady Turton. But I'd simply love to. When shall I come?"

Her head went up and she hesitated, frowned, shrugged her shoulders and then said, "Oh I don't care. Any time."

"How about this next weekend? Would that be all right?"

The slow narrow eyes rested a moment on mine, then travelled away. "I suppose so, if you wish. I don't care."

And that was how the following Saturday afternoon I came to be driving down to Wooton with my suitcase in the back of the car. You may think that perhaps I forced the invitation a bit, but I couldn't have got it any other way. And apart from the professional aspect, I personally wanted very much to see the house. As you know, Wooton is one of the truly great stone houses of the early English Renaissance. Like its sisters, Longleat, Wollaton, and Montacute, it was built in the latter half of the sixteenth century when for the first time a great man's house could be designed as a comfortable dwelling, not as a castle, and when a new group of architects such as John Thorpe and the Smithsons were starting to do marvellous things all over the country.

Neck

It lies south of Oxford, near a small town called Princes Risborough—not a long trip from London—and as I swung in through the main gates the sky was closing overhead and the early winter evening was beginning.

I went slowly up the long drive, trying to see as much of the grounds as possible, especially the famous topiary which I had heard such a lot about. And I must say it was an impressive sight. On all sides there were massive yew trees, trimmed and clipped into many different comical shapes—hens, pigeons, bottles, boots, armchairs, castles, eggcups, lanterns, old women with flaring petticoats, tall pillars, some crowned with a ball, others with big rounded roofs and stemless mushroom finials—and in the half darkness the greens had turned to black so that each figure, each tree, took on a dark, smooth sculptural quality. At one point I saw a lawn covered with gigantic chessmen, each a live yew tree, marvellously fashioned. I stopped the car, got out and walked among them, and they were twice as tall as me. What's more the set was complete, kings, queens, bishops, knights, rooks and pawns standing in position as for the start of a game.

Around the next bend I saw the great grey house itself, and in front of it the large entrance forecourt enclosed by a high balustraded wall with small pillared pavilions at its outer angles. The piers of the balustrades were surmounted by stone obelisks—the Italian influence on the Tudor mind—and a flight of steps at least a hundred feet wide led up to the house.

As I drove into the forecourt I noticed with rather a shock that the fountain basin in the middle supported a large statue by Epstein. A lovely thing, mind you, but surely not in sympathy with its surroundings. Then, looking back as I climbed the stairway to the front door, I saw that on all the little lawns and terraces round about there were other modern statues and many kinds of curious sculpture. In the distance I thought I recognized Gaudier Brzeska, Brancusi, Saint-Gaudens, Henry Moore, and Epstein again.

The door was opened by a young footman who led me up to a bedroom on the first floor. Her ladyship, he explained, was resting, so were the other guests, but they would all be down in the main drawing room in an hour or so, dressed for dinner.

Now in my job it is necessary to do a lot of week-ending. I suppose I spend around fifty Saturdays and Sundays a year in other people's houses, and as a result I have become fairly sensitive to unfamiliar atmosphere. I can tell good or bad almost by sniffing with my nose the moment I get in the front door; and this one I was in now I did not like. The place smelled wrong. There was the faint, desiccated whiff of something troublesome in the air; I was conscious of it even as I lay steaming luxuriously in my great marble bath; and I couldn't help hoping that no unpleasant things were going to happen before Monday came.

The first of them—though more of a surprise than an unpleasantness—occurred ten minutes later. I was sitting on the bed putting on my socks when softly the door opened, and an ancient lopsided gnome in black tails slid into the room. He was the butler, he explained, and his name was Jelks, and he did so hope I was comfortable and had everything I wanted.

I told him I was and had.

He said he would do all he could to make my weekend agreeable. I thanked him and waited for him to go. He hesitated, and then, in a voice dripping with unction, he begged permission to mention a rather delicate matter. I told him to go ahead.

To be quite frank, he said, it was about tipping. The whole business of tipping made him acutely miserable.

Oh? And why was that?

Well, if I really wanted to know, he didn't like the idea that his guests felt under an obligation to tip him when they left the house—as indeed they did. It was an undignified proceeding for the tipping and the tipped. Moreover, he was well aware of the anguish that was often created in the minds of guests such as myself, if I would pardon the liberty, who might feel compelled by convention to give more than they could really afford.

He paused, and two small crafty eyes watched my face for a sign. I murmured that he needn't worry himself about such things as far as I was concerned.

On the contrary, he said, he hoped sincerely that I would agree from the beginning to give him no tip at all.

"Well," I said. "Let's not fuss about it now, and when the time comes we'll see how we feel."

"No, sir!" he cried. "Please, I really must insist."

So I agreed.

He thanked me, and shuffled a step or two closer. Then, laying his head on one side and clasping his hands before him like a priest, he gave a tiny apologetic shrug of the shoulders. The small sharp eyes were still watching me, and I waited, one sock on, the other in my hands, trying to guess what was coming next.

All that he would ask, he said softly, so softly now that his voice was like music heard faintly in the street outside a great concert hall, all that he would ask was that instead of a tip I should give him thirty-three and a third per cent of my winnings at cards over the weekend. If I lost there would be nothing to pay.

It was all so soft and smooth and sudden that I was not even surprised.

"Do they play a lot of cards, Jelks?"

"Yes, sir, a great deal."

"Isn't thirty-three and a third a bit steep?"

"I don't think so, sir."

"I'll give you ten per cent."

"No, sir, I couldn't do that." He was now examining the fingernails of his left hand, and patiently frowning.

"Then we'll make it fifteen. All right?"

"Thirty-three and a third, sir. It's very reasonable. After all, sir, seeing that I don't even know if you are a good player, what I'm actually doing, not meaning to be personal, is backing a horse and I've never even seen it run."

No doubt you think I should never have started bargaining with the butler in the first place, and perhaps you are right. But being a liberal-minded person, I always try my best to be affable with the lower classes. Apart from that, the more I thought about it, the more I had to admit to myself that it was an offer no sportsman had the right to reject.

"All right then, Jelks. As you wish."

"Thank you, sir." He moved towards the door, walking slowly sideways like a crab; but once more he hesitated, a hand on the knob. "If I may give a little advice, sir—may I?"

"Yes?"

"It's simply that her ladyship tends to overbid her hand."

Now *this was* going too far. I was so startled I dropped my sock. After all, it's one thing to have a harmless little sporting arrangement with the butler about tipping, but when he begins conniving with you to take money away from the hostess then it's time to call a halt.

"All right Jelks. Now that'll do."

"No offence, sir, I hope. All I mean is you're bound to be playing against her ladyship. She always partners Major Haddock."

"Major Haddock? You mean Major Jack Haddock?"

"Yes, sir."

I noticed there was a trace of a sneer around the corner of Jelks's nose when he spoke about this man. And it was worse with Lady Turton. Each time he said "her ladyship" he spoke the words with the outsides of his lips as though he were nibbling a lemon, and there was a subtle, mocking inflection in his voice.

"You'll excuse me now, sir. *Her ladyship* will be down at seven o'clock. So will *Major Haddock* and the others." He slipped out of the door leaving behind him a certain dampness in the room and a faint smell of embrocation.

Shortly after seven, I found my way to the main drawing room, and Lady Turton, as beautiful as ever, got up to greet me.

"I wasn't even sure you were coming," she said in that peculiar lilting voice. "What's your name again?"

"I'm afraid I took you at your word, Lady Turton. I hope it's all right."

"Why not?" she said. "There's forty-seven bedrooms in the house. This is my husband."

A small man came around the back of her and said, "You know, I'm so glad you were able to come." He had a lovely warm smile and when he took my hand I felt instantly a touch of friendship in his fingers.

"And Carmen La Rosa," Lady Turton said.

This was a powerfully built woman who looked as though she might have something to do with horses. She nodded at me, and although my hand was already halfway out she didn't give me hers, thus forcing me to convert the movement into a noseblow.

"You have a cold?" she said. "I'm sorry."

I did not like this Miss Carmen La Rosa.

"And this is Jack Haddock."

I knew this man slightly. He was a director of companies (whatever that may mean), and a well-known member of society. I had used his name a few times in my column, but I had never liked him, and this I think was mainly because I have a deep suspicion of all people who carry their military titles back with them into private life—especially majors and colonels. Standing there in his dinner jacket with his full-blooded animal face and black eyebrows and large white teeth, he looked so handsome there was almost something indecent about it. He had a way of raising his upper lip when he smiled, baring his teeth, and he was smiling now as he gave me a hairy brown hand.

"I hope you're going to say some nice things about us in your column."

"He better had," Lady Turton said, "or I'll say some nasty ones about him on my front page."

I laughed, but all three of them, Lady Turton, Major Haddock, and Carmen La Rosa had already turned away and were settling themselves back on the sofa. Jelks gave me a drink, and Sir Basil drew me gently aside for a quiet chat at the other end of the room. Every now and then Lady Turton would call her husband to fetch her something—another martini, a cigarette, an ashtray, a hand-kerchief—and he, half rising from his chair, would be forestalled by the watchful Jelks who fetched it for him.

Clearly, Jelks loved his master; and just as clearly he hated the wife. Each time he did something for her he made a little sneer with his nose and drew his lips together so they puckered like a turkey's bottom.

At dinner, our hostess sat her two friends, Haddock and La Rosa, on either side of her. This unconventional arrangement left Sir Basil and me at the other end of the table where we were able to continue our pleasant talk about painting and sculpture. Of course it was obvious to me by now that the Major was infatuated with her ladyship. And again, although I hate to say it, it seemed as though the La Rosa woman was hunting the same bird.

All this foolishness appeared to delight the hostess. But it did not delight her husband. I could see that he was conscious of the little scene all the time we were talking; and often his mind would wander from our subject and he would stop short in mid-sentence, his eyes travelling down to the other end of the table to settle pa-thetically for a moment on that lovely head with the black hair and the curiously flaring nostrils. He must have noticed then how ex-hilarated she was, how the hand that gestured as she spoke rested every now and again on the Major's arm, and how the other woman, the one who perhaps had something to do with horses, kept saying, "Nata-*li*-a? Now Nata-*li*-a, listen to me!"

"Tomorrow," I said, "you must take me round and show me the sculptures you've put up in the garden."

"Of course," he said, "with pleasure." He glanced again at the wife, and his eyes had a sort of supplicating look that was piteous beyond words. He was so mild and passive a man in every way that even now I could see there was no anger in him, no danger, no chance of an explosion.

After dinner I was ordered straight to the card table to partner Miss Carmen La Rosa against Major Haddock and Lady Turton. Sir Basil sat quietly on the sofa with a book.

There was nothing unusual about the game itself; it was routine and rather dull. But Jelks was a nuisance. All evening he prowled around us, emptying ashtrays and asking about drinks and peering at our hands. He was obviously shortsighted and I doubt whether he saw much of what was going on because as you may or may not know, here in England no butler has ever been permitted to wear spectacles—nor, for that matter, a moustache. This is the golden, unbreakable rule, and a very sensible one it is too, although I'm not quite sure what lies behind it. I presume that a moustache would make him look too much like a gentleman, and spectacles too much like an American, and where would we be then I should like to know? In any event Jelks was a nuisance all evening; and so was Lady Turton who was constantly called to the phone on newspaper business.

At eleven o'clock she looked up from her cards and said, "Basil, it's time you went to bed."

"Yes, my dear, perhaps it is." He closed the book, got up, and stood for a minute watching the play. "Are you having a good game?" he asked.

The others didn't answer him, so I said, "It's a nice game."

"I'm so glad. And Jelks will look after you and get anything you want."

"Jelks can go to bed too," the wife said.

I could hear Major Haddock breathing through his nose beside me, and the soft drop of the cards one by one on to the table, and then the sound of Jelks's feet shuffling over the carpet towards us.

"You wouldn't prefer me to stay, m'lady?"

"No. Go to bed. You too, Basil."

"Yes, my dear. Good-night. Good-night all."

Jelks opened the door for him, and he went slowly out followed by the butler.

As soon as the next rubber was over, I said that I too wanted to go to bed.

"All right," Lady Turton said. "Good-night."

I went up to my room, looked the door, took a pill, and went to sleep.

The next morning, Sunday, I got up and dressed around ten o'clock and went down to the breakfast room. Sir Basil was there before me, and Jelks was serving him with grilled kidneys and bacon and fried tomatoes. He was delighted to see me and suggested that as soon as we had finished eating we should take a long walk around the grounds. I told him nothing would give me more pleasure.

Half an hour later we started out, and you've no idea what a relief it was to get away from that house and into the open air. It was one of those warm shining days that come occasionally in midwinter after a night of heavy rain, with a bright surprising sun and not a breath of wind. Bare trees seemed beautiful in the sunlight, water still dripping from the branches, and wet places all around were sparkling with diamonds. The sky had small faint clouds.

"*What* a lovely day!"

"Yes—isn't it a lovely day!"

We spoke hardly another word during the walk; it wasn't necessary. But he took me everywhere and I saw it all—the huge chessmen and all the rest of the topiary. The elaborate garden houses, the pools, the fountains, the children's maze whose hedges were hornbeam and lime so that it was only good in summer when the leaves were out, and the parterres, the rockeries, the greenhouses with their vines and nectarine trees. And of course, the sculpture. Most of the contemporary European sculptors were there, in bronze, granite, limestone, and wood; and although it was a pleasure to see them warming and glowing in the sun, to me they still looked a trifle out of place in these vast formal surroundings.

"Shall we rest here now a little while?" Sir Basil said after we had walked for more than half an hour. So we sat down on a white bench beside a water-lily pond full of carp and goldfish, and lit cigarettes. We were some way from the house, on a piece of ground that was raised above its surroundings, and from where we sat the gardens were spread out below us like a drawing in one of those old books on garden architecture, with the hedges and lawns and terraces and fountains making a pretty pattern of squares and rings.

"My father bought this place just before I was born," Sir Basil said. "I've lived here ever since, and I know every inch of it. Each day I grow to love it more."

"It must be wonderful in summer."

"Oh, but it is. You should come down and see it in May and June. Will you promise to do that?"

"Of course," I said. "I'd love to come," and as I spoke I was watching the figure of a woman dressed in red moving among the flower beds in the far distance. I saw her cross over a wide expanse of lawn, and there was a lilt in her walk, a little shadow attending her, and when she was over the lawn, she turned left and went along one side of a high wall of clipped yew until she came to another smaller lawn that was circular and had in its centre a piece of sculpture.

"This garden is younger than the house," Sir Basil said. "It was laid out early in the eighteenth century by a Frenchman called Beaumont, the same fellow who did Levens, in Westmorland. For at least a year he had two hundred and fifty men working on it."

The woman in the red dress had been joined now by a man, and they were standing face to face, about a yard apart, in the very centre of the whole garden panorama, on this little circular patch of lawn, apparently conversing. The man had some small black object in his hand.

"If you're interested I'll show you the bills that Beaumont put in to the Duke while he was making it."

"I'd like very much to see them. They must be fascinating."

"He paid his labourers a shilling a day and they worked ten hours."

In the clear sunlight it was not difficult to follow the movements and gestures of the two figures on the lawn. They had turned now towards the piece of sculpture, and were pointing at it in a sort of mocking way, apparently laughing and making jokes about its shape. I recognized it as being one of the Henry Moores, done in wood, a thin smooth object of singular beauty that had two or three holes in it and a number of strange limbs protruding.

"When Beaumont planted the yew trees for the chessmen and the other things, he knew they wouldn't amount to much for at least a hundred years. We don't seem to possess that sort of patience in our planning these days, do we? What do you think?"

"No," I said. "We don't."

The black object in the man's hand turned out to be a camera, and now he had stepped back and was taking pictures of the woman beside the Henry Moore. She was striking a number of different poses, all of them, so far as I could see, ludicrous and meant to be amusing. Once she put her arms around one of the protruding wooden limbs and hugged it, and another time she climbed up and sat sidesaddle on the thing, holding imaginary reins in her hands. A great wall of yew hid these two people from the house, and indeed from all the rest of the garden except the little hill on which we sat. They had every right to believe they were not overlooked, and even if they had happened to glance our way—which was into the sun—I doubt whether they would have noticed the two small motionless figures sitting on the bench beside the pond.

"You know, I love these yews," Sir Basil said. "The colour of them is so wonderful in a garden because it rests the eye. And in the summer it breaks up the areas of brilliance into little patches and makes them more comfortable to admire. Have you noticed the different shades of greens on the planes and facets of each clipped tree?"

"It's lovely, isn't it."

The man now seemed to be explaining something to the woman, and pointing at the Henry Moore, and I could tell by the way they threw back their heads that they were laughing again. The man continued to point, and then the woman walked around the back of the wood carving, bent down and poked her head through one of its holes. The thing was about the size, shall I say, of a small horse, but thinner than that, and from where I sat I could see both sides of it—to the left, the woman's body, to the right, her head protruding through. It was very much like one of those jokes at the seaside where you put your head through a hole in a board and get photographed as a fat lady. The man was photographing her now.

"There's another thing about yews," Sir Basil said. "In the early summer when the young shoots come out . . ." At that moment he paused and sat up straighter and leaned slightly forward, and I could sense his whole body suddenly stiffening.

"Yes," I said, "when the young shoots come out?"

The man had taken the photograph, but the woman still had her head through the hole, and now I saw him put both hands (as well as the camera) behind his back and advance towards her. Then he bent forward so his face was close to hers, touching it, and he held it there while he gave her, I suppose, a few kisses or something like that. In the stillness that followed, I fancied I heard a faint faraway tinkle of female laughter coming to us through the sunlight across the garden.

"Shall we go back to the house?" I asked.

"Back to the house?"

"Yes, shall we go back and have a drink before lunch?"

"A drink? Yes, we'll have a drink." But he didn't move. He sat very still, gone far away from me now, staring intently at the two figures. I also was staring at them. I couldn't take my eyes away; I *had* to look. It was like seeing a dangerous little ballet in miniature from a great distance, and you knew the dancers and the music but not the end of the story, not the choreography, nor what they were going to do next, and you were fascinated, and you *had* to look.

"Gaudier Brzeska," I said. "How great do you think he might've become if he hadn't died so young?"

"Who?"

"Gaudier Brzeska."

"Yes," he said. "Of course."

I noticed now that something queer was happening. The woman still had her head through the hole, but she was beginning to wriggle her body from side to side in a slow unusual manner, and the man was standing motionless, a pace or so away watching her. He seemed suddenly uneasy the way he stood there, and I could tell by the drop of the head and by the stiff intent set of the body that there was no laughter in him anymore. For a while he remained still, then I saw him place his camera on the ground and go forward to the woman, taking her head in his hands; and all at once it was more like a puppet show than a ballet, with tiny wooden figures performing tiny, jerky movements, crazy and unreal, on a faraway sunlit stage.

We sat quietly together on the white bench, and we watched while the tiny puppet man began to manipulate the woman's head with his hands. He was doing it gently, there was no doubt about that, slowly and gently, stepping back every now and then to think about it some more, and several times crouching down to survey the situation from another angle. Whenever he left her alone the woman would start to wriggle her body, and the peculiar way she did it reminded me of a dog that feels a collar round its neck for the first time.

"She's stuck," Sir Basil said.

And now the man was walking to the other side of the carving, the side where the woman's body was, and he put out his hands and began trying to do something with her neck. Then, as though suddenly exasperated, he gave the neck two or three jerky pulls, and this time the sound of a woman's voice, raised high in anger, or pain, or both, came back to us small and clear through the sunlight.

Out of the corner of one eye I could see Sir Basil nodding his head quietly up and down. "I got my fist caught in a jar of boiled sweets once," he said, "and I couldn't get it out."

The man retreated a few yards, and was standing with hands on hips, head up, looking furious and sullen. The woman, from her uncomfortable position, appeared to be talking to him, or rather shouting at him, and although the body itself was pretty firmly fixed and could only wriggle, the legs were free and did a good deal of moving and stamping.

"I broke the jar with a hammer and told my mother I'd knocked it off the shelf by mistake." He seemed calmer now, not tense at all, although his voice was curiously flat. "I suppose we'd better go down and see if we can help."

"Perhaps we should."

But still he didn't move. He took out a cigarette and lit it, putting the used match carefully back in the box.

"I'm sorry," he said. "Will you have one?"

"Thanks, I think I will." He made a little ceremony of giving me the cigarette and lighting it for me, and again he put the used match back in the box. Then we got up and walked slowly down the grass slope.

We came upon them silently, through an archway in the yew hedge, and it was naturally quite a surprise.

"What's the matter here?" Sir Basil asked. He spoke softly, with a dangerous softness that I'm sure his wife had never heard before.

"She's gone and put her head through the hole and now she can't get it out," Major Haddock said. "Just for a lark, you know."

"For a what?"

"Basil!" Lady Turton shouted, "Don't be such a damn fool! Do something, can't you!" She may not have been able to move much, but she could still talk.

"Pretty obvious we're going to have to break up this lump of wood," the Major said. There was a small smudge of red on his grey moustache, and this, like the single extra touch of colour that ruins a perfect painting, managed somehow to destroy all his manly looks. It made him comic.

"You mean break the Henry Moore?"

"My dear sir, there is no other way of setting the lady free. God knows how she managed to squeeze it in, but I know for a fact that she can't pull it out. It's the ears get in the way."

"Oh dear," Sir Basil said. "What a terrible pity. My beautiful Henry Moore."

At this stage Lady Turton began abusing her husband in a most unpleasant manner, and there's no knowing how long it would have gone on had not Jelks suddenly appeared out of the shadows. He came sidling silently on to the lawn and stationed himself at a respectful distance from Sir Basil, as though awaiting instructions. His black clothes looked perfectly ridiculous in the morning sunlight, and with his ancient pink-white face and white hands he was like some small crabby animal that has lived all its life in a hole under the ground.

"Is there anything I can do, Sir Basil?" He kept his voice level, but I didn't think his face was quite straight. When he looked at Lady Turton there was a little exulting glimmer in his eyes.

"Yes Jelks, there is. Go back and get me a saw or something so I can cut out this section of wood."

"Shall I call one of the men, Sir Basil? William is a good carpenter."

"No, I'll do it myself. Just get the tools—and hurry."

While they were waiting for Jelks, I strolled away because I didn't want to hear any more of the things that Lady Turton was saying to her husband. But I was back in time to see the butler returning, followed now by the other woman, Carmen La Rosa, who made a rush for the hostess.

"Nata-*li*-a! My dear Nata-*li*-a! What *have* they done to you?"

"Oh shut up," the hostess said. "And get out of the way, will you."

Sir Basil took up a position close to his lady's head, waiting for Jelks. Jelks advanced slowly, carrying a saw in one hand, an axe in the other, and he stopped maybe a yard away. Then he held out both implements in front of him so his master could choose, and there was a brief moment—no more than two or three seconds—of silence, and of waiting, and it just happened that I was watching Jelks at this time. I saw the hand that was carrying the axe come forward an extra fraction of an inch towards Sir Basil. It was so slight a movement it was barely noticeable—a tiny pushing forward of the hand, slow and secret, a little offer, a little coaxing offer that was accompanied perhaps by an infinitesimal lift of the eyebrow.

I'm not sure whether Sir Basil saw it, but he hesitated, and again the hand that held the axe came edging forward, and it was almost exactly like that card trick where the man says "Take one, whichever one you want," and you always get the one he means you to have. Sir Basil got the axe. I saw him reach out in a dreamy sort of way, accepting it from Jelks, and then, the instant he felt the handle in his grasp he seemed to realize what was required of him and he sprang to life.

For me, after that, it was like the awful moment when you see a child running out into the road and a car is coming and all you can do is shut your eyes tight and wait until the noise tells you it has happened. The moment of waiting becomes a long lucid period of time with yellow and red spots dancing on a black field, and even if you open your eyes again and find that nobody has been killed or hurt, it makes no difference because so far as you and your stomach were concerned you saw it all.

I saw this one all right, every detail of it, and I didn't open my eyes again until I heard Sir Basil's voice, even softer than usual, calling in gentle protest to the butler.

"Jelks," he was saying, and I looked and saw him standing there as calm as you please, still holding the axe. Lady Turton's head was there too, still sticking through the hole, but her face had turned a terrible ashy grey, and the mouth was opening and shutting making a kind of gurgling sound.

"Look here, Jelks," Sir Basil was saying. "What on earth are you thinking about. This thing's much too dangerous. Give me the saw." And as he exchanged implements I noticed for the first time two little warm roses of colour appearing on his cheeks, and above them, all around the corners of his eyes, the twinkling tiny wrinkles of a smile.

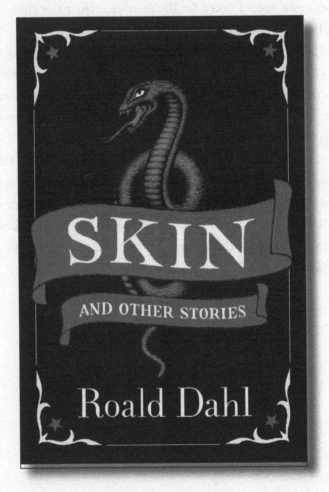

978-0-14-131034-3

Read These Other Wonderful Books
by **Roald Dahl!**

There's more to Roald Dahl than great stories...

Did you know that 10% of author royalties* from this book go to help the work of the Roald Dahl charities?

THE
ROALD DAHL
FOUNDATION

The Roald Dahl Foundation supports specialist pediatric Roald Dahl nurses throughout the UK caring for children with epilepsy, blood disorders, and acquired brain injury. It also provides practical help for children and young people with brain, blood, and literacy problems—all causes close to Roald Dahl during his lifetime—through grants to UK hospitals and charities as well as to individual children and their families.

The Roald Dahl Museum and Story Centre, based in Great Missenden just outside London, is in the Buckinghamshire village where Roald Dahl lived and wrote. At the heart of the Museum, created to inspire a love of reading and writing, is his unique archive of letters and manuscripts. As well as two fun-packed biographical galleries, the Museum boasts an interactive Story Centre. It is a place for family, teachers and their pupils to explore the exciting world of creativity and literacy.

THE **ROALD DAHL** MUSEUM AND STORY CENTRE

www.roalddahlfoundation.org
www.roalddahlmuseum.org

The Roald Dahl Foundation (RDF) is a registered charity no. 1004230.
The Roald Dahl Museum and Story Centre (RDMSC) is a registered charity no. 1085853.
The Roald Dahl Charitable Trust, a newly established charity,
supports the work of RDF and RDMSC.

* Donated royalties are net of commission